6/23

YOU
CAN'T
STAY HERE
FOREVER

YOU CAN'T STAY HERE FOREVER

A Novel

KATHERINE LIN

HARPER

An Imprint of HarperCollinsPublishers

YOU CAN'T STAY HERE FOREVER. Copyright © 2023 by Katherine Lin. All rights reserved. Printed in the United States of America. No part of this book may be used or reproduced in any manner whatsoever without written permission except in the case of brief quotations embodied in critical articles and reviews. For information, address HarperCollins Publishers, 195 Broadway, New York, NY 10007.

HarperCollins books may be purchased for educational, business, or sales promotional use. For information, please email the Special Markets Department at SPsales@harpercollins.com.

FIRST EDITION

Designed by Kyle O'Brien

Library of Congress Cataloging-in-Publication Data has been applied for.

ISBN 978-0-06-324143-5

23 24 25 26 27 LBC 5 4 3 2 1

For Ben, who not only said that I could, but that I should

YOU
CAN'T
STAY HERE
FOREVER

Chapter One

I was waiting for the J train when I found out my husband was dead. I had left work earlier than usual, and the underground Embarcadero Muni Station, which was so jammed during rush hour that it was difficult to walk down the platforms, was nearly empty. My phone had only one bar of reception, and the ringing from my phone had startled me. The screen read "San Francisco, CA" below the unknown number.

"Mrs. Anderson?" said the voice on the phone.

"Yes?" I said, remembering the first person who'd called me that: the bellhop at the hotel where we stayed on our honeymoon, only a few months ago. I'd been startled when he spoke. Who? I wanted to say. Who is Mrs. Anderson?

When I had told Mable how upsetting it was for me to be called "Mrs. Anderson" a day after the wedding, she said, What did you expect when you changed your last name? You've erased yourself on two fronts. As a woman and as an Asian American woman.

The train whirred past me, and I was tempted to hang up. I was impatient to get on with what I felt the night should look like: getting on the Muni, walking to the bar that almost always smelled like ammonia, having drinks with Mable, which meant getting drunk or at least earning a respectable buzz, and then somehow making my way back home.

"Where are you? Are you sitting down?" the man asked, letting out a small cough between the questions.

"No," I said. I had been listening to music when I picked up the call, the ringing interrupting the song, and now I pressed my headphones more firmly into my ears.

"Are you driving?"

"No. I'm sorry, who is this?"

"I'm afraid I have some bad news. Your husband was in a serious car accident. He's dead." He spoke clearly and firmly, as if underlining each word twice. He gave me his name and the name of the hospital he was calling from, one I recognized from its association with a medical school. On the other end of the line, I could hear him shuffling papers, and I imagined him as a young resident, likely trained to deliver news from some mnemonic device or protocol. He began to list the names of procedures (all intended to be lifesaving, but all ultimately unsuccessful) and then repeated those words again, He's dead. He repeated the name of the hospital and told me to come in as soon as I could. I said nothing, just hung up.

I found myself leaving the station. I could smell urine as I headed toward the stairwell to the exit, the daylight streaming ugly through the Muni street opening. A pigeon by my feet had curled up its left leg so it looked like it was dancing instead of limping. I dropped my phone at the top of the stairs and the screen shattered.

"Sucks," a teenage boy said as he passed. The back of his head was dyed pink.

The phone still worked somehow, though, and I requested an Uber to the hospital. A car was just around the corner, and I felt thankful when it arrived. It was a dirty Camry whose driver grunted at me as I buckled myself in. I wondered if Ian had been wearing a seat belt when he died. The car made a few turns on local roads and then turned onto a freeway on-ramp.

Even though Ian and I were young and barely married, I had already spent at least a handful of hours wondering what it would be like to receive this kind of news. This imagining usually happened as I was curled up next to him while he slept, a mound of comforter rising and falling like a metronome. I felt I'd first deny it, swear up and down that they had the wrong Mrs. Anderson. It couldn't be him, I'd say, I just saw him this morning. There are a million people with this last name. And then, after I'd accepted my fate, been forced to after identifying a splotchy birthmark on his hip, I would start to plan the funeral. I ran through lists of our friends, deciding whom I'd ask to speak, who would send flowers instead of attending, and who would show up but eventually disappear from my life. The images that would go through my mind were clichéd, drawing from the scenes that Mable and I made fun of in movies and television shows.

But my imagined reaction was nothing like my real one. Even though I was gutted, sickened, wanted to hurl myself out of the back seat of the moving car or curl myself into something so small it no longer existed, I didn't question the fact of it. Two words made me so certain: car accident. Ian had always driven like a maniac. When we first started dating, I'd pretended I found it frightening, gasping whenever he cut across four lanes of highway traffic to pull off at an exit, the sounds of car horns following us. But really, I loved it. I thought it made him different from the other lawyers I'd met, whose pleated khakis created unflattering mounds and lumps where they shouldn't be.

From the Uber, I called my mother, who picked up after two and a half rings.

"Did you see Carol's invites?" she asked. "I swear they used the exact same vellum we did."

"He's dead," I said. The driver caught my eye in the rearview mirror.

"What? What did you say?"

I repeated myself three times, then told her I was already on the way to the hospital. Even though she was in Ohio, I gave her the hospital address, too. She started crying and shouting until I said, "I just got here, I have to go now."

"I'm sorry," said the driver as I hung up and exited his car. Inside, a main desk receptionist directed me to an elevator in which a man lay under a thick blanket on a gurney, his eyes closed. Next to the gurney stood a doctor in a white coat who was using his thumb to scroll through a social media app on his phone, only slowing down to study pictures of someone's vacation. There were shots of a beach, a man holding a frosted cocktail. A woman with coral red lipstick, a parrot on her arm, was midscream when another photo was taken. It was supposed to be a playful picture, but it looked frightening to me. The man on the gurney whimpered and the doctor glanced down.

"Almost there," he said.

On the Emergency Department floor I spoke to someone behind a desk. She typed his name into her computer and then looked up briefly at me and back down at her keyboard. She said, "Hold on, let me get someone for you." I realized then that the news of his death might've been hours old when it reached me. He could've been dead when I was eating lunch, picking shrimp tails out of my salad and laying them in a spiral on my napkin. Or this afternoon, when I'd closed my door and pretended to be on a conference call but really just texted with Mable to make plans.

The woman got up from her desk and walked down the hallway. She wore a set of pink scrubs, and on her collar there was a pin of a smiling cartoon bear holding a bunch of multicolor balloons. I saw her speaking to a group of people wearing blue and teal scrubs. When she returned, she said, "It won't be much longer."

A man standing with the group of people she had just spoken to came up to me and introduced himself as the doctor who had called me. I said, "You look older than you sound."

"Let me take you somewhere quieter," he said.

He led me into a small room off of the waiting area, where he had me sit down on a small couch and took a seat opposite me. He explained that my husband had arrived at the hospital after suffering serious injuries from a car accident. He once more listed all the procedures they had done. There was nothing we could do, he kept saying. The entire time he was speaking I had to stop myself from leaning across the couch and shaking him, even striking him. It seemed appalling that he could say such words to me. Instead, I asked to see Ian's body, and the man told me he'd take me to the morgue.

As I followed him out, my phone buzzed. My mother had texted that she'd be on the next plane out to San Francisco, and sent me her flight number. Mable had sent me a string of question marks, and I realized that I hadn't canceled our drinks date. I imagined her sitting at our table at the bar, the one equidistant between the door and the bathroom, positioned so we wouldn't catch the cold breeze outside or have to hear the toilet flushing. She still had the luxury of not knowing. She was still on the other side.

Chapter Two

When I picked up my mom at the airport, shortly after dawn, I found her waiting by the curb. Before she spotted me in the car, I saw the flash of the silver hairbrush she always had with her as she ran it through her hair. She looked thinner than the last time I'd seen her. Next to her on the ground was a small carry-on. My mom was a supreme packer, with the ability to fit multiple outfits into what looked like an overnight bag. I could imagine the neat coils of cashmere and the sensible cottons, the socks tucked into each corner. There would be something for her to wear out to dinner at a casual restaurant, another outfit appropriate for a place that called them "entrées," not main courses. I went through my mental catalogue of her closet and tried to guess what she'd chosen for the funeral.

We hugged, and I took in a deep breath. I could feel her do the same.

"This is horrible," she said.

I helped her put her luggage in the trunk. She offered to drive, but I had already gotten back into the driver's seat. As we pulled onto my street, I realized I had forgotten to close the garage door when I left for the airport. We could see it sitting empty from down the block. I pulled my car into the garage, tight against the right side of the wall, though Ian's car wasn't in its usual space on the left.

Inside the house my mom took off her jacket to reveal dark navy slacks with an ivory-colored sweater with visible ironing lines on the arms. She folded the jacket and laid it on a kitchen chair, then said, "The kitchen looks different."

"We got it painted a few months after you last visited," I said. She hadn't been to San Francisco since May, when Ian and I had gotten married, and it was now early September.

I put the car keys on the kitchen counter and said, "I'm going back to bed, if that's all right with you."

She nodded and said, "I've got plenty to do here." I padded to the bedroom, whose shades were drawn so that it was almost dark, and shut the door. I hadn't been in this room since yesterday morning, when Ian was still alive. I heard the snap of latex gloves over her wrists, the spray of the cleaning bottle, the movement of picture frames and plants on the top of shelves.

For about an hour I lay in bed, trying to fall asleep, but eventually gave up and took out my phone. I opened the browser and reread the first page of results from my recent search: "police report, san francisco, how long." All the links on this page were light purple, indicating that I had already opened them.

Yesterday, on my way home from the hospital, I'd called the police department's main number and asked for details about the accident. They transferred me through to multiple departments before I reached someone who informed me that I would have to wait until the police report was created. He had been in the middle of explaining how to order a copy of the report when he suddenly stopped and said, Are you okay? I said, I'm sorry, I'm really trying not to cry. I asked him to repeat the directions. There was a long pause, and he said, Listen, let me grab this for you and do my best to rush it. He asked for my name and number and said he would call me as soon as he could. It's important, I said. I need to know. He repeated my number back to me and I heard the *click-click* of a pen. Okay, he said.

I realized now that I hadn't gotten his name and had no way of following up with him. I went to the second page of the results pages and methodically opened each link.

The sun was glaring through the window when I heard the front door close a few hours later. I pictured my mom in the produce aisle of the nearest grocery store, gripping the oranges with one palm, shaking open the plastic bag with the other. She wouldn't know that San Francisco now charged for bags. Only a few cents, but she'd be peeved nonetheless.

Why here? she asked when I told her that Ian and I planned to take the California bar. You always go on about how there's so much more on the East Coast. You've spent nearly three years here already. Aren't you sick of sitting around and talking about how much you hate tech?

Ian and I had been about to graduate from law school at Stanford, and it was the beginning of summer. After the bar exam, I would be heading to Washington DC for two clerkships, each a year long, but I planned to join Ian after that in San Francisco, where he was going to be an associate at a midsize firm. I hated the idea of Ian and me being apart, but there was no question that I would accept the clerkships. Clerking was the most prestigious job a law school grad could get, and the two judges who had hired me were among the most coveted. When they each called and offered me a position, Ian and I had been in the middle of declaring our intention to be barred in California, and I felt as though they had anointed me through the phone.

My mom leaned her elbows on the rickety table in our law school apartment, something we'd found for forty bucks at a garage sale and fashioned into a kitchen table. Whenever we dropped our heavy textbooks onto it, the legs had shuddered, and Ian and I would joke that even it found various legal subjects tiresome. I'd told my mom months before that we were planning to stay in California, but this was the first time we had actually discussed the fact that I wouldn't be coming back to Ohio, or moving somewhere closer like New York City. I shrugged. We like it here, I said. My mom shook her head and said, You mean Ian likes it here. No, I said. I don't mind it. I don't care all that much where I live.

She knew that this last sentence was meant to hurt her. I'd never considered moving back to the Midwest, and especially not to Beachwood, the suburb of Cleveland where I grew up and where she still lived.

I regretted saying it, but I didn't apologize. At the time, the only thing I really thought about my mother was that being around her made me feel vaguely resentful, which also made me feel guilty because I was aware of how unfair my resentment was. Earlier that week I'd seen my name, for the first time, next to Ian's on a legal document: MONTH-TO-MONTH LEASE AGREEMENT. We'd found a small apartment in San Francisco where we planned to study for the bar together after graduation. As soon as we picked up the keys, the world seemed to align for the first time. It felt satisfying, like finally wiping the window free of streaks, or curling the loose tail of a ribbon with a scissor's blade.

The rental apartment was in Noe Valley, the same neighborhood where we would eventually buy our house a few years later, after I'd paid off my loans and Ian had made partner. Neither of us had lived in San Francisco before, just spent a few Saturday nights in the city while we were in law school. Our first apartment there was inside an older building, where all the floorboards had centimeter-length spaces between them, wide enough so nothing ever looked quite clean. Our front door was new, though: Ian had somehow convinced the landlord to get rid of the mail slot in the door and install a dark gold mailbox in the hallway for us. The landlord had first offered to nail down the slot, but Ian got him to buy an entirely new door, this time in a color we chose. It's weird when people just stick their hand into your house, Ian had said. There was a half bathroom at the front of the house. It was minuscule, and the toilet was almost always running, but having one made me feel distinctly adult, knowing that someone who came over for dinner wouldn't have to see our shampoo bottles on the edge of the shower, our toothbrushes on the counter.

And right when I started to feel pride in my adult home, I felt shame, too. This is exactly what you hated about her, I thought. I fell backward into memories of my mother pushing me into etiquette classes at age seven, held at a community center where an old out-of-tune piano sat covered in a black blanket. Throughout elementary school, there were the frilly socks over the patent leather shoes, the glorification of meals that were only steamed fish and vegetables, with plain fruit for dessert. My tender childhood memories are rarer: standing with her in the bathroom, watching her put two fingers into a pot of cold cream then hold her palms together, warming the cream with her hands until it reached the temperature of her body. It smelled like cucumber, and when she wasn't looking, I would push my finger into the open jar and pull out a dollop that looked like a soft peak of just barely whipped egg whites.

It wasn't until I was fifteen that I saw my mother as others did. I was sleeping over at a friend's house, watching a soapy teen drama set in a wealthy New England town. The mother in the show wore a pink suit with pearls—that's the classic Chanel suit, my friend had said. WASP-y. I asked her what that meant.

It stands for "White Anglo-Saxon Protestant," she said. That's my mom, I said. She'd totally wear something like that. No, she said, sucking popcorn into her teeth. It's "*White* Anglo-Saxon Protestant." And you have to be rich to be a WASP, anyway.

I spent that night fidgeting in my sleeping bag. So, my mother wasn't even a WASP, but something worse. She was someone who aspired to be a WASP. Even though, as I eventually learned, no self-respecting WASP would ever consider her one of their own. A single mom, barely getting by, Taiwanese. After my father died, not long after she found out she was pregnant, she told me she had thought about going back to Taiwan. But they had worked so hard for their student visas, both of them—their names already tinged in awe by their families—that she felt it would be a second tragedy to come back with nothing to show for it but me.

And so when Ian and I got our first place together, in both our names, I felt only the familiar current of resentment work through my blood. I should be able to enjoy this moment, I imagined myself saying to her. I am in a fulfilling and, most important, equal relationship. I am with a man who admires my mind and my career and my ambition.

But when Ian and I went to sleep that night, on a mattress that had just been delivered, I was unable to escape. For all my attempts at distancing myself, I felt I had somehow absorbed her ideas, like osmosis, when I was in the womb. Sometimes I imagined her in labor at the hospital, alone, waiting for a single other family member to finally join her in America: me.

Chapter Three

The front door opened and I heard three footsteps and then a thump of grocery bags hitting the floor. "Ellie," my mom called, "Wake up. I'm home."

I found her in the kitchen putting away groceries, her back toward me. Her hair was pulled up in a ponytail, one of the few times I had ever seen it not falling past her shoulders. Each time she finished putting the contents of a paper bag inside the fridge, she'd fold the bag into thirds and place it on the kitchen island.

I sat down on a stool by the island. It was made of a dark, hard material and had never been comfortable. I put my palms over my eyes.

"How'd you sleep?" she asked, glancing back at me.

"Horribly."

"Barely anything?"

I nodded even though her back was turned to me now. She closed the fridge and put her hand on top of the stack of brown bags. "Remind me again where the recycling is."

The week before our wedding was the first time she'd come to stay at our new home, which was only a few blocks down from where we'd been renting. Before we had closed on the house, she had called me a few times, always asking the same few questions about the mortgage and the state of our finances. Don't worry, I remember saying to her, often while leaning back in my office chair. You won't believe how much Ian makes now that he's partner.

Of course, it helped that he'd had a windfall. During law school, I went with him to upstate New York to oversee the selling of his childhood home, which had sat unoccupied for a few years after his parents' deaths. The sale was thrilling to him, in that he would no longer have any law school loans and would have the beginnings of a down payment, even in a city as expensive as San Francisco. It took us almost three hours to drive to his hometown from the nearest airport, and he kept making jokes about how the flight from California was almost as long. By this point, I could tell when he was using humor to deflect from the way he was feeling, and I found his sensitivity endearing. When we got to his town, he spent a long time pointing out his elementary school, the community pool where he learned to swim. Isn't it getting late? I asked when he drove us to a baseball field where he'd played Little League. Shouldn't we call it a night and head to your place? He said, Oh God no, we're not going to stay there tonight. I booked us a hotel.

Now, I pointed my mother to the lower cabinet opposite the sink, where she stowed the brown paper bags before turning her attention to the dirty dishes in the sink, left there from the night before last. She used up the remainder of the dish soap and tossed the bottle into the recycling bin. I got up from the stool and walked over to her. As she placed clean plates and utensils on the counter by the sink, I dried them and put them away. There was a working dishwasher next to the sink, but it went unspoken that she wouldn't use it. We'd used ours as a drying rack when I was growing up in Beachwood. Then she picked up a mug with the Golden State Warriors logo on the front. Inside, a brown coffee stain ringed the middle.

"Don't wash that one," I told her.

She held up the mug, a question on her face. "Yeah, that one," I said. "He used it yesterday morning." I took it from her, holding the mug hard against my stomach. She held a hand against my neck, and I felt hot water and soap dribbling down the back of my shirt. We stayed like that for a moment before she said, "Call Mable. Tell her to come over."

I told Mable about Ian the night before. At that point I had dozens of missed calls from her, and when I called her back, she picked up by saying, Dude, I got wasted at the bar by myself waiting for you. I told her what happened, and she said she was going to come over right away so I wouldn't be alone, but I said I was going to close my eyes and then would call her if I woke up before needing to go to the airport to pick up my mom, who was landing in only a few hours anyway. When I woke up, it was almost dawn, and I was lying on the living room couch, still wearing my shoes and coat.

When Mable arrived, I let my mom answer the door. I was lying on the bed reading through all the text messages Ian and I had exchanged in the last few weeks. Most of them were brief and economical, conveying practical information. The last text he'd sent to me was "Coming home late. Start dinner without me." A few texts earlier, I'd informed him that we were almost out of dish soap. I

held my phone so my thumb covered the date that appeared above
his last message.

I exited out of my text conversation with him and opened my
messages with Mable. Before she had sent me the string of question marks the day earlier, she and I had been texting back and
forth about what we were going to order at the bar. Neither of us
ever drank anything fancy, but Mable had screenshotted the most
expensive part of the menu, as if we could order only from that section. One of the priciest wines was from 2008, and she sent a picture
of Obama's campaign poster that read: Hope. Action. Change. It's
2019 now, I had responded, and the new administration will kill
us all. You're no fun, she replied. She followed up with a GIF from
Obama's "Yes We Can" speech.

"Mary," I heard Mable say in the living room. "Hello." When
we first met, Mable had found it fascinating that I sometimes referred to my mom not just by her first name, but also her chosen
American one. She told me that I was the only Asian daughter she
knew who did that, and that her parents would find it the epitome
of disrespect. When she then found out that my mom and I spoke
to each other only in English, and that I knew little if any Manda-
rin, I braced myself. But she just said that wasn't that rare given
that my mom had come to America for her undergraduate degree,
as opposed to her own parents, who'd arrived well into adulthood.
Her nonchalance comforted me, yet another testament to Mable's
power.

"Mable." I could hear more murmurs.

The bedroom door opened, and Mable climbed into bed next
to me and pulled the covers up to her chin.

"Do you two need anything?" my mom asked, as if we were middle schoolers having a sleepover. We shook our heads.

"I'm guessing she's kept busy herself since landing this morning?" Mable asked as soon as my mom was out of earshot.

"Exactly." I thought for a moment. "It's nice to have her here right now. She's good at these things."

"Weddings and funerals, your mom can do it all."

I shifted to lie belly-down on the bed, my face flat on the pillow. Mable did the same, and we peeked at each other through our curtains of hair. "Mable," I said, my voice muffled.

"I know," she said. She was lying on Ian's side of the bed, and it was both jarring and comforting to see her face buried in his pillow. "I'm so sorry, Ellie."

"Tell me something. Anything."

"Anything, really?"

"I don't care. I can't keep thinking about Ian."

She began to recount her latest disagreement with Alex, a co-worker of hers whose signature look was a flannel shirt tucked into tapered khakis. Mable's theory was that he dressed this way in an attempt to seem both corporate and alternative. "He asked me if I knew what South by Southwest was," Mable said. "As if he was the first person who's ever fucking gone to it."

Alex and Mable were desk mates at a tech start-up where she'd been working as a recruiting coordinator. She'd been there just over a year, one of her longest professional stints since graduation, and she'd picked this particular start-up because they had a famous award-winning chef cook all their meals. This was something Mable found particularly evil. Every employee is a moron, yet they somehow get to eat nicer food than the vast majority of human be-ings in the history of civilization. She usually then launched into a takedown of tech, then capitalism, and then her belief that the human race was unworthy of living on Earth. That she worked for a tech company was something she didn't mention, and I often wondered if she had moved to San Francisco and gotten this job in order to get more firsthand evidence to bolster her dinner party arguments about the state of the world. How could the engineers or product managers have anything to say in response when she was there, too, working on the inside?

I listened to her story but not really, more the sound of the words. Or, really, her voice. Mable's voice was my favorite thing about her. It was a rumble of a thing, a car engine that woke you up in the middle of the night.

That voice was the first thing I knew about her; my ears met her before my eyes ever did. Freshman year at Northwestern, my roommate dragged me to an a cappella concert. Twenty minutes in, a group of frat pledges behind us had begun chanting obscenities to the soloist performing. Show us your tits, show us your tits, they screamed. After a few seconds it became only the last word—tits tits tits—and then a meaningless syllable. The singer started crying but stayed onstage, and it seemed as if no one was going to do anything until we heard something that sounded like a pack of hounds. But it was a voice. The boys didn't stop, and then the voice began to get louder, shouting and cursing so much that eventually the the-ater's manager was called out from backstage. Wearing a maroon-colored vest, he walked through the seat rows, calling for silence, but no one paid him any attention. When the doors opened, light flooded in, and I saw the dirty white sneaker soles of a person being dragged out by their elbows. What the fuck? the voice kept saying. I'm trying to do your fucking job.

The next day in Allison Dining Hall, I heard the voice again, this time at a neighboring table. I couldn't believe it could belong to such a small girl. She had bleached hair and was wearing a black choker. I went up to her and said, You were at the show last night, weren't you? She rolled her eyes hard. I was the one telling them to stop, she said, and yet I'm the one who gets thrown out? Does that seem fair to you? No, I said and introduced myself to her. She said: I'm Mable Chou.

We hung out almost every day after that. It turned out that she lived in the same dorm as me, although the walls of her room were almost completely covered in posters, pictures cut out from magazines and newspapers, even some pages from books, their passages underlined so heavily it was hard to read the text. The only clear surface was the ceiling. My room, on the other hand, was neat and orderly. I thought I had been discerning with my bedspread, picking a dark pattern that conveyed some sort of edge instead of the cream- and pastel-colored sheet sets that my mom kept pushing on me. But when I saw Mable's room, it felt obvious that all my choices had been made standing in the aisle of a department store. Our outsides, it seemed, matched our insides, and Mable's were much more interesting. She was from Northern California, a suburb called Saratoga, a place that seemed exotic to me because it was in California, no matter how much she denied it.

Mable, I soon realized, was always engaged in a debate, discussion, or disagreement. The first few months of our friendship mostly consisted of her turning to me and saying: Don't you *agree*, Ellie? I have trouble remembering what I said back; it felt unremarkable. Once, she missed a day of classes in order to continue an argument with an anthropology major in our dorm who had asserted that the only books worth reading were nonfiction. The problem with you, she'd told him, is that you think being contrarian gives you a personality. But it doesn't. I'd heard her say a variation of this to people who talked about being able to live only in New York City or some other coastal metropolis. Each time these conversations would start, I would remain rooted in place, my duties well defined, as if she were a boxer and any moment she would need me to give her a water bottle, a fresh towel to wipe her face.

At some point it became clear to me that we weren't exactly hanging out together, more that I was following her around and she let me. I felt like an observer to her life, and almost felt compelled to take notes, as if I were a ghostwriter on assignment. She had strong beliefs about seemingly every subject, and possessed the kind of knowledge that set apart her opinions from the kind of well-intentioned but ultimately naive ones usually held by college students. She was intimidatingly smart, to the point that I worried about taking the same classes as her. It felt impossible to imagine her anywhere but at college, or someplace in which she was only responsible for talking about abstract ideas, like the only role suited to her was a philosopher-king in ancient times.

In her view, everything had some sort of flaw or intractable issue. Name any industry, political party, idea, argument, or even person we knew and cared about, and Mable would lay out their problems with unnerving clarity. When she was finished, you had to admit to yourself that her arguments were sound and logical, that getting an MBA was likely morally void, and so on. Being around her always reminded me that nothing was good enough, and while she never said anything directly to me about my own choices, I couldn't help but turn this attitude inward.

I, on the other hand, had spent my whole life being called "good" by teachers, and "nice" by classmates. During my freshman year, I found myself frequently being asked to dinner by classmates I wasn't particularly close with when their family was in town, because I was the kind of person who could talk to anyone. I spent that year sitting next to a lot of grandparents. And the thing is, it's not that I didn't feel like I had anything important to say. I actually felt like I always had things to say. The problem was I thought too much about when and where to say them, and by the time I had decided, the conversation had usually moved on. When I became friends with Mable, people naturally compared us, and my square-ness became even more stark. It just felt easy for me to slip into this role, as if I had been waiting my whole life for her to bring me into focus. At times, I would ask myself whether this was really who I was, or just who I decided to be because it was there, like someone had left an outline of a personality for me on my bed one morning and I slipped it on without another thought.

• • •

At dinnertime, my mom left to pick up takeout from a place just a few blocks away. "Seventeen dollars for an appetizer?" she'd said before putting on her coat. When she discovered there was a delivery fee, too, she told me she'd get it herself.

While she was out, Mable convinced me to take a shower and put on new clothes. When I came out of the bathroom that adjoined the bedroom, my hair still hanging limp and wet in the middle of my back, she said, "You look different." She was sitting cross-legged on the bed.

I was wearing an old pair of Ian's boxers and one of his T-shirts. I said, "They're Ian's clothes."

"It's not just that. Your hair, too."

"I didn't brush it."

"It's tangled," she said. "In all my years of knowing you, you've never left it like that."

"You sound like Mary," I said. Before she could respond, my phone rang. I immediately recognized the number as belonging to the police department.

"Do you want me to get it?" asked Mable.

"I can do it." I turned my head so I was no longer facing her and picked up and said hello.

"Mrs. Anderson? I'm calling from the San Francisco Police Department."

"Oh, yes. Right. Of course," I said.

"You called me to get details from the police report on the accident." I could hear faint office noise behind him: someone talking, a phone ringing. "With your husband," he added.

"Yes."

"The accident occurred in the morning, close to eleven a.m. Looks like he was driving about twenty to thirty over, and visibility wasn't great. Also, because of the rain from the day before, the road was slick. Not ideal conditions."

Ian regularly drove eighty mph or higher on the freeway. I walked to the doorway even though I had no intention of leaving the room.

"Where was it, exactly? Where did the accident happen?" I asked.

"Exit Fifty-Two, on Two Eighty North."

I closed my eyes thought back to the last time I'd used Exit 52, which I almost always took to get back to the city. Two Eighty was one of the freeways that connected San Francisco to the southern part of the Bay Area. Almost every time I'd been on it these last few months was during rush hour, when the cars were going barely above twenty mph.

"What?" I asked. "Can you repeat that?" I was now facing Mable, who had swung her legs around to me. I could see the whites of her eyes.

"North, Mrs. Anderson. Two Eighty North."

When Ian made partner, his already packed schedule became even more hectic. Every Sunday morning, we would have what Ian called "our week in preview." We'd tell each other which nights we'd be home and what time, if there was any window for us to see each other before heading, bleary-eyed, to bed. From the past Sunday's week in preview, I knew that he had no in-person client meetings this week. There was no reason he would've been anywhere besides the office, let alone on a freeway returning to the city.

The police officer was still speaking, telling me something about the state of the car. I felt my body sliding onto the carpet, as if an invisible force was pushing me down by my shoulders.

Mable crouched down next to me. "What's wrong?" she kept saying. "What is going on?"

I hung up the phone and told her.

"Well," she said. She opened her mouth again and then stopped, so her lower jaw hung in the air, open enough that I could see her tongue.

"Well, what?" I didn't wait for her to answer. "What was he doing down in South Bay? I mean, we go there sometimes on weekends. But it was a workday."

"Does he have a client down there?"

"I don't think so, but I guess I could be wrong."

"Could be," she said. "Maybe his schedule changed last minute. I don't think you need to torture yourself about it."

"I can't believe you, of all people, are saying that," I said. "I need to know. I can't just not know."

She was now fully sitting on the floor next to me, and some water from my hair had dripped onto her feet. "Okay, then. If you have to know, you have to know."

Chapter Four

Debra was Ian's administrative assistant at the firm. Or as she said, his "secretary." I disliked that term, and Mable hated it, but it was Debra's preference. I'm of the generation that doesn't care about that stuff, honey, she told me once. She had coiffed chin-length hair with a deep side part, and a wide face with two blue pinpricks for her eyes. She owned a closetful of solid, jewel-tone dresses that went to the middle of her calf, and always kept a cardigan draped over her chair because the office was kept at a cool sixty-eight degrees. Ian told me that once when the firm hosted an outing in Napa Valley and everyone was in shorts and sandals, she wore shiny pantyhose.

The first time I met her, I'd just moved back to San Francisco from DC, and had dropped by Ian's office one afternoon. She cupped my face in her hands and exclaimed, Eleanor! Ian gushes about you. You seem marvelous. I breathed in her scent, a mix of hairspray and something sweet, and I wondered whether Ian had asked to work with her on purpose. I thought maybe he missed his mother.

"Debra? It's Ellie Anderson," I said when she picked up. When

Ian had been rushed to the hospital for an emergency appendectomy a couple of years ago, he'd given me her number so I could let her know.

"Oh, Ellie." Her voice was already breaking.

"Listen, I was wondering if you could tell me something." Mable was still next to me on the floor, and I gripped her hand. "Did Ian have a client meeting in the South Bay yesterday morning?"

"Oh—oh, Ellie." There was a long pause and she said, "It's only been a few months since your wedding." She was crying now. "The last time I saw you two together."

"I know, I know." I didn't know how long I could hold my focus without getting caught under her wave of grief. Mable squeezed my hand harder. "It's important. Can you tell me?"

There was another pause filled only with her raking breaths. Finally, she said: "It's all my fault, Ellie. I'm so sorry."

"What do you mean?"

"I mean, it's my fault that he's gone."

"You mean you sent him down there?"

"No, I mis-calendared the partner meeting at eleven. I had meant to make it bimonthly, but I screwed up. They just updated that version of Outlook and I didn't realize—the command changed."

"What? The partner staff meeting? Isn't that in the office?"

"I just didn't put it on his schedule for the day and didn't realize it until ten forty. I called him right when I realized it, because he wasn't there, and he said he'd be right over. And I—"

"What do you mean he wasn't there? He wasn't at the office?"

"He said he was running an errand for you. Something about how you were sick and needed a prescription picked up?"

"He said I was sick."

"Yes, that's right."

I dug my nails into Mable's palm and let out a small sound, almost as if in agreement.

"Are you mad at me?" Debra asked. "I'm so sorry. I understand if you are, I—"

"No, of course not. Really." We exchanged a few more phrases before I said I had to go and hung up.

"You weren't sick," said Mable.

"No," I said.

"Could he have been confused?"

"No."

By then my mom had gotten back with dinner and had knocked on the door. In the dining room, a plate of still-steaming stir-fry in front of me, I sat listening to my mom and Mable talk. Oddly enough, the two of them got along very well. I think she saw my friendship with Mable as something amusing and harmless, while Mable treated her as if she was the subject of a study that she'd just been given a large grant of money to complete, with no strings attached.

"Any new prospects?" my mom asked her.

"Prospects?" Mable said. "What do you mean?"

"In boyfriends."

Mable laughed, her voice deepening the way it did when the laugh came from her belly. "Oh God, wait until you hear this one," she said. "The last guy I went out with works at some organization that's supposed to dismantle the capitalist tech industry." She paused and said, "We aren't together anymore."

"How long did this one last?" asked my mom.

"Six weeks?"

"Six weeks," my mother repeated. "And did he dismantle the tech industry?"

They both laughed and Mable said, "If he did, he didn't do a very good job. Apparently they wanted their organization to be completely flat. No bosses, no hierarchies. No way for anyone to implement any decision or be effective in any way."

"How's your new job, though? Ellie tells me you're a recruiter at a company here."

Not bothering to stop chewing, Mable said, "It's boring. Stupid. But it gives me the headspace to focus on my writing."

"Have you had anything published yet?"

"No," Mable said.

"I thought you were working on some project—I can't remember what Ellie said. A short story, wasn't it?"

"I told you I wasn't sure," I said to my mom, trying to keep my tone, even though it came out stern.

"I'm working on a few of them actually," said Mable.

"A series, then?"

Mable wiped her mouth with her napkin and said, "Maybe. I don't know."

During this exchange, I made sure to hold my face so it conveyed no emotion. Mable rarely, if ever, spoke about her writing, and as a result, it was a subject of fascination for anyone close to her. In college, I sometimes had seen little scribbles of her almost illegible handwriting on her desk when we lived together starting sophomore year. But these things didn't seem altogether serious to me; it felt like this was just the part of her that came hand in hand with being so intelligent, the way that some professors in the microbiology department were also fantastic violin or cello players, or ran marathons in their spare time. It didn't ever occur to me that writing was something she needed or wanted to work at.

This writing project of Mable's seemed relatively new, something she just started mentioning in the past year or so. All I knew was that she considered it a series of related stories, but nothing more. When I dared to ask her about it, she'd only say that it was "shit," and that they were "stories." Soon, "Shit Stories" became a shorthand between us.

"Ellie?" said my mom, now turning her attention to me.

I didn't look up from my plate, but she continued.

"I spoke to some people today about the funeral arrangements. I can have it done at that funeral home just a few blocks from here, but I stopped by earlier, and I don't know how I feel about the pictures they showed me." She took out her phone. "I took some pictures of the flowers and coffins if–"

"Mom." I pushed back my chair, as if I was about to leave.

"You need to make some decisions."

I shook my head. "I told you already, you can decide. About everything."

For our wedding, I'd let her take over everything, too busy at my new firm to care that she was so pleased to arrange flowers, create seating charts. I had no doubt that she still had the number of local florists handy, maybe even a caterer.

"But what about what he should wear? And where he should be buried?"

"We made all these decisions months ago, remember? We told you." I had insisted on squaring away end-of-life decisions before the wedding. So romantic, Ian had said, two lawyers about to get married figuring out in precisely what circumstances they'd be willing to die. I grinned, because it was funny then. Do not resuscitate, we both checked. We set up a trust to avoid probate court, and joked about forgetting everything we'd learned in Property Law.

"Still, you're going to have to do some things. I don't know where to announce the details, so people can come. Also, figuring out who should speak, all of that." My mom began to pile up the used plates. I had taken at most three bites of my food, and I pushed my almost full plate over to her.

"I don't want to," I said.

"Ellie, come on."

"I can help," said Mable.

Before my mom could say anything else, I told them both I would pass along the document Ian and I had created. Mable left soon after that, and when she said goodbye, she hugged me and whispered in my ear: "Don't worry, we'll figure it out together. Promise."

The next day, she came over early, and she and my mom sat side by side in the dining room, going through the document together. Mable had brought her laptop, and at times my mom would reach for it, squinting at the screen. A couple of times, they called me in from the living room, where I sat watching television, the channel turned to a network that was playing reruns of a popular reality TV show. They'd ask me to confirm a decision, until they realized I had little to no opinion on anything. Mable found our wedding guest list from only a few months ago and read aloud to my mom the names of those closest to us both, as contenders for funeral speakers. My mom wrote them down and then checked that we still had their contact information from sending the wedding invites. When they left to go to the funeral home to finalize everything, I realized I'd been on the couch for at least six hours, still in my pajamas.

The funeral was the next day. That morning, I came out of the shower to see that my mother had laid out a black dress I'd never seen before on my bed. I was grateful. I felt like I was a child again, putting it on, followed by the earrings and necklace she'd carefully placed next to it. The shoes were at the foot of the bed. By the time I was fully dressed, I realized everything was new. She must've purchased a full funeral outfit for me when she was out with Mable yesterday.

I'd told my mom I wasn't prepared to speak and she understood. A few of Ian's friends from home gave short remembrances, as well as two colleagues from his firm. The whole service, I could feel everyone staring at me and I didn't care. Mable and my mom eventually pushed me into a chauffeured black car that took us to the gravesite, the place Ian and I had picked out just a few months ago. I cried and cried, and when they put him in the ground I ran up to the coffin. I wanted to bash my head in or grab the mechanism that lowered his body, so I could feel each piece of cartilage in my fingers smash open.

The reception was at our place, and for about an hour I sat on a couch while people lined up to say things to me. I found that each conversation went more quickly if I gave them my hand and they could hold it for a moment. I could then signal that the exchange was over by pulling my hand back to my lap. After each person passed, they stood around the living room and kitchen, where caterers my mom had hired passed around food and plastic cups of wine. My mom was by their makeshift bar, helping to hand out drinks to passersby. Small piles of white cocktail napkins had been placed on the dining and kitchen room tables, end tables, and the kitchen counter. Soon semicircles formed that corresponded with people Ian and I knew from every stage of our lives: college friends, law school friends, friends from work.

An hour or so into my receiving line, a white woman with a long, slicked-back, low ponytail approached me, wearing a dark suit. I'd seen her at a Women in the Law event just a few weeks before.

"Cat," I said. I knew I must've said her name in a different tone because Mable, who was sitting next to me on the couch, perked up for the first time since the line had started.

"I'm so sorry about all this," she said.

"Oh," I said. "Yes, it's a lot."

"He was really wonderful." She hunched over and for a moment I thought she was going to hug me. But instead she began to cry.

I nodded, but realized I hadn't given her my hand and thus had no way of ending the interaction.

Mable said, "Can you remind me where you know Ellie from?" Her voice was a pitch higher than usual, which I imagined she thought came across as kind or sweet. To me, it sounded almost sarcastic.

Cat shook her head and said, "No, no. I'm the one being rude." She gestured to where a few of my close friends from the firm were standing by a tall bookcase, all of them in dark suits that I'd seen in depositions and courtrooms. "I heard our colleagues talking about it, and I wanted to come. I hope that's okay."

"So you know Ellie from work," said Mable. She hadn't dropped the pitch of her voice.

"We worked together on a case over the summer," I said, nodding at Cat, whose breath had become more even. "Our flight to LA got canceled at the last minute, and we had to drive all the way down to make it for a deposition."

For some reason, this memory set Cat off again. "Ellie was so nice to me," she said. "It was my first time taking a deposition, and she was my second chair. She didn't have to offer me the opportunity to take the deposition. She could've done it herself, but she gave it to me."

Mable handed Cat a tissue from the coffee table.

"It's okay," I said. "It's been a lot today."

Cat nodded and then said, "It was nice to see you, Ellie. I'm so sorry again." She leaned in once more, this time to hug me. When she did that, all I could think about was how different our bodies felt. She was soft in a way that I wasn't. I had the absurd urge to ask her whether if it was because her mom hadn't taught her to scrutinize the way her legs and stomach looked under fabric, like mine had. This thought led me to imagining Cat's mother. I wondered what this person would do if her daughter, who was single as far I knew, got married and widowed within the same year.

When Cat finally rose and walked away, her ponytail swung back and forth like a pendulum.

After the line receded, I took a break on the small balcony off our living room. Ian and I had opened a bottle of champagne out there the day we moved in. The sun had just been setting, and it was one of those rare evenings in San Francisco when it was still warm outside. We could see the rolling hills in the southern area of the city, the multicolored houses dotting them like flowers. The champagne bubbles had made me feel like I could've fallen straight off the balcony and down to the street below.

I'd only been standing there for a few minutes when the door clicked open behind me. It was Jim, a senior partner at Ian's firm who'd championed him to the other partners. Ian had been mesmerized by him.

"How are you?" he asked.

"You know," I said. "Just thinking about jumping off."

"Oh," he said. He was holding a plastic cup of wine that was stacked on at least four other empty plastic cups.

"But the thing is, if I did, I would probably only break a leg. We're not high enough for any real chance at death." After a moment I said, "I'm just kidding."

"Well," he said. "It's undoubtedly a terrible time. I do wish you all the best."

How many emails has he sent in his life with the words "All the best" above his name? Corporate-speak was probably the only way he knew how to convey emotions. I made a mental note to share this thought later with Mable as Jim and I talked a bit about the service, and he told me how impressed he was with so-and-so who said such-and-such. I nodded along, pretending to care.

"I think some of them were on their phones," I said. "The lawyers. I saw them checking email during the service."

"Well, that's fucking rude," he said loudly, making a slashing motion with his right arm. "I can't believe that."

I shrugged. He said, "Do you know who did that? Because I'm happy to say something." He rubbed his hand on the side of his face, where he had a five o'clock shadow. One of Ian's female colleagues once told me her theory that Jim thought not shaving made him look rugged. His lips were stained red from wine.

"I don't know," I said. "It's okay, though."

There was a long pause, and I could tell he was searching for words. "Like I said, it was a lovely service."

"I know."

"Really lovely."

"Right."

"That first speech, by Ian's friend Roger."

"You liked the story about Ian playing Little League."

"I did, I did." He leaned against the railing, and when he did, his suit jacket became unbuttoned. His dark green tie was now free to blow in the wind.

"You know, you can always come to me if you need it. Ian used to do that." He fingered a loose thread on the sleeve of his shirt.

"Okay," I said, and nodded. "Thanks."

"He was a great guy, Ian. We were saying that all yesterday. There was no better guy than him. Got along with everyone."

"Yes." I shifted my weight from one leg to another. "I think a good number of your colleagues came. They're all still inside."

He took a step forward toward me, and I saw a glint in the air, his wedding ring catching the light above the door. It moved toward me and then onto my shoulder. It moved up and down and then back up again. He was caressing my forearm. I thought about a nature program I had seen a few weeks ago. They had shown a fox's bloody paw in a hunting trap and explained that animals would gnaw off their own limbs to save their lives. It hadn't struck me at the time but now it felt like the most reasonable, wise action any living being on the planet could make.

"Friday night? We could grab dinner. Talk more about him," he said.

"Maybe. I'll let you know."

"Come on. I'll make reservations somewhere downtown."

"Not sure if I'll be in the mood to go out."

"Of course, I get it," he said, and paused briefly. "I could come here and bring you takeout? A night in?"

I took a step back. "What are you doing?"

"What?"

"Yes, what are you doing?" I was proud of how easy it was to make my face impassive.

"I don't understand the question. I'm just trying to be there for you."

"Like at The Battery?"

The Battery was an exclusive social club located in the financial district. Ian's firm had hosted an event there in June, soon after we'd returned from our honeymoon. I had worn a short dress, and I remember Ian telling me how proud he was to have me walk in with him. I preened. Later that night, after we'd each had too much to drink, Ian went to use the bathroom while I waited by the door. Jim sidled up to me and put his hand on my lower back as he made small talk with me. I'd seen his wife moments earlier, still seated at a table. I could've easily moved away from him, but I didn't, and I even leaned into his body. When Ian came out, it was as if his hand had never even been there.

Inside our Uber home from the event, the only light was a small halo emanating from the driver's phone. The driver had said nothing when we got in, only turning up the music, some kind of EDM, too loud to make ourselves heard. Sitting down had raised my hemline a few more inches, and I slid Ian's right hand between my legs. He was surprised, I could tell, and he leaned into my ear to say something. I couldn't hear but I knew it was a question, so I nodded and told him, Yes.

On the balcony, Jim seemed to start to understand that I had no interest in him and I could see him trying to backtrack. "The Battery? What's that supposed to mean?"

"You know what it's supposed to mean," I said. Mable would've had a better response, but it was the best I could come up with. "Don't act stupid," I added.

I tried to push past him to the door, but he didn't move. There was no path to leave without touching his body.

"I'm just trying to be nice, and you're acting like I'm some kind of creep."

"He's barely cold in the ground, you know."

His face began to take on a pinkish tinge. Blotches appeared on his skin, making him look almost speckled. I thought of how he had come out on this balcony, thinking that he had a chance, that I would've been taken with his splotchy face, and I began to laugh. It was the first time I'd been able to since Ian died, and the sound came pouring out of me. I grabbed the railing and gasped with laughter.

"You're obviously not in a good place right now. You're not well," he said. This only set me off further, and my sides began to hurt. My face ached. I hoped I looked like a maniac.

He leaned toward me so that his face was next to mine. I could see now that the red wine stain covered only the middle portion of his upper and lower lips. The creases were still pale pink. "You know he was with someone else this entire time, right? He was pretty open about it with me."

I was no longer laughing, but my body suddenly seemed too light, as if I could float away at the next gust of wind. I clutched the railing harder and let out a few short breaths, then finally said, "Oh."

"You think a guy like that didn't have other choices?"

"No," I said. "I don't think that."

He opened the door and left the balcony. He didn't close it behind him, and Mable was standing on the other side of the door, talking to someone. She caught my eye and came outside, shutting the door behind her.

"What's wrong?" She had her arm around me. "You don't look like yourself."

I told her what Jim had told me, and by the time I was finished she'd led me to sit on the small outdoor couch Ian and I had bought just a few weeks ago.

"Oh my God," said Mable. She repeated that phrase a few more times.

"What do I do?" I finally got out.

She looked at me for a long time. "I don't know."

Chapter Five

I saw him on the first day of law school orientation. There was a happy hour thrown by the faculty, and I was standing by the bar with a woman I'd just met in my section. It being California, the event was outside. The sun was just setting, and we had to shade our eyes to talk to each other.

He was leaning against the building, his left foot tucked over his right in what looked like an uncomfortable position. He wasn't talking to anyone, just observing, but it was obvious to me how nervous he was. I could see a tan line on his neck, a band of red peeking out of a blue shirt. He must've recently gotten a haircut, since the skin just above the tips of his ears was slightly lighter than the rest of his face. His hair was dark blond, almost brown.

He wasn't looking at me, but I was looking at him.

"Who is he?" I nudged the woman. "I didn't see him at the other events."

She shrugged. "I think some people from the waitlist just arrived this morning. He must be one of them."

I had become aware of his existence only a minute before, but I felt that I could imagine his entire life outside of this moment. I could see him eagerly waiting for an update on his status, refreshing his inbox in the hope of an email from the admissions office.

I saw him for the third time later that week in the library, huddled over a stack of books. The second time had been the day before. He'd still been moving boxes in and out of Munger, one of the law school dorms. For some reason if you held the door of Munger open for longer than a minute, the alarm would blare incessantly, even if it was the middle of the day. I was near the end of my run when I saw him bent over, holding the door open while trying to shove a large, half-open cardboard box inside. I kept my feet moving, running in place, and asked if he needed any help. No, he said, but we sure know this door is secure now, hahaha. Yes, I said, we'll sleep well tonight. Safe and sound. He patted his hand against the door, which was still screaming. I put my fingers in my ears and pretended not to hear him. We both laughed, and then I waved goodbye.

"Hey, there," I said, having approached his table in the library. "Did you move in all right?"

He looked up from his Criminal Law textbook, and I could tell he was surprised to see me. Highlighters in a range of colors lay in a row next to the open page. "Yeah, but my eardrums may never recover."

Up close, he was even more handsome. He had one of those faces that my mom would've called "classic Hollywood" and that Mable would've called "boring."

"That's a tort, right?" It was a stupid joke, and I thought of what Mable would've said if she'd heard it. Really, Ellie? I could imagine her saying. And to that guy, of all people?

But he nodded. "Intentional infliction of emotional distress. Has to be. Why else would they make that alarm so loud?"

"Well, for the security. And besides, didn't you choose to keep that door open? That's your own fault."

"Okay, I fold." He grinned, and when he did, I noticed a few faint white spots around the bridge of his nose, and a thin white line on each temple. They might've been from sunglasses, or maybe he usually wore glasses and recently switched to contacts. The image of him standing at his bathroom mirror, a lens case open on the sink, felt more important to me in that moment than anything else that had ever come before in my life.

A few days after that, we discovered that we had the same Civil Procedure professor, albeit in different sections: he had class in the morning, and mine was in the afternoon. For weeks we remained friendly, chitchatting whenever we ran into each other late at night in the library, or in the morning purchasing coffee from the stand near our class building. Isn't it weird how much Professor Sim clears his throat? Did you get caught in that rainstorm yesterday? These morning conversations always took place between the time we ordered our coffee and the time we finished pouring in the cream and sugar. I began to take my time with that step, as if I had to make sure my coffee was properly mixed before I could even consider taking a sip. Sometimes I would look for a napkin, or an extra stirrer—illusory tasks performed to keep the conversation going. We discussed only light topics, and for a while I thought nothing more would never happen. Once, his hand brushed mine when he handed me my coffee, and I lived off that touch for days.

Two months into the fall quarter, however, I was sick in bed with what felt like an interminable cough when I saw an email from him. *Hey. I saw you haven't been around. Here are my notes from civ pro today.* It had been several hours since his class had met, and I wondered if he'd taken the time to pretty up his notes, cleaning up punctuation and clauses before he emailed them to me. I opened the document and, even in my exhausted state, I felt a rush of adrenaline. I had a window into his mind from the hours of eleven ten and twelve thirty that morning. What did he think when they discussed that case? Did he agree with the outcome? How had he known I was sick? Did he ask around about me?

I was halfway through the notes when I noticed something. *World-Wide Volks. v. Woodsen, 444 U.S. 286—established minimum contacts/personal jdx for corp if fair play and substantial justice exist.* I checked the notes I'd taken the night before while I was doing the reading. And then, to be safe, the casebook. He was wrong. That holding applied to another case. I scrolled farther down in the document and noticed that a later case's holding had been swapped with the earlier one. I pulled up tomorrow's list for the cold call, a classic law school educational technique in which a professor would call upon a student at random and interrogate them about a case in front of the rest of the class. This professor was nice enough to list the potential cold call pool of students for each lecture, but he also never missed an opportunity to grill a student, even if it meant spending most of the class on one person while the rest of us watched. Ian's name was the first one on the list. I debated it for least an hour before starting to compose an email.

Thank you so much for thinking of me. I really appreciate it! I added an anecdote about how I'd been missing our professor's assortment of tweed jackets. *I couldn't help but notice a small clerical error, something I do all the time! Just wanted to make sure you didn't get mixed up tomorrow in class.* I pointed it out, and thanked him once again. When I reread the email for the third time, I added a few more exclamation marks. And then another story about how I, also, had made the same mistake, even though it wasn't true.

I didn't receive a response that night or the next morning, and began to panic.

"Should I not have done that?" I asked Mable over the phone. She was living in New York then, and it was almost noon her time. "I don't want him to think I'm annoying. Or aggressive. I guess in a way it's rude for me to correct him after he did me a favor?"

"Of course not, Ellie." I could hear faint honking sounds in the distance. "Let's not have a repeat of Jeremy." Jeremy was a serious boyfriend in college, and even though we had broken up senior year and I had dated other people since then, Mable still held a grudge about him.

"Jeremy just needed to figure his shit out."

"The shit he needed to figure out, Ellie, was how to treat you like an actual person. You know, the same species and of equal intelligence, et cetera."

"Come on, he wasn't *that* bad."

"Jesus, are we doing this again?" I could imagine her on the other end of the line, scanning the news while we talked. She was working as a temp then, with a different employer every couple of months: a large bank, a series of publishing houses, a nonprofit. Mostly, she found the jobs boring, looking forward to spending most of the day scrolling social media on her phone and using the office's computer to read entertainment gossip. She was obsessed with TMZ, E! Online, *People*, and the *Daily Mail*. You've got to have the lowbrow to have the highbrow, Mable said. I contain multitudes. In college, someone we knew said they felt celebrity gossip contributed to the downfall of the United States, to which she said, It must be exhausting to have to perform your intellect all the time.

Mable said, "Forward me the email you sent him." I obeyed, and waited for the pinging sound of the email notification on her end. "Ellie, my God. If he gets offended by this, he's delusional. It's insanely nice. Too nice."

"I know, I know. It's just I don't want to come off as—"

"You don't come off as anything. Besides, if he can't be corrected by a woman, then fuck him."

I cleaned my room, distracted myself with television. Every time I was away from my phone or computer, I felt my resolve deepen. I finished up the rest of my reading for the week, taking care to use the color-coordinated highlighting system I'd devised. Blue for holdings, or the case's ruling, green for facts, and purple for case analysis. I made dinner with my roommates, did my laundry.

I forced myself not to check my email until the next day, proud of how long I'd held out. His name was in bold, a new message at the top of my inbox. *Good catch. I'm so glad I fixed that before class. Obviously I'm going to need your help studying. Are you busy tonight?*

His response was better than good. It was fantastic. I called Mable in a frenzy to tell her. Good, she said, though he doesn't sound as smart as you are. At that point, I couldn't have cared less what she said. He wanted me, all of me, including my mind. He wasn't Jeremy.

On our first date, the waitress messed up my order, a fillet of salmon. "That's not what you got," Ian said, pointing at the steaming catfish tail in front of me.

"Don't worry," I said. "I don't mind at all."

But he called the waitress back over. "Not your fault," he said in a soft voice. "Must've been a mix-up in the kitchen."

She smiled and so did I, and after she had taken my plate away and I'd repeated that it really wasn't a big deal, Ian looked me straight in the eye and said: "You deserve to get what you want." It undid me.

At the beginning of dinner, we discussed the classes we were taking, some of our classmates, and a bit about our future plans. Then he asked me about my childhood, and I told him something I hadn't yet told any other person in California: that my father died before I was born. He, in turn, told me about how he'd lost both his parents and that, like me, he was an only child. A brief silence passed between us before we started eating again, and it was like we had crossed a threshold together, made a mutual decision to cross a gate side by side.

When we walked back to his car that night, his hand shook when he held my face and leaned in toward my lips. He seemed so vulnerable, I felt like I could've cried. I thought about the small number of people who had seen this side of him. When we finished kissing, he immediately looked down at the ground, and I remembered feeling powerful. By the time he caught my gaze again, I felt I could live inside his eyes forever, transformed into someone I always wanted to be.

From that point on, everything was so easy. That's what I re-

member the most about that time, how easy it was to be with him.
He was charming and playful, qualities that made him immensely
popular in our class. For Halloween parties, he would dress up as
one of our professors and give a fake lecture, to the delight of all
the guests, who stood listening, their plastic cups in hand. It was
amusing but not at all mean. Ian wasn't like that, I remember thinking; he isn't mean. He never crossed the line, never mimicked the
female professors or the minority professors, of whom there were
only a handful anyway. It was always the old white male professors,
the ones who were stodgy or difficult or who seemed to take pleasure in cold-calling and catching someone off guard. And even
then it was gentle, a joking homage.

Being with him, I knew I seemed more amiable than I really
was, more interesting and funny and sociable. You're so lucky, other
women in our class would say to me, Ian seems so *nice.* I would shrug
and tell them that we had as many issues as other couples—garden-
variety ones, disagreements over how to load the dishwasher when
he would stay over at my dorm, differing preferences for movies
and TV shows—but inside I glowed. Yes, I am lucky. Yes, he *is* so
nice.

Near the end of our first year, I found myself in a Contracts
study group made up of eight of us who spent equal time studying
and meandering off topic. For one session, we were all on the floor
or couch in my dorm's living room, the coffee table covered with
snacks. I was wearing dark gray sweatpants I'd bought at the law
school bookstore, and half of the white letters spelling out "Stanford Law" on my right leg were covered in the orange-blue dust of
Cool Ranch Doritos. The discussion turned from which professors

we thought had the most fascinating personal lives to the sex lives of our classmates. Soon we decided that we'd each individually list the hottest people in our class, and then share the list with the rest of the group.

"Are we doing this alphabetically?" I asked.

"Of course not," said Kelly, who, like me, had gone straight to law school from undergrad. We frequently commiserated about spending the first half of our twenties in such a traditional environment. She scrunched her face so that her glasses looked too big. "What a stupid question."

For a few minutes there was only the sound of everyone typing out their lists, the key-clacking punctuated with snorts of laughter. We then each took an oath that nothing, absolutely nothing, would leave this circle. Such was the bond of classmates who were subsisting solely on Kettle chips, Lay's, Ruffles, and Doritos. Josh, who had spent the last few years as a naval officer, made us swear on a half-used roll of paper towels, while I drafted a mock NDA. Then Kelly clapped her hands together and said, "Well, what are we waiting for?"

One by one, we read our lists aloud. Ian had made the top of everyone's list of men, and he was the only entry for Susan, a bookish, quiet girl who wore the same pair of white Keds every day. Susan had almost unnaturally porcelain skin, so pale that you could clearly see each fork formed by the blue-green of her veins, and when she said Ian's name a deep blush raced into her face, the dumping of red Kool-Aid powder into water. She turned to me and quickly said, "Obviously this doesn't mean anything."

I shook my head and waved a hand. "Don't even sweat it," I said. "He's number one on my list, too."

In the meantime, finals permeated every aspect of our lives. We shuttled between the dorm, the classroom, the library, and back to the dorm. During our first year at Stanford, we'd rarely gone off campus, and anyone and anything outside the sphere of law was put on hold. People had stayed home during the holidays to get ahead on finals. Besides Mable, I'd drifted away from many of my friends outside of law school.

Few people say this about that time, but for me, law school was where I found my home. I excelled at it. The linear thinking suited me, as did the rigor of the schedule. I found it natural to engage in legal analysis, to draw inferences and conclusions from the thousands of pages of cases we needed to read every month. I earned awards given to the top students in each of our subject classes. A professor asked me to help him research a white paper.

For Ian, though, it couldn't have been more different. He made frequent mistakes, his struggle with details an almost fatal flaw in a discipline that required perfection. Ian also had trouble saying anything besides a regurgitation of the basics of any case: facts, procedural posture, holding, dicta. He struggled with any higher analysis, and he had no new ideas. He'd talk to law professors for hours in their offices, trying to ingratiate himself. He always seemed to be engaged in some effort or campaign to receive a higher grade.

I can memorize anything, he'd once said to me. But I can't go beyond that. It's a problem. This isn't at all a problem, I had said. You won't need this type of skill outside of academia, out of certain legal jobs you don't want anyway. He had tried to agree with me, telling me that he wanted to work at a firm. Besides, I'd told him, you are the most popular person in our class. Beloved by everyone. He had shaken his head at this and said, Not the professors. They like you, not me.

My only exposure to the world outside of law school was Mable calling to tell me about her life, always with a story. One man texted her back only when it was convenient for him. She eventually found out she was the other woman. Another confided to Mable that some of his female colleagues had approached him to tell him they were sick of him stealing their ideas and talking over them in meetings. Can you believe that? he had said to her. She said she could, and they broke up. And one man had begged to see some of her writing, and she had finally relented, sending him something that was only a few pages long, a very short story from several years before that she no longer cared about. I had felt jealous of this guy when she told me, but I didn't have time to think about it because of what happened next. He waited almost three weeks to read it, and when he did, he had sent her back a blank email with a single attachment. It was her document, with edits in Track Changes.

Then there was the white guy who seemed to be so nice and so good until he told her he'd only ever dated Asian women. They're the only ones I like, he had said, shrugging. What's wrong with having a preference? Discussing this point, of course, Mable and I were vicious. When we were finished, there was nothing left of his memory except for a few streaks of blood.

By then, Ian and I were a couple of years into our relationship, and any issues I had with him seemed small in comparison. I felt

lucky next to her. Facing this sea of undeserving men seemed impossible. Her description of the awkward sex, the lacking one-night
stands, made me appreciate Ian's affection all the more. The truth
was that all through college, when our group of girlfriends talked
about our sex lives, it sounded like we were all persuading each
other—and ourselves—that we were having good sex. There was
a lot of nodding along, like we were in some sort of group therapy circle. Mable was the only one who was honest about it, and
we were all relieved. We weren't stupid enough to think it was supposed to look like it did in porn, but it also wasn't at all like any
movie or song or book we'd encountered and that discrepancy
was confusing. It wasn't that it was *bad*—most of us enjoyed it and
wanted more of it, always. All the same, though, we were nineteen
or twenty, and it often felt like sex was something that was largely
more pleasurable for men.

But the first time I slept with Ian, I felt like I finally understood,
that if he asked me what my name was during sex, I wouldn't be
able to come up with the answer. It seemed clear to me that I should
devote the rest of my life to making sure I could feel this way whenever I wanted to. Once, when he was inside me, I told him that I felt
like he had taken my virginity. I was embarrassed when the words
came out of my mouth. But then the look on his face made me feel
like I could have asked him to do anything and he would've done it
twice over and then asked me for more.

I told Mable about the sex I was having with Ian, but the only
thing she said was that women always had better sex as they got
older. I agreed with her but still thought he was deserving of credit.

After graduation, Ian found that grades, after all, had meant nothing. He excelled at his first-year firm job. He was smart enough to get by, and charm and the ability to get along with everybody was key in the world of corporate law. This power he felt at work seemed to project itself onto me, too. Even from thousands of miles away, his charm worked its way through the phone to DC and inside of me. I was funnier around him, more cheerful, more enjoyable to be around. He could make the weekends we spent together feel drenched in possibilities. I wasn't in his shadow, I got part of his spotlight.

After my clerkships ended and I moved back to San Francisco, I was submerged in the new Ian, whose time at the firm had allowed him to sharpen and perfect himself. Debra loved him, telling him all about her lunches with the other assistants, the ones in which they railed on the attorneys. The partners trusted him with their gossip, even turned to him for advice. He was the golden boy, the one every partner wanted to work with and every associate tried to emulate. He got the plum assignments, flying across the world to take this expert's deposition, or to make this oral argument. They were grooming him for partner, and he knew it.

He even looked better at this point, as if his body was readying him for ascent. He now had money for a personal shopper. He began working out every morning, something that he said cleared his mind. He found someone he liked to cut his hair, and he went back every few weeks.

In San Francisco, I chose a prestigious law firm that had a reputation for being filled with lawyers from top schools and clerkships, and joined the general litigation section, thinking I would eventually find a passion and specialize in it. But a few months into the job, it was obvious I was barely getting by. The happy hours, the schmoozing, taking an interest in the partners' lives—I was not only uninterested in it, I was inept at it. I would blow off firm events so I could go back to my desk, miss lunches with partners so I could eat alone in front of my computer, more worried about my work product then getting to know anyone. I'd forget so-and-so's daughter's birthday; I'd mispronounce the name of some luxury destination that the client had just visited.

I knew that I should look for something else, but I had never quit anything in my life, and it felt nearly impossible to do so now. It's not that I'm not doing well, I told myself, it's just that I need to work harder. A couple of years passed. It turned out that inertia was an easy position to maintain. Plus, the firm had a name that made people pause at cocktail parties, look at me differently. I imagined that all of us were walking around with flags, ready to unfurl when someone asked us what we did for a living. The firm's flag was a burden to carry around, but the idea of another, lesser flag felt intolerable. I knew of classmates who were happier at nonprofits, academic gigs, and smaller, less competitive firms. But nothing paid better than the type of firm I was at, not even in-house law jobs at tech firms, and San Francisco was mercilessly expensive. I conveniently ignored the fact that after Ian had sold his family house, and we had our combined firm salaries, we had easily paid off all our student debt. Once Ian was a partner, I would say, I could leave and find something I was actually good at. When he did make partner, I told myself that I should wait until he had earned at least one year's salary. Then we bought our home, and I decided internally that I would leave when we paid off half of the mortgage. In the meantime, I never applied to anything but had informational lunches with my classmates at legal aid societies or on tenure tracks. All of these ideas were buoys I could barely make out, floating in the faraway distance.

It was during this time that Ian proposed. At the Village Pub, a Michelin-star restaurant we had been going to once a year since law school, he got down on one knee with his eyes wide open, so ready for my response. He was smiling in that way that reminded me of the first time he had kissed me, when his hand was shaking. A man behind me gasped and a woman began to cry. I felt like I would never die, that I would live forever.

Chapter Six

At breakfast the day after the funeral, Mable announced to my mom that she and I were planning to go to the spa in the afternoon, a cover story we'd come up with on the balcony the day before. Mable had ended up sleeping over after the reception, spending the night in bed on Ian's side, as my mother had taken the guest room.

"What a good idea," my mother said. "That's exactly what Ellie needs."

I felt guilty knowing that this excuse would work on her, but telling her the truth meant telling her what Jim had said, and I wasn't ready to do that. I needed time to figure out exactly how I wanted to present it to someone else. Mable, of course, didn't count as someone else.

As a child, I discovered there was a small list of topics that were safe to talk to my mom about: mainly shallow things like clothes, design, exercise, and foods that were low in calories. Even when I got older, things like current events, relationships, or my dim view of the firm, I imagined, would only be met with judgment. My phone calls home to her lasted at most twenty minutes. When I started dating Ian, he was added to the list of safe topics, mainly because my mom took to him so quickly that it felt safe to talk about him to her. I remember when I first realized that Mable talked to her brothers about her favorite books and movies, her political opinions. It was a shock to me that a family member could take so many roles in one's life: friend, confidante, sparring partner. It's not like I could do this with my parents, Mable said once when I told her how I envied her intimacy with her brothers. You know as well as I that you can't do that with Asian immigrant parents. I do know that, I said, but I don't think the reason my mom and I don't talk like that is that she's an Asian immigrant.

Around three in the afternoon, I finally put on a worn pair of leggings and a large sweater. I wiped off my makeup from the night before and tied my hair up in a ponytail. We said goodbye to my mom and went out to the garage. Mable was driving, and as she adjusted my car's driver's seat and mirrors to her liking, I stared out into the empty space of the garage where Ian's car usually sat.

"You really think she might've been involved with him?" Mable asked while we drove to the financial district. Late last night, when my mom was asleep, I had convinced her that investigating Cat was the right thing to do, and it had been so odd, me persuading Mable to do something illicit and not the other way around.

"It doesn't make sense that she came to the funeral."

"Maybe it's just that you meant more to her than you imagined."

"Outside of the time we worked on that case together, we've spoken maybe once. And I'm sure it was only about work."

"You said she liked to ask you for advice. She might've seen you as some sort of mentor figure."

"I guess that could be true," I conceded, even though I was doubtful.

We pulled into the parking lot of my office, and Mable started circling slowly. Because it was after the lunch rush, none of my colleagues were around, which was a relief. I didn't want to have to explain to anyone why I was there the day after my husband's funeral, instead of at home taking the firm's generous bereavement leave.

"There it is. That one," I said, and she pulled up to Cat's green Prius.

I'd often seen her rolling up to the firm in this Prius, almost always parking as close to the exit as possible. Her car had a bumper sticker on the back that said: COEXIST, different religious symbols placed to look like letters. Mable noticed the sticker, too. "What *is* it with white women?"

"What isn't it?" I said.

"What kind of name is 'Cat' anyway?" Mable was always fascinated with names, probably because she hated hers. I think my parent wanted to name me Maybelle, she explained to me when I first knew her. But they messed it up. Now I'll forever be Mable, like table, she would say.

"Is Cat short for Catherine?"

I shook my head. "I think it's just Cat."

"So her parents are idiots then."

"Must be."

Mable turned off the car engine, but her phone was still playing a Phoebe Bridgers song through the car's speakers. We talked again about Jim, and Mable made me reenact his arm-rubbing again. I was getting good at it by now. "Fucking perv," she said. I remembered my insight about his email sign-off and told her. Then she asked me to show her how he'd touched my lower back at the holiday party. I told her I felt guilty about this one, since Ian had been there and I hadn't moved away, and in fact had enjoyed it.

"Whatever," she said. "You're still a woman, even if you're married."

"I know, but it's not the same when you're married. You're supposed to tell each other these types of things."

"The way he told you about his affair?"

Over the past twenty-odd hours, the news started to seem easier and easier to accept. It was the same feeling I had when I decided to call the police department for details about Ian's death. It was cold and vague, but it was there; I couldn't deny its existence. But it's not like I had thought he was cheating on me when he was alive.

"Why do you think that is?" I asked Mable after I elaborated this to her.

"That you just knew?" she asked. I nodded. She gave me a funny look.

"*You think a guy like that didn't have other choices?*" I repeated.

"Plural."

"I noticed that, too. *Choices.* But I don't think that's right. He barely had time to sleep. He had just made partner at a law firm, for Christ's sake." I paused for a bit to take off my seat belt. I had taken off my shoes already and now I hugged my knees into my chest. "Maybe Jim was just saying that because I'd just rejected him."

I told her to pull up ahead a bit so we'd be farther from Cat's car. I had worked with Cat long enough to know that she liked to leave before the worst of the commuting traffic, drive home, and then log back on to work for a few more hours. I knew that Cat lived outside the city, but I wasn't sure where, and our firm's internal database didn't list any addresses. As if on cue, at four o'clock sharp, she exited the parking lot elevator and walked toward her Prius.

"Damn, you're good." Mable said. From my side mirror, I watched Cat get into the car, and after a moment, I gestured for Mable to follow her.

After exiting the parking lot, we followed her on the local roads, Mable gritting her teeth in concentration. Even though there wasn't a ton of traffic, the financial district was still busy enough that it would've been easy to lose the Prius, and it took about twenty or so minutes for us to get through the worst of the city.

Depending on Cat's next turns, we could've been getting on the highway that took us from San Francisco to the East Bay, meaning she lived somewhere like Oakland or Berkeley. But then she turned onto the exit for 280 South. Mable said nothing, just pulled off behind her and kept her car in our sights, which wasn't hard given that the highway was pretty empty. Mable's phone was now playing some top 40 hit I didn't recognize. I turned it off, afraid the heavy bass beat would launch me into a panic attack.

After about twenty minutes, Cat turned off at an exit for Pacifica, a small, picturesque sea-side city where I'd been only once, hiking with Ian. I had forgotten a hair tie and had to use a rubber band we found in the car to keep my hair off my neck. This memory made me feel sick, so I rolled down the window and stuck out my head, not even worrying that Cat would see me in her rearview mirror. The air did me some good, and by the time we saw her turn into the driveway of a small ranch house, my stomach felt more settled.

Mable pulled up to the curb a few houses down the block, and we watched Cat get out of her car and unlock the house's front door. "Well," Mable said, then paused. "I know this isn't the point, but I can't believe she can afford to buy something here. Didn't you say she had only been at your firm for a year? She just graduated law school, right?"

"It must be family money or something," I said. "I know she mentioned once how lucky she felt because she didn't have loans."

Mable had loads to say on the topic of generational wealth, but instead of launching into it, she said, "What do we do now?"

"Pull into the driveway."

"You sure?" she asked, but she had already put the car into drive. I could tell that she was just as angry as I was. Her left hand was clutching the steering wheel hard, her chipped dark green polish accentuated by the whites of her fingernails. She pulled off the large jacket she'd been wearing, tossing it into the back seat as if she was preparing for a confrontation in which she would need full arm mobility. She pulled into the driveway, and I got out of the car. I rang the doorbell, and when Cat opened it, her face told me everything I needed to know.

She began to cry, wiping at her tears with the sleeve of her dress. I studied her closely, as if I had never seen her before, like she was a stranger. She looked nothing like me. She was small and soft, like a baby animal. She had issues speaking up in firm meetings, and I had coached her once on raising her volume. You'll never come off as shrill, I said to her. I thought of how, on the way back from LA, she'd told me how intimidating she found me at first. She was acutely aware, she said, that the firm didn't usually hire from her law school, which was routinely on the bottom of the first page of law school rankings. You did two clerkships, she went on, her eyes comically large. I told her that no one cared where she went to law school, even though we both knew that was a lie. I felt embarrassed by how flattered I was by her comments.

And then I remembered that the night when Ian had first met her, at my firm's most recent holiday party, he'd turned to me and said he was surprised she'd been hired. Good for the firm, he'd said, the culture has got to change.

"I'm so sorry, Ellie," she said. I pushed my way in and Mable followed, shutting the door behind us. I was in her living room. The room was filled with colors I would've never used, dark purples and mauves. There was a forest-green accent wall behind a large TV. An overstuffed couch sat next to a black coffee table that looked too small for the room. For some reason, her difference in taste from mine made me furious.

I began to scream, knocking books from a nearby bookshelf onto the floor. I walked into her kitchen and opened and closed cabinets, as if I was looking for something. I emptied out cupboards, threw cans of food onto the floor. I shouted, said nasty and foul things. Did you two fuck here in this room? What about here? Fucking slut, fucking homewrecker. It was a litany of swears and any horrible thing I could think of.

She took it silently. Her head was bowed, and her arms were crossed against her chest. I could see her stomach heaving under the dress. I didn't care. I wanted to hurt her more than I could even comprehend. I wanted her to suffer in unimaginable ways. I began to pull out entire drawers and empty them onto her floor, pushed a vase off her kitchen table. I reveled in the sound of it smashing against the floor. Mable stood with her back to the front door, never taking her eyes off me. When I started toward the bedroom, she walked over and grabbed my arms from behind.

"Come on, Ellie."

Something in her tone of voice made me stop. It was stern but also kind; I knew she agreed with everything I was doing and that she must be feeling like it was too much for Cat. For Mable, this type of pity was rare, and I knew then that I really should stop.

I relented and we headed back to the living room, where Cat was now crouched on the floor. She looked like a puddle. I stopped and stood a few inches in front of her.

"Tell me how long. You owe me that," I said.

She didn't look up and I saw her steadying herself with one hand on the floor. "How long?" she asked.

"You know what I'm asking."

"Since March." Her voice was small. "Two years ago." I wanted to scream at her to speak up.

"How is that even possible? You hadn't met him until this past December, at the firm's holiday party." Even though I was standing above her, my voice sounded like a child's, thin and pleading.

"I interviewed at his firm in my last year of school. He was in my second-round interview," she said. "I didn't get the job."

Two years ago in March was before we were engaged, only months after I had come back from DC.

I'd seen a bathroom off the living room and I ran to it now and threw up, heaving three times over the toilet bowl. Mable held back my hair for me. When I was finished, I walked out through the front door, not bothering to look back at Cat.

"Bitch," Mable said when slamming the door shut. I knew Mable despised that word, hated what it meant to women. I was glad she used it.

Chapter Seven

A day later, I'd decided I was going to tell my mom about Cat. Are you sure? Mable asked. I wasn't, but I also knew that there was no way I would be able to get through any more days of pretending that I was experiencing a more uncomplicated grief. The choice was either to tell her, or to impale myself with one of the plastic knives we had accumulated from the last few days' takeout.

Do you want me there? Mable wanted to know. No, it's better if it's just me, I said. Even though Mable was like my sister, she wasn't my mom's daughter. I didn't want my mom to say something she could never take back, and for Mable to hear her say it. I guess I still wanted to protect each of them from the other.

I told her that night over takeout from a Taiwanese restaurant in Inner Richmond. My mom complained about the dearth of authentic Taiwanese food in Cleveland, and so I had ordered it, thinking that it would perhaps somehow soften the blow. When I finished the story about Cat, she sat there unblinking for what felt like an entire minute, then finally said: "Don't tell anyone else."

"What do you mean?"

"Keep this between us. And Mable, since I'm guessing she already knows."

"Who else was I going to talk to?"

"It doesn't matter who it was, just don't."

"That's your reaction?" I had been using a fork to push food around my plate, and now I put it down and laid my palm flat against the table.

"Oh, Ellie. Of course, I feel sorry for you. Of course."

"Of course?"

"Yes, I am your mother, you know."

"Really."

"Yes, really. And listen, do you want to know *why* I think this? Because it will be hard enough as a young widow. You don't need other people, other men especially, thinking you are a widow who was cheated on, too." I wondered what my face looked like at that moment. And then she said, "I know you don't like my answer, but there it is. And that's the truth. It's something only a mother would tell you."

"You love that phrase."

"What?"

"*Something only a mother would tell you.* You said it all the time when I was growing up. If an outfit made me look fat, or when my hair didn't look right," I said. "You probably think he would've left me."

"I can't know that. You might've worked things out."

I let out a small laugh. "Worked it out? After he slept with someone else—my colleague—for years?"

"Yes. That is forgivable, you know."

"Everything is forgivable to you in a relationship."

"Right," she said. We were almost finished eating, but when she got up, it still felt abrupt. She went straight into the guest room, and I could hear her pulling her suitcase out of the closet and unzipping it.

"Mom?" I followed her and leaned on her doorframe. I hadn't yet been inside the room when she was staying there. Even now, I felt uninvited.

"It's okay." She had taken a dress off a hanger and folded it in half inside her luggage. "But I think I should go back home."

"No, stay. Please."

"I want to go home." She didn't look at me as she started to pack up all her jewelry from the counter in the adjoining bathroom.

"I see," I said. It was all I could get out.

"And Mable will be here. You'll be looked after."

• • •

My mom was able to get on a flight later that evening, one open middle seat near the back of the plane. I drove her to the airport, neither of us saying anything to the other. Eventually, I started playing music over the car speakers to cover the silence. At the curb I helped her take out her luggage from the trunk. She and I traded goodbyes, and without even checking that she had made it into the airport, I drove off.

The next morning, I decided to cut my bereavement leave short and go back to work. You know this is a sign of something, Mable said when I told her. I technically had ten more days of leave, and if

I had wanted, I could've easily asked for more. A sign of what? I had asked. Not sure, but it's not a good thing, she said.

Even when I emailed HR and my litigation team to tell them I was coming back early, they asked me if I was sure. *Yes*, I said, *a thousand times yes*. I had once heard a female character on a television show say that when a man was down on one knee, and I thought it would be a funny reply, even though there was no way anyone else would get the reference. It seemed like since Ian's death, my jokes were funny only to me.

There was nothing else for me to do once my mom left, I figured. Mable was back to her own job and I didn't want to talk to anyone who didn't know what had happened with Ian and Cat, even the many friends who reached out to check in on me. Instead, I fantasized about going back to something that was so machinelike and cold. I didn't want to feel anything anymore; my only wish was to disappear into the billable hours that were expected of me by corporate America, categorizing my movements into the six-minute increments required by my employer instead of thinking about my dead husband, who had been cheating on me.

I arrived absurdly early on the first day back at the firm, at six in the morning. No one else was there, and as I walked through the office, the motion-sensor lights flickered on in the darkened hallways. Even though the building was silent and it was barely light outside, I closed my door when I got to my office and drew the shades.

I turned on my computer and checked my email for the first time since Ian died. My inbox was full of condolence notes from the outgoing summer associate class. Earlier in the year, in February, I had volunteered to be the associate lead for the summer associate class. My job was to make sure they each had an enjoyable summer, so that if they were offered a place at our firm by the end of the ten weeks, they'd accept. Even though the associates were technically interning for us, it was mostly a cushy recruitment program. When Mable heard I had signed up, she had said, Why? I thought you said the only lawyers who did that were the ones who actually had a chance at making partner. I'm a confused overachiever, I'd replied. I don't know when to give up.

I scrolled through their emails and then pulled up the messages I had sent the summer class starting in early June, when I had gotten back from our honeymoon. I reread my welcome email to them, and the subsequent ones from throughout their ten-week internship at the firm. Our class was composed mostly of second-year law students, many of them who were just a few years younger than me, and they were paid close to four thousand dollars a week.

The majority of my emails to them included links to memes, viral posts, and articles about pop culture. More often than not, I used GIFs. I'd spent a great deal of time on each email, trying to force a relaxed tone on everything I was announcing, whether an upcoming long weekend or a request for work via a partner. Some emails took me almost an entire day to compose, and I would minimize the draft every few hours to attend to other work, only to return to it later and reedit my message. When a particular email was giving me trouble, I'd pretend to be Mable.

Rereading the emails now was excruciating. The worst ones were when I thought I had been funny. I could only skim those. As I read some of the longer emails, I used my cursor to highlight certain phrases I'd used, and cringed at them. When I was finished with each email, I deleted it, then went to my Trash folder and permanently deleted them all.

Eventually, I made my way to the top of my inbox and spotted a message from yesterday evening that Cat had sent to the entire litigation team, announcing that she would be working from home full-time for a few weeks. She'd sent this email only a few hours after I'd told HR I was cutting my leave short and heading back to the firm. Our firm had never required much face time if you satisfied your billable-hours minimum, but it was still odd for someone to work fully from home. I imagined her lying to her case teams about why she couldn't come into the office anymore. I thought of a few of the more aggressive partners pushing back, and Cat lying even more.

I left my office and walked down the hallway to Cat's office. I stood for a few moments in her doorway, taking a long look at her empty chair.

A few days into my return to work, I got an email from someone in HR from Ian's firm. It seemed that Ian had signed up for life insurance—something he'd mentioned to me in passing but that I hadn't remembered until now—and that I was the sole beneficiary. The email was a few paragraphs long and explained how the firm calculated a new partner's worth, the forecast they'd given to his future earnings. Attached to the email was a PDF that I had to fill out, sign, and then send back to them. *After the paperwork is finalized, the money shall be transferred to the account by the insurance company in approximately four to six weeks*, the email concluded. I scrolled back up to the top of the email, and looked again at the amount I would be receiving. Ian had signed up for only the most basic plan, and although I wasn't getting enough that I could think about never working again, I could pay off the rest of our house if I'd wanted.

There was no one else for it to go to, of course. The morning of our wedding, Ian's second cousin had emailed to tell us he wouldn't make it after all. His flight had been canceled, and he said nothing about finding another. That was the only relative of Ian's with whom he was still in touch, and I realized sadly there would be no one he was related to at the ceremony.

While my mom buttoned up the back of my wedding dress, she had told me I was lucky that Ian had so little family. What is that supposed to mean? I'd asked. She ran her hands through my hair, shaking out some of the curls. I mean that Ian has no real family, my mom said.

I said, I know what you mean. I *mean*, what are you implying? You'll understand when you're older, she replied. It'll just be easier for you, that's all. I pushed her hands away. Jesus, Mom.

At the time, I had found her comment cruel and nasty. But now, as I thought about Ian breathing in Cat, Cat letting in Ian, the two of them wrapped around each other's bodies, I found it hysterical that I had been so angry at my mother just a few months ago. It was a hilarious joke: I'd defended my husband against my mother, only to find out that it was him all along who was the horrible one. The joke was on me, written by me, executed by me. I almost choked on my own spit, that's how hard I laughed.

Chapter Eight

It took only a week back at the office before I realized that something was wrong with me. I thought that I was pushing out the same kind of good-quality, if unexceptional, work I had done at the firm for the last year or so. Then Marcus, one of the partners, came to see me. I had just sent him a draft of a brief we planned to file within a few days. One of our arguments had no case law that was directly relevant, and so we needed to cobble together some sort of authority using cases that were instructive but still, technically, unrelated to the point we were trying to make. The closest I had gotten on my draft before Ian died was finding a case from 1948 that had to do with maritime law, while we were working on a securities case for a Fortune 500 company. Our team had gone back and forth about how best to frame our position, and I'd been tasked with writing the first draft.

"You all right?" Marcus asked now, standing in the doorway of my office.

"Sure."

"Really?"

"Is this about something in the brief?"

"Yes. There's something a bit odd about it."

"Was it that one section about weighing–"

"Can I come in? There's something I want to talk to you about. It's important."

I leaned back into my chair, pretending that I'd anticipated whatever he was going to say. "Come in."

Marcus was a popular partner whom I usually sought out opportunities to work for. At this point, I'd memorized the line of family pictures behind his office chair: a Halloween photo in which he and his young children had all dressed up as Marvel characters; he and his wife on their honeymoon in the Maldives; Marcus sitting in the middle of a large couch, his parents and older brothers on either side of him; he and his youngest child laughing on a dock with a comically small fish, the size of a sardine.

He closed the door and took a seat opposite me at my desk. He laid a copy of the draft brief in front of me. "Take a look, Ellie."

I glanced through the document for a few seconds before I realized there was something wrong with the connection between my eyes and my brain. Specifically, that I was having trouble comprehending any of the words on the page. I knew I was reading–that is, I could feel my eyes running over the words. But my brain wasn't processing them. I understood each individual word, but not the way they were arranged.

"I'm sorry. I'm not feeling very well. I can't seem to make any sense of this. Maybe I have a fever or something." I put the back of my hand on my forehead, the way my mom would when I was young, but my temperature felt normal.

"Ellie," he said, looking concerned. "Some of the sentences . . .

they don't make any sense. I don't mean that they aren't strong arguments. They don't make sense, full stop."

I gripped the sides of the paper and tried to compel my brain to make sense of the words, like forcing myself to dry swallow a pill. *Plaintiff requests firmly for remedy to court.* I blinked and tried to reread the sentence. I couldn't tell anymore whether it was my inability to read, or his suggestion of my inability to write, that was troubling me.

"I'm— I— I don't know what to say." I stared straight down at the paper. I had a feeling that if I looked directly at him, I would start crying.

He pulled the paper gently from my hand. "Look. It's only been a little while since Ian died."

I looked up. "You think this is related?"

He shrugged, but his face gave me the answer. "I know you decided to cut your bereavement leave early and come back to work. But maybe that was a mistake. You should consider taking some more time for yourself."

"I was just having an off day, I think, when I wrote this. It was late. I hadn't slept. I haven't been sleeping."

"Think about it."

Now that my mom was gone, the house was empty during the day, though Mable was still staying over every night. "That's kind of you, it is. But I really don't think it's necessary."

"Would you be willing to reconsider?"

"It's just one brief. We have plenty of time to rewrite it."

"It's not just this one."

My face made itself into a small knot, and I knew that if I made any movement at all, it would be undone. I thought Marcus would look uncomfortable, but instead he just seemed very sorry for me. This made me feel worse, and then I actually started to cry.

"I'm sorry. I don't mean to get upset," I said.

"It's okay, really. No big deal."

"Everyone must've been redoing my work. And not even telling me." I let my hair fall in front of my face. I had already forced myself to accept that I would never be a star at the firm. But I had never been bad at my job before.

"Nothing that was too terrible. Besides, we just get to bill more to the client, right?" He gave me a small smile. Marcus had laid his phone on my desk when he sat down, and it lit up now with a notification. His phone background was a screenshot of his son's soccer team photo, and it felt profoundly unreasonable that this hardworking family man should have to sit here while I apologized for my poor work product. I knew also that he was lying; there was no way the firm would've billed any client for my hours in the last week if my output was this poor.

"Listen, you don't need to decide right now. Think it over. We'll always want you around," he said, getting up to leave. He put his phone back in his pocket.

"Okay," I conceded. As he left my office, I turned back to my computer screen, pretending to get lost in an email.

• • •

At home that night, Mable lay in my bed using my laptop to search for "sudden onset of illiteracy" to see if it connected to key words like "depression," "anxiety," "grief," and "fucked-up men."

"There are some promising hits," she said after a few minutes.

"Maybe my brain decided to end itself when it learned about all that's wrong with my life," I said.

Mable didn't answer, instead focusing on the screen. Her hair was half up, one piece of it in her mouth, and she'd put her feet on the pillow next to my head.

It was an unspoken agreement that Mable would continue to stay with me, given that I needed her and that she hated the four-bedroom apartment she shared with three random roommates in the Mission. She'd found it when she moved here from New York two years ago, vowing that she would find her own apartment in five months, tops. Yet last month she had gone in with her roommates on the purchase of a couch, even though she still complained that the walls were so thin she could hear everyone's business at night.

We rarely hung out at Mable's place since at least one of her roommates was always in the common spaces and her room couldn't fit much more than a full-size bed and a dresser. A few months after she moved in, however, we were on the way to brunch when she realized she had forgotten her phone at home. We headed back to her place, and while she searched for it, I noticed that she'd placed a small café table in the corner of her room. Unlike all the other surfaces, it wasn't covered with dirty clothes or open compacts of makeup. I also spotted a folding chair that was lying flat between her dresser and the wall.

"I can't find anything totally definitive about the sudden inability to read," she said now, then paused. "But you know what I'm going to say."

"That I should look for a therapist?"

"Yes."

Mable had been in therapy for as long as I'd known her. It had been easier when she was on her parents' health insurance, but after she'd turned twenty-six, whenever she considered switching jobs, she would closely review any potential new employer's health insurance policy to make sure therapy was covered. Each time she changed doctors, either because she moved or because of a change in insurance, she and I would do extensive online research on the candidates before she made an initial appointment. Mable was very open about therapy, frequently calling me to recap after a session with her current doctor, who was based in Oakland.

"It's just, you know," I said. "I feel like Mary would find it weird."

"And haven't you spent most of your life trying prove that you're not anything like her?" She looked up from the screen at me.

"Right, I get it." I broke eye contact with her to grab the remote control from the nightstand and turn on the television. "I'll think about it, I promise. And it's not that I don't think therapy will help. I know it will. But I'm afraid what they'd say to me."

"Well, that's healthy."

"Indeed," I said. When we were in college, we had an American history professor who, though he always seemed to be half asleep, would say "Indeed" to whatever any of us said. It cracked us up then, and like many inside jokes between close friends, it persisted but mostly as a function of our former selves, a nod to who we once were. I wasn't sure whether we'd find it funny if it happened now.

I clicked through various streaming apps until I settled on a travel show that Ian and I sometimes watched. The newest episode opened with an overly tanned woman on a yacht, gesturing to a beach in the near distance. She told us she was in the South of France, and that behind her was a luxury hotel called the Hotel du Cap-Eden-Roc.

"You should really go talk to someone. Not just about Ian or Cat, but also yourself, your own life outside of them." I could feel her eyes on me again, but I just stared at the television.

"I said I'd think about it."

"I can have my therapist give me a recommendation for you. Or, if you're okay with it, you could see him, too." I imagined the doctor thinking during our sessions that Mable was psychologically more sophisticated than me, and how if it ever came up, I would have to tell him that I agreed.

Instead, I said, "I don't want to share a therapist with you."

"Then I'll get him to give me some names." She said it like I had already agreed to it.

I turned up the volume and nodded to the woman on the screen. "You think she likes her job? Traveling to all these nice places."

Mable and I sometimes created fantasy trips together. We kept a list of destinations in a shared Google document we both edited, adding in hotels or restaurants we'd read about during the day when we were bored at work.

"Probably sucks." She was now looking at the TV as well. "At some point, even this must start to feel like work."

"I wouldn't mind it."

"Me either. Would be better than what I'm doing." Mable, as far as I could tell, was still using the early mornings and evenings to write, though the most I could get out of her about these moments was a stray comment about Shit Stories. Sometimes, when I was feeling bold, I would ask her more about her work in progress than she liked. Are the stories autobiographical? Are they about your-self? Our friends? Us? But all I'd get was a sort of noncommittal answer. Once she told me that the belief that all writing was some sort of self-confession on behalf of the author was a mark of an un-serious reader. I had no comeback; I only knew that I felt oddly jealous when she spoke about her writing.

"So quit your job," I said. "You're always saying you will, and you never do it." Earlier that night she'd been telling me how much food she took home from the cafeteria, something that was explic-itly forbidden. They had a whole training session on it during ori-entation, she said, which was what had given her the idea to steal in the first place.

"I will. Right when you start seeing a therapist."

I got up from my side of the bed and lay down next to her on my stomach, my feet on the pillow next to hers. "How much do you think it would be for us to go to this hotel?"

She shrugged, and I grabbed my laptop from her to look up Hotel du Cap-Eden-Roc. I only had to type a few letters before the name auto-completed in my search engine.

"You've looked up this place before?" Mable asked.

"For our honeymoon, actually. I'd forgotten about it until now." Ian had told me about this hotel when were in the middle of wed-ding planning. I'd been in our kitchen trying to butterfly a whole chicken. I had made him stand next to me and read me the in-structions from my phone. There's this great hotel we could go to,

Ian said. He said the name aloud slowly, with a comically heavy American accent. You're going to have to say it right or the French will murder us, I remembered saying. I began slicing along what I thought was the chicken's backbone and I said, Isn't this romantic? Planning our first trip as a married couple while I dismember a carcass? In the end, we'd decided on Turks and Caicos instead.

The website told me that the Hotel du Cap-Eden-Roc was in Antibes. I was still having trouble reading for some reason, and it took me a few blinks to pull up a new browser window and type the name of the city into the search bar. "We can fly to Nice," I told Mable. "It's a short drive from there."

"Oh, so we're going, are we?"

"Yes, we are." I found a flight that left tomorrow from SFO, with a layover in Paris. The only seats left were in first class.

"That price is fucking wild," she said, looking down at the laptop screen. "Even if it's all for fun."

The woman on the travel show was now walking around the hotel's grounds. It was the kind of place where she had to say that she was walking on the "grounds," because that was how many buildings there were. Everyone around her looked famous or famous-adjacent. No one was even slightly unattractive. Soon, she was listing all the celebrities who had stayed there: A-list movie stars, models, musicians. With the mention of each name, Mable would offer a running commentary. He *would* stay there, she said, or Guess she still has money left over from that franchise.

Back on the hotel's website, I looked up the room calendar, in which you could indicate your length of stay, and highlighted the rest of September to see what was available.

"There's availability for the next three weeks," I told her. "Two bedrooms and a sitting room."

"What if I wanted more than one sitting room?" she asked me.

"You'll just have to make do."

"Indeed." We both laughed this time.

I pulled up our shared document and added the information about the flight and hotel to it. "Can you imagine if we ever did do something like that?" Mable asked. She was now watching the show more intently. "What do you think these people's tax rate is? Don't answer that. Not high enough is the answer. Fucking criminal, really."

"Do you have your passport? Is it more than six months before it expires?" Mable turned her head slowly to stare at me.

"You can't be serious."

"I am."

"I know you and Ian had money, obviously," she said, and gestured around the bedroom. "You own a house in San Francisco. But this is a whole new level. And for three whole weeks?" She pulled the laptop toward her. The cost of the hotel was such that even a weeklong stay would take us into the five figures.

"Ellie."

"What?"

"This is completely unreasonable."

"So?"

"So?" She sat up now. "You're starting to sound like me."

"Is that a bad thing?"

She grinned hard. "I don't think I'd be a good friend if I told you to blow all your savings on an ultra-luxurious trip that I get to go on, too."

"It's not all my savings." I explained to her about the life insurance money. "I'll be getting it in a few weeks."

She let out a high-pitched laugh. "I can't believe you're serious about this."

"I've never been more serious."

"Why? Why do you want to do this?"

"Why did Ian sleep with Cat? Why am I a widow at twenty-nine? Let's not go down the road of asking 'Why.'"

"Okay, but what about work? You can't just take a spontaneous three-week vacation from a law firm."

"I'll figure it out. Marcus already said he wants me to take a longer leave," I said. "Like you care about my job anyway."

"I don't care about it; I care about you. And you care about your career."

"It'll be fine—they don't want me around right now. And now you have an excuse to quit."

"I guess it's not like anything is holding me back," she said. "I can always get some other entry-level gig somewhere." She also had no qualms about leaving employers with little to no notice, more than once quitting on a Wednesday and leaving that Friday.

"Right," I said. "And isn't this such a 'fuck you' to Ian? Using an irresponsible portion of the money that his firm calculated to be roughly the value of his life on some stupid vacation. Also on something as ridiculous as these first-class seats." I clicked over to the browser tab with the flight information.

She laughed. "Okay, I'm in."

"If we do it, though, it has to be soon. Leaving tomorrow. If I think about it for too long, I'll lose my nerve."

"Got it." She took the computer from me and began to fill in our personal information. "Flight leaves at noon. That work?"

"Yes," I said. I got up from the bed, grabbed my wallet, and tossed it to her. She ceremoniously took out a credit card, holding it high over her head and then laying it gently next to the laptop.

"Wait," I said. "I want to do it."

Mable moved to make room for me again on the bed, and I typed in each number on the card into the hotel website, and then the flight website. Every time I entered a digit, Mable said the number aloud, like some sort of declaration. Soon she began to chant the last few digits of my card, like it was a religious ritual.

When we had it all booked, Mable said she was going to go back to her place to pack. "Okay," I said. "But don't take too long. I might talk myself out of it."

Chapter Nine

Mable got an Uber to and from my place, and by the time she returned with her packed luggage, about an hour and a half later, we were both very giddy. I told her that I thought we might both be experiencing manic episodes, which made me wonder whether I was having a nervous breakdown. Mable said it was probably a folie à deux.

We split a bottle of wine, and Mable composed and sent her resignation email with a satisfying swoosh. "Your turn," she said to me, handing me my work phone. It was an older version of my personal one, and it had taken a few months of my being at the firm before I became used to constantly checking two phones. I'd worry about accidentally sending a drunk text on my work phone, Mable once said. That's probably the only reason you're not a lawyer, I told her.

"Well, I'm not actually quitting."

She wasn't listening, instead rooting through a drawer looking for a corkscrew to open another bottle.

I typed out and erased an email to Marcus three times, still unsure whether my words made any sense. Mable had gone into the guest room at some point, and being alone in the room was making me more anxious about the idea of taking another leave. Even though I had set this trip in motion, I didn't actually want to take time away from the firm. It made me feel untethered. It also made me feel vaguely unfeminist, as if having Ian die and finding out about his affair was now causing me to fail at my career. The firm wasn't right for me in the long run, but I still wanted to leave on my own terms, unrelated to Ian and Cat. I knew Mable would have a lot of thoughts on this, but I also didn't want to ask her for them, because I felt like I would just do whatever she said and think whatever she thought. I wanted to maintain some control over my own life, or at least, the illusion of control.

On the fourth try, I came up with this: *Marcus, Thanks again for your kindness earlier today. I've taken some time to reflect on what you said, and I think I will be fine continuing to work, although I hope to be able to proceed on a part-time schedule for the next few weeks. I will also be working remotely in Antibes, France, in the hope that a change in scenery will do me good.*

At least, this is the message I had in mind. I still didn't trust my brain to be able to write it clearly, but I hit Send before I could change my mind. I hadn't heard of any attorneys reducing their schedule after a death in the family, nor relocating to the French Riviera, but there were certainly lawyers at the firm who had gone part-time after having children. I doubted anyone would push back on my decision so soon after Ian had died.

Almost immediately, my phone pinged with a response from Marcus. *I am so glad to hear that you are taking some time for yourself. I'll let the rest of the team know of your new schedule. Below*

are some restaurants I enjoyed the last time I was in the area. Hope
you try them out, and I am wishing you all the best, Ellie.

I walked out to the living room and announced that I was offi-
cially now part-time and working remotely. Mable said nothing. It
was unlike her to censor herself, and I wondered how bad I must
seem if she felt like she needed to wear kid gloves around me.

While she sprawled across the couch, I began to pack for myself,
wandering around the rest of the house looking for shoes, summer
clothes, various toiletries. As I opened drawers and closed doors in
the other rooms, each movement reminded me of Ian.

When I was in middle school, my favorite field trip was one we
took to Hale Farm, a historical property just about an hour outside of Cleveland. I ran my hands against the sides of walls, doors,
any surface that seemed vaguely unrenovated. This person once
touched this part of the windowsill, and now I am, too, I remembered thinking. Or they once stood at this exact spot and saw how
the light came into the window. I had the same feeling as I walked
through our house. Ian was here, and there, and also here. I took
off my socks, feeling the wood and rugs beneath my feet. I ran my
toes through the loops of the mat in the bathroom off the bedroom.

If this were a museum, they could install a small plaque by our
dining room table: Site of Ian and Ellie's last dinner. Just two weeks
ago, I had met with a partner who always confused me with Brenda
Li, another Asian female associate, no matter how many times I'd
corrected him. This could've been almost funny to me, how deriv-
ative and uncreative this type of garden-variety racism was, except
that I also found myself wishing this particular partner knew me,

relied upon me, valued me. That I both hated this man and desired his attention made me feel despairing. I called Ian from a bathroom stall after the meeting, waiting until all the other stalls were empty to cry. That night, he came home early for once and spent the rest of the evening doing a spot-on impression of the partner. It was like law school all over again, except it was better because the only audience member was me.

It took me a long time to finish packing, but Mable didn't really notice because she was deep into the next bottle of wine. By the time I was done, she was half asleep.

"I'm glad you're coming," I said, taking a seat at the end of the couch and putting her feet in my lap. "I know it's asking a lot of you to drop everything."

As soon as I said this, we both started laughing. "Please," she said. "Like I needed an excuse to quit my job."

"Are you going to write while we're there?" Even though I was drunk, too, I took care to use an uninterested tone.

There was a pause and then she said, "Yep. Time to put more shit in the Shit Stories."

"They need more shit."

"I thought there wasn't enough shit. Turns out I was wrong."

"Unbelievably so."

"Wasn't at maximum capacity."

"Not even close."

We went back and forth like this for a while, until she fell fully asleep on the couch and I went back to my bed.

• • •

I woke up to a text message from the airline telling us that our flight to Paris had been delayed until the evening.

"Fuck," I said after I went into the living room to wake Mable up and tell her. "Maybe this is a sign we shouldn't be going."

"Or maybe this is a sign that flights get delayed," she said. She was already on hold with the airline to confirm we could get another connecting flight to Nice.

"I have a feeling we shouldn't go," I said, pacing the living room.

"What kind of feeling?"

"I don't know. Just a feeling."

"I think this is just the first time you're doing something that doesn't really make any sense. And it scares you." She'd put her phone on speaker and the hold music blared from it.

"Yeah, well, I'm really, really scared."

A woman finally picked up the other end of the line, and Mable began to speak with her about our connection. After she got confirmation of our new flight to Nice, Mable hung up and said, "Listen, let's get out of here. I mean, out of your place. Bad vibes all around."

I didn't think I would feel any better out of the house, but I was at the point where I just wanted someone to tell me what to do, so I got dressed and followed her outside and down the street. It was cold and foggy, and within a few minutes we were both shivering. Neither of us had thought to wear a thicker jacket. We were also nursing bad hangovers from the wine the night before, and even though it wasn't very sunny out, we both wore dark sunglasses.

"I can't just go to a random coffee shop and wait," I said, guessing what Mable was going to suggest. "I'll chew my fingers off."

We walked around the neighborhood for a bit longer, popping in and out of random shops and looking at things we didn't need. I was close to telling her that we should just go back to my place—and also that I wanted to cancel the entire trip—when she got an idea.

"Let's go to the de Young."

"You want to go to look at art? That's also kind of far."

She nodded. "It's the middle of the workday, and I'm sure any museum will be empty. And it's warm and there's a café if we get hungry."

Mable used my phone to call an Uber, and we got to the de Young about twenty minutes later. She'd been right about the crowds: besides a few senior citizens, no one else was there. The museum had a new exhibit on Monet's later years, and Mable decided to get the guided audio tour, but the thought of going at a predetermined pace through the exhibit made me feel even more panicked, so I chose not to.

At the beginning of the exhibit, I read a sign with a short blurb about how Monet had taken a self-imposed break from painting after he suffered a series of personal tragedies, including the death of his wife. These paintings, it explained, were some of the work he produced when he returned to art two years later. Also, during this period he was dealing with cataracts that impaired his vision. When I got to the end of the paragraph, I realized that this was the first time in twenty-four hours that I'd been able to read consecutive sentences without any difficulty. I took it as a sign of progress.

By the time I reached the third painting, I felt something stir at the base of my stomach. At first I thought I was going to be sick, or that it was related to my hangover, but then I realized that the sensation wasn't altogether unpleasant. It was as though someone had injected me with a tempering liquid that was now spreading through all my veins and blood vessels, mixing together with my blood and bones and making me slow and tired. I wondered whether I was experiencing a precursor to fainting. I would've asked Mable for help, but she was in another area of the exhibit, and I didn't feel capable of walking at any pace other than the one I was using now.

As I continued through the paintings, I began to feel increasingly sedated. I was so exhausted at one point that I had to stop and sit down next to an older woman using a walker. The blues and purples and lavenders of the painting in front of us blended together in the reflection of the sky in the pond. There were water lilies, too, but I focused only on the reflection. What was in the sky above Monet that day? What was he seeing? For some reason, it comforted me that we couldn't know and that the only thing we were certain of was this blurry mirror image. I had the sudden urge to touch it, to feel the canvas under my fingers. I clenched my hands, got up from my seat, and walked on.

In the next room, the colors changed to oranges and browns. I imagined Monet outside his home in Giverny, painting while the sun set. Then I thought more about his hiatus from painting. I imagined him alone, mourning his wife, his vision compromised. He must've been terrified that he could never paint again, and yet instead of testing out that theory, he forced himself to do nothing. He indulged in the pain, in some way. I wondered which painting he started first after he returned to work.

It was at this point that I realized I had been crying. The older woman with the walker had been going at about my pace, and she gave me a sympathetic look, as if she knew it wasn't about Monet at all. I avoided her gaze and went over to read a passage on the wall that described the artist's volatile moods, how he was known for slashing or burning some of his own paintings. They quoted a letter he wrote to a friend in which he described how much he suffered from his work, the pain that it caused him. I read and reread this quote many times, ensuring that I committed it to memory. *Ah, how I suffer, how painting makes me suffer!*, it said. *It tortures me. The pain it causes me!*

When I reached the last room of the exhibit, Mable was done and waiting for me. Her audio guide was fifty minutes long, so I must have taken longer than I thought.

"You look funny," she said. "Are you going to be sick?"

"No, I'm not. I actually feel better than I have in days."

• • •

That evening, we confirmed that our flight was on time and headed to the airport. When we boarded in the first group, a flight attendant took our jackets and hung them up in a small closet at the front of the plane. On each seat, there lay slippers, a small bag filled with luxury brand toiletries, and a folded pair of soft pajamas that I ran my hands across. Even though people were boarding around us, Mable took off her shoes and socks immediately and put on the slippers. After we sat down, the flight attendant introduced herself. She already knew our names, and offered us each a glass of champagne and an extensive food menu.

"Damn, did you see all the movie options?" Mable said, catching the flight attendant's attention to ask for a second champagne after downing the first.

This was my maiden voyage in first class, but Ian and I had flown business a few times, including last fall, when we had gone to London. He had needed to go for work, and my firm had a London office I could easily work out of for a week. When we had walked through the first-class cabin to get our seats, Ian had said that the next time we flew to Europe, we'd splurge. It's fine, I said, business class is already nicer than anything I've ever been in. It's not the same, he responded.

As soon as the seat-belt sign was switched off, I immediately positioned my seat so that I was lying flat, and Mable began to lean down and whisper surly remarks to me about everyone else in the cabin. Doesn't it bother you that there're so many more men than women in this category; don't you think if the plane does a straight nosedive it's fitting that we would be the first ones to die, and so on. She had bought a stack of celebrity gossip magazines at the airport, and they now sat on her lap on top of the novel she had brought.

It didn't surprise me that Mable was in an ecstatic mood. Mable loved beginnings. Quitting things always made her happy; it made her feel like she was starting over. She also liked that she was in the caretaker role, mostly because she loved me, but also because I knew a part of her enjoyed being the more put-together, competent one for once.

She started whispering about one first-class passenger who was talking loudly to the person next to him despite the silence in the rest of the cabin. Normally, I would egg her on, but I was feeling increasingly not myself, much like the beginning of our visit to the de Young. I felt tender and volatile, and worried that if I thought about anything too hard, it would make me upset.

"I'm going to try to sleep through the flight," I told her. I sat up briefly to grab the blanket by my seat and pull it over me. I turned so I was now facing the window and Mable was behind me. Before I fell asleep, I thought of how Ian had been afraid to fly, but even more afraid to tell anyone about his fear. On business trips with colleagues, he would take a Xanax in the airport bathroom before boarding. I don't think it's anything to be embarrassed about, I'd said to him; you can't be the only one. I'd read that flying was one of the most common fears around, up there with public speaking and clowns. But he refused to tell anyone except me, and for a long time I'd seen that as a good thing; I was his keeper of secrets, his chosen one. I was special.

Chapter Ten

We landed in Paris in the late afternoon and made our re-scheduled connection to Nice. I felt like a small child as Mable shuttled me through Charles de Gaulle, even buying me a snack because she was worried that I'd eaten too little on the overnight flight. On the short flight to Nice, she tried to keep me awake so that I could start adjusting to the time zone, and I felt fussy and tired like a toddler. At the car rental agency, I sat passively until it came time for payment, then felt a rush when they charged my credit card, glee that Ian's life insurance money was being drained for something as stupid as this trip. Once we got to the car, Mable took the driver's seat and reminded me to buckle up. We didn't talk much as she drove to the hotel, the reassuring female voice of the Google Maps intermittently interrupting the music she'd set up to play through the car's speakers. A HAIM song changed into a song by Drake, and then Google Maps told us to turn into the hotel entrance. "No matter where we are in the world," Mable said, "the hands of capitalism will guide us in a soothing American accent."

Before entering the hotel's grounds, we had to stop at a security checkpoint, where a uniformed guard asked our names and confirmed we were guests. We then headed down a long driveway until we reached the hotel's main building. Mable put the car in park and we both just stared. There had been teases of splendor on the drive from the checkpoint to the hotel, but now we took in its full grandeur. The cream-colored building looked to be three stories tall and was surrounded by lush green life, some of the trees and bushes full and round, others trimmed with surgical precision into sharp points. Ahead of us were two parked cars, both foreign brands I didn't know. The closer one had its trunk halfway open, revealing a set of matching designer luggage resting upon light tan, unblemished leather. Uniformed staff strode briskly and with great purpose up and down the driveway and the stairs leading to the hotel doors.

A man wearing gloves opened Mable's door. She wasn't used to valet service, and I could tell she felt embarrassed by not knowing exactly what to do, and also because she was against the entire concept of someone parking your car for you. Another set of men took our luggage silently, and we followed them up the steps of the building and through the front doors into a striking entrance room, where a large chandelier hung next to a glass elevator. It smelled faintly of lavender and citrus, and the blast of air conditioning was a shock to our systems. We exchanged brief, nervous glances while we shivered.

All the guests walking by us in the lobby were like what we had seen on television: clearly wealthy and very attractive. I thought I might have spotted a well-known model and maybe an actor, but would need to confirm with Mable to be sure.

A short man with a small lilt in his walk approached us. He was wearing a suit in a different color than the men outside, and a shiny lapel pin introduced him as JEAN-MICHEL. I wondered if that was really his name or if they had made him choose it because Americans could pronounce it. He led us both to a small couch and gestured for us to sit down, then asked for our passports, which he handed to another man in a suit, who went to make copies of them. When we confirmed that our stay was three weeks, he smiled wide at us. "Wonderful!" he said. "A long stay for two lovely ladies."

"Yes," Mable said. "We are lovely, aren't we?" Jean-Michel found that funny and began to tell us about all the luxuries we could find at the hotel, including the spa and its many services, and all the yachts, cars, and jets we could rent.

"Jets?" Mable asked.

"That's right," he said, and began to expand on the various options. I could tell Mable was remembering things to comment on later.

I sat there without saying anything. I could see Jean-Michel's eyes flicker to me a few times, like I was some sort of dangerous animal. When his colleague returned with our passports, Jean-Michel asked us what credit card we wanted to use for our charges while at the hotel. They had already charged me a portion of our stay when I booked online. I took out a different credit card in case this would exceed the limit of the other one I'd used, and said, "My husband will be paying for this."

"How wonderful! And where is he?"

"He's dead."

"Excuse me?"

"He's dead. I mean, he's in San Francisco, California, physically, if that's what you're asking. But that's his body."

He gave Mable a confused look, but she didn't give him any indication that I was kidding. She seemed amused but also like she felt very sorry for me.

After I signed a series of documents, Jean-Michel told us to wait one moment for someone who would show us to our room. As we waited, a white woman and Asian man exited the glass elevator. The man wore a fitted T-shirt and a pair of linen pants. He was tall and square-jawed, and it was obvious that he was in very good shape, his clothes just tight enough around his arms and legs that you could catch a glimpse of his muscles moving. He had a towel under one of his arms, and his Panama hat was pushed up on his forehead. It felt good to take all of him in at once.

The woman he was with had on a pair of large sunglasses over a small, pointed nose and carried a wide-brimmed sun hat under one arm. She was saying something with such great emphasis that she needed both hands to explain it. It didn't look quite like they were arguing, but it didn't seem like they were agreeing either. Her dark blond hair was pulled back into a neat, low bun, and an expensive-looking straw tote hung over one shoulder. I thought about how rich she must've been to have a designer bag that was just for the beach.

I'd thought the man and woman were both the same age, and the man looked only slightly older than Mable and me, probably barely even thirty. But when she adjusted her sunglasses, it was clear from her hands that she wasn't as young as I first thought. My guess was early forties, although her beauty did a superb job of camouflaging what I took to be a decade between her and her partner. Her sunglasses were so dark that I couldn't be sure, but I thought we locked eyes for a moment.

Despite the air conditioning, a damp sheen of sweat was forming between my thighs and between my legs and the seat of the couch. I pulled at the collar of my oversize shirt, feeling a trickle of wetness roll down my back. I didn't think anyone had overheard my exchange with Jean-Michel, but nonetheless I imagined the woman with the straw bag somehow had heard everything. I took out my sunglasses and put them back on.

"Maybe we should change our clothes," I said to Mable.

"I think we should rent our own jet every day. Except the days we rent a yacht."

"I'm serious," I said.

"I know you're already footing the bill here but . . . what's a few thousand more, Ellie? It's a rounding error at this point, really."

"Look at everyone else and look at us."

"We look fine. We only just got here. After two flights, including an international one."

"You look good in anything," I said. "It's not the same for me."

"That's not true. And you're only feeling this way right now because you're exhausted."

"I feel horrible," I said.

"Like emotionally?"

"Obviously."

The man who was to show us the hotel grounds arrived just then, and we followed him to the back of the lobby and past the glass elevator into another space that was just as intimidating. The walls were two or three stories high. Off this area was a small bar awash in soft lighting. "This would be a very fine place to have a cocktail before dinner," he said.

"Very fine, yes," Mable said. From this place, the man led us outside and began to point out the various gardens, the tennis courts, and the other buildings, in a very clear and measured manner, like a docent in a museum. One of the buildings he showed us was small and could be accessed only by using a large, medieval-looking key that opened a glass door rimmed with gold. The carpet inside was thick, as if we were the first people ever to walk on it.

As he led us down the hallway, I was struck by how such a vast piece of land could feel so intimate and secluded. Once we'd driven past the hotel's security checkpoint, the memories of the neighboring town were completely smudged out. I thought of how Mable and I had waited in line at the airport bathroom in Nice behind a woman and her three young children. All of them had passed around a travel-size plastic Kleenex packet, picking out a tissue and blowing their noses one by one. The shape of this memory seemed irregular to me now, and I wondered if they had ever existed at all. It seemed ridiculous that Mable and I had ever stepped foot inside an airport, utterly preposterous that earlier that day we had ever seen anyone who wasn't gliding by us on a manicured lawn, a sweating drink in their hand.

It was impossible not to notice the hotel guests. They were all stunning. In the lobby, at the bars, walking the hallways, the clientele hailed from various parts of the world, but their differences disappeared in the face of their great commonality: spectacular wealth.

Our guide told us he was now going to lead us to our rooms, which were located on the third floor in the main building. He and Mable had not stopped talking once during the tour, and I could tell he wasn't just laughing because he needed to be polite. She'd somehow been able to make cracks about the other guests without being offensive, and made it clear that she was on the side of the staff without saying so directly.

Our rooms were composed of a large suite and a connecting bedroom. The suite had two bathrooms and a sitting room, and the adjoining room had its own bathroom. The pictures online hadn't done it justice. The rooms were much more luxurious and beautiful than either of us could have imagined. As the man showed us around, I nodded along, pretending like I stayed at places like this all the time.

Mable touched everything he showed us, petting the robes, as if testing out the quality, and opening and closing nearly every drawer. She undid the shutters and poked her head outside. They were now chatting about the places the man liked to frequent in the area, what he considered to be the best cocktail at the hotel bar, while I remained standing in the middle of the sitting room, as if I had found something about the space really interesting.

When he left, we both stared at each other.

"Jesus," said Mable. "This is really fucking nice."

"I know."

She walked into the connecting bedroom and threw herself onto the bed. I walked into the main suite and began to unpack, all the while listening to her go on about how soft the bed was, how the pillows were a dream. She described the feel of the slippers she was trying on, and her voice felt comforting, like the white noise of the beach.

"There's no Bible in my nightstand," she said.

I checked mine. "Me neither."

"Well, what really would've been the point with this crowd? There's only one place they'll go, really. Or should I say, we'll go." She pointed toward the carpet.

I know she was trying to make me laugh, so I managed to get something out, although it sounded like a cough.

When I'd finished putting a few things away and changed out of my travel clothes for the hotel robe, Mable said it was my turn to open and close all the drawers and shutters and doors in the rooms. I want you to really experience it, she explained. She found the spa menu and read aloud to me about all the different massages and facials and wraps and soaks we could have.

"You can do a lot of things with caviar," she said. "I mean, not just eat it. You can have it rubbed into your skin."

"Mmm" was all I could get out. I was feeling more and more tired, and I wanted to think it was jet lag, but I wasn't sure.

"Do you think they use the same type you can eat?"

I said nothing and climbed onto my bed.

"Come on, Ellie. Let's go outside." She was sitting on the edge of my bed, and again I felt like her child, but a sickly Victorian-era one. I just buried my head deeper into one of the pillows.

She tugged at my shoulder, but I didn't look at her, just said: "I'm exhausted."

"You slept on both of the flights."

"It's the time difference."

"It's almost dinnertime here, so it's morning in California. You should feel awake. Don't go to sleep, so you get used to French time." When she said "French time," she waved her fingers.

I didn't respond, and Mable said, "Are you okay? Should I ask them to get you something? An Advil? Or whatever the equivalent of that is here?" She said "Advil" in a comically French accent.

"It's okay. Just go out. Try the bars and tell me which ones are good. Make friends, all that stuff you're good at."

She protested for only a few more seconds before getting up. "Come find me if you want dinner, okay?"

I nodded.

I was able to sleep for only a few hours, but I stayed in bed even after I woke up, breathing in the cold, recycled air. The air conditioning was on too high, but I didn't get up and change the thermostat. I could hear the faint opening and shutting of doors, someone cutting grass outside. When at least another hour had passed, the sun began to set and the streams of light that had made their way through the window shutters started to fade. Soon the sounds and the darkness took over me, and I felt like I was in some sort of meditative state. I thought of Ian, Cat, my mom, and myself. I actually was thinking about myself a lot more than I really ever had, and soon it felt like I was standing over my own body, taking impersonal but exacting notes. Here lies the subject, in a too-expensive bed, making some sort of statement about her dead husband. How unoriginal and uninspiring she is, and how much should we pity her when she already pities herself so very much? I sat up briefly, untying my robe and throwing it onto the ground. I lay down again and burrowed back under the covers to hide my body from the view in my mind's eye. I was shivering harder now. My narrative voice began to get crueler, and I let it. She will blame her mother for it all, won't she? Now there was a group of individuals, all made up of me, all commenting on me. They were a hostile group, and the subject was something they had grown weary of, I could see.

I tried to shut out the voices, and the only way I could do it was to think of Ian. My whole body yearned for him with such a fervor that my skin felt painful, itchy. At the same time, I was ashamed that I wanted him, that I missed him so much. I wanted badly to grieve, and yet I also hated that I wanted to, given what I knew. I felt like my body was trying to split in two: one half that stayed in the past, was ignorant of Cat, and could be nothing but the widow; and the other half that could think only of Cat and betrayal, that felt a small but distinct sense of pleasure that he had died in large part because of his affair. Somehow this sense of having two Ellies was very much real, as if I had never before been alive in quite such a definite way.

I checked the time on my phone when I heard the door to Mable's adjoining room open. It was close to one in the morning, and Mable was trying to be quiet but was doing a terrible job at it. I wondered if she was drunk. Soon I heard nothing, just the silence of the night. It was a while before I finally fell asleep.

Chapter Eleven

I woke up before Mable the next morning and took a shower, and by the time I was done, she was awake and on the sitting room sofa. I waited for her to launch into a recap of last night, but she said, "Let's go get breakfast first. I'm so hungover."

I started to go through my clothes, but Mable handed me one of my T-shirts and a pair of denim shorts that were purposefully unhemmed and slightly unraveling. She was wearing a similar outfit. "We'll change into real clothes later," she said, "but first we need sustenance. Jean-Michel didn't tell us about any dress code for breakfast, anyway."

Breakfast was served in a building at the end of a wide gravel path just opposite the lobby doors. To get there, we walked past a terrace where guests could order drinks and look at the ocean that the guide had showed us the day before. Mable was unusually quiet, and I realized that she was as awestruck by our surroundings as I was. The only sound was the soft crunch of gravel beneath our sandals.

No matter where you stood on the gravel drive, the view was stunning: the ocean on one side and the main building on the other; the tennis courts placed in the middle of the rich lawn; the curated greenery and trees that flanked the sides of the path. That morning, the sky was mostly clear, except for a few clouds that were so fluffy and thick they were almost cartoonish. The air was warm and gentle against our skin. I ran my hands through my hair, still damp from the shower, so I could feel the wind against my scalp.

When the path ended at the ocean, we turned to the right and entered another, smaller cream-colored building and went to the second floor, where breakfast was being served in a partially covered area. A man asked us for our room number and names and then led us to an open table overlooking the sea. He took our drink orders, and after Mable confirmed twice that breakfast was included in the cost of the hotel room, she ordered two teas and a coffee.

"Very good," he said neutrally. He had no reaction to anything she said, including her questions about money.

When he was out of earshot, she leaned toward me. "'Very good.'"

We headed to the buffet tables in an adjoining room, and as we filled our plates, Mable leaned in and asked me if I could believe, like really believe, that there were this many types of eggs and bacon and cured meats and croissants. At a table with platters of fruit, she almost squealed at the angular pieces of mango, laid out like some sort of modern painting. She loaded up her plate with almost half of the mangoes on offer, ignoring the other guests, who were openly staring at her.

The sound of the waves drowned out the low music from the hotel speakers, and I began to feel optimistic that I would like it here. I imagined my feelings about Ian and Cat evaporating from my skin on our walk to breakfast, and then being gently deposited at the mouth of the ocean.

This was the first time when Mable and I could really study the hotel's clientele. Most everyone staying here was white—something Mable remarked upon yesterday—and a good portion of them American. She'd tried to make me guess whether the other guests would identify us as visitors from America or China. There's no right answer here, I'd said. Obviously not, she said.

There was no dress code for breakfast and yet there seemed to be unspoken rules that everyone else knew. All around us, guests were dressed in white or off-white, and even though it was already very hot out, the only other people in shorts were small children. A baby at a nearby table stared at us, the puckered sleeves of her white dress waving back and forth like a flag of surrender.

"I knew we should've dressed up for breakfast," I said.

Our waiter returned with the drinks, then gestured to the menu and asked if we wanted to order anything.

"Food?" I asked. "I thought it was just the buffet."

"No, those are just some sides, if you want some. But you can order something off the menu. Most guests do." He took great care not to look at our plates, which were piled high with pastries and fruit and meat. Mable had even placed two hard-boiled eggs on top of a chocolate croissant.

"I think we are fine for today," she said. "But tomorrow. Tomorrow, be prepared." She flashed him one of her signature smiles, and he gave us a low bow and left, smoothing the white napkin that hung over one arm.

Mable finally started to tell me about the previous night. She had met a man at the bar and gone to his room. He was much older, she said, in his sixties, and had been wearing a bow tie.

"I can't make this shit up," she said. "A real-life bow tie out in the wild. With no sense of irony."

"Is he here?" I asked. "At breakfast?"

"He was checking out this morning, actually." She smoothed a dollop of deep red jam onto a piece of toast.

"Oh, that sucks."

"No, it's actually why I decided I was fine sleeping with him. I didn't want him hanging around the rest of our trip."

"So you knew he was leaving before you slept with him?"

"Yes. He told me everything about his life: his kids don't talk to him, the people who work for him don't appreciate him, et cetera, et cetera." She took a bite of her toast and then began to load more jam onto it before taking another.

"What does he do?"

"What do any of these people do? I'm sure he just moves money around and tries to look important. Anyway, I was pretty drunk."

"What was his name? Do you remember?"

She shrugged. "God, I'm just so glad he was leaving. It would've been a nightmare otherwise."

I could tell she was waiting for me to agree with her, but I didn't have much to say on this point. Mable and I had extensively covered her love life. She had a string of boyfriends in college, none of them lasting longer than a few months, and all so different that the only thing they had in common was her. Different majors, looks, personalities. It's like she was trying each person to get just a taste of their outlook on life, only to find it boring or stupid a few weeks later. One of her longer relationships in college was with a tall Literature major with a shaved head who'd told me between beers one Sunday afternoon that he felt reading obscure works by some even more obscure author fed him even more than food did. Mable and I had shrieked about it for weeks after.

"I know he's flying back to London," Mable went on. "So I guess that'll be my first clue when I have to track him down to tell him about the pregnancy. I hope he's okay with moving to America. Our love child shouldn't have to grow up in the shadow of a morally indefensible monarchy."

The baby at the next table was making gurgling noises, and I made a face at her and she smiled. "Good one," I said, still looking at the baby, who had a blue-and-white striped bow on her bib.

We went back and forth for a while, the baby and I, and I felt myself beaming each time I was able to get her to laugh. The parents, both tall and blond, smiled at me.

"Don't, Ellie," said Mable after a bit.

"What?"

"I know what you're thinking."

"Oh, really?" I forced my attention back toward Mable, and the baby made a yelp of protest.

"Yes. And I think it's only going to make you feel worse, if you go down that path."

I picked up one of the English-language newspapers that the waiter had arranged on our table and pretended to be interested in the story above the fold.

"I am right, aren't I?" she asked after a moment. "You two had just talked about having kids, right? A few weeks ago."

"Not for a few years. That was the plan."

"The plan," she repeated.

"He wanted one of each, a boy and girl. Even though you know I wasn't sure if I wanted kids at all."

A server came by and refilled her coffee. She waited until he left to say, "I thought you did want kids."

"I did. Or I do. But, I guess, it always feels like there's this future version of myself, the one with children, and I have some sort of block on how to get there. I could see this person, a few years older than me, taking folic acid pills and all that. And then, after that, the kids. They're always faceless." I stared at the newspaper as I spoke. "But I didn't know how to get there. The person in between."

"You'd have to be a fool not to be at least a little afraid of pregnancy and childbirth. Why wouldn't you be? It feels like a punishment."

"Well, the pain of childbirth *is* a punishment. According to the Christian doctrine."

I looked up as I said this, and she was laughing. "You're right," she said. "So is sex before marriage. Good thing I'm still a virgin."

"Was last night good, by the way?" I asked.

"It was better once I showed him what I liked."

"Did he unseat Chamber Pot Guy in your top five?"

"No way."

A few years ago, when Mable was still in New York, she met a man who lived in an industrial-space-turned-loft-turned-art-studio that didn't have reliable running water. On days the toilet didn't work, he pissed in a bucket, Mable told me after their first night together. When I had come up with the name Chamber Pot Guy,

Mable had said, It's canon now, and had even changed his name in her phone. Chamber Pot Guy was very good at sex, so much so that Mable decided she could put up with his lack of plumbing for a while. What's annoying, though, is that he knows he's good, Mable said once. Whenever he's done eating me out, he looks up at me like he's ready to be awarded the Nobel Peace Prize.

"God, I haven't thought about him in ages," she said, laughing loudly. An older couple a few tables over shot us a severe look, although they were too far away to hear what she was saying.

"That's sacrilegious," I said. "His name lives in infamy."

"Of course."

"I do have one question I never got to ask about him, though."

"Please, go ahead," she said.

"Given that he knew the medieval method for disposing of his waste, I'm curious about his other skills. Did he know how to shoe a horse?"

"Obviously," she said. "That was his trade. He was known for towns over."

"Ah, so he was the local blacksmith."

"A steady income."

"I'm guessing he wore a codpiece," I said.

"Such is the fashion. He gave me the gift of six children before I turned twenty-three, and I almost died in childbirth each time," she said. "So let that be a warning to you. It's good you and Ian didn't have kids." She paused for a second, then said, "Chamber Pot Guy would be happy we're taking the seaside cure for our womanly problems."

"Consumption?"

"Hysteria, actually."

Soon, Mable left to use the bathroom, and the couple I'd seen in the lobby yesterday entered the breakfast area. They were both dressed head to toe in white, though the woman had on red lipstick so perfectly mapped she must've used a lip pencil. Maybe even a magnified mirror, too. I found the idea of putting on lipstick for breakfast very shallow, and I started to feel strongly that she couldn't be a good person. As they passed our table on the way to theirs, I noted her clean scent, and that both of them wore sandals that looked expensive.

A few tables away, they ordered food from the menu without even glancing at the buffet. The woman's voice had the flat tones of an American news anchor, her accent was that general, and the man sounded American, too. When he was finished ordering, he glanced over at her, as if waiting for her to start the conversation. But she only leaned back in her chair, which was placed on the edge of the covered patio, and let her head hang off the back of her seat. She smiled wide, and I could see thin lines, like a calm ripple, around her eyes and lips. Now I was sure she was in her forties, at least a decade older than her partner. She was saying something so quietly I couldn't make it out, and suddenly I wanted to know very badly what it was.

When Mable returned, we finished our food and got ready to leave. On our way out, I nudged her and said, "Don't look back, but did you see that woman?"

"Who?"

I didn't know quite how to describe her without making her sound like everyone else, so I just changed the subject.

• • •

We spent the day by the hotel pool, which was located two stories above the beach. The man who greeted us there prepared our lounge chairs and umbrella, and asked us how much sun we wanted.

"None for me," I said.

"Good, more sun for me," said Mable, pulling her chair a bit away from mine.

On this point, I adhered strictly to my mother's religious belief that sun was to be avoided at all costs. This was something Mable's mother also felt, but Mable made a point to disagree with her about it. This is all rooted in colorism, Mable always said. All that skin-lightening makeup sold in Asia. I agreed with her in theory, but asked her once if she worried about skin cancer or wrinkles. You're really missing the point, she said.

I had spent a few weekends with Mable's family when she moved back to San Francisco. Saratoga, the suburb where she grew up, wasn't far from Stanford, and when I had accepted my offer there I'd thought that maybe I'd get to see a bit of Mable's family. I already knew a fair deal about her two younger brothers, Kevin and Will, who worshipped her and called her incessantly throughout college, often late at night, asking her to help them with all sorts of problems. She always took them seriously and never laughed at their questions.

As for her parents, Mable had always put a great deal of intellectual rigor into the way she spoke about them, in a way I found almost unnatural, whether about her disagreement with certain parenting philosophies of theirs, or identifying the attachment issues she believed they'd given her brothers. She spent a year obsessed with the idea that her parents needed to go to therapy, either individually or as a pair. I don't think she ever conveyed it to them, though.

So when I would spend the night with Mable at her childhood home, I felt as if I was already part of the family. Her parents would rib her, telling her to be more like me and apply to law school; I felt proud of this fake sibling rivalry. At night, the two of us would lie on the carpet next to her bed and go through her old yearbooks, and read entries from the journals she'd kept since childhood. Her parents had fruit trees in the back of their house, and when we would leave to go back to the city, they would push a bag of persimmons, freshly picked, into our hands. For some reason, whenever this happened I felt an urge to cry, and when I got home I would put that bag on my kitchen counter, staring at it as if it contained some important message.

"*Mesdemoiselles, alors,*" a server in a stiff uniform greeted us when it came time for lunch. "What will we be having today?"

Mable ordered sandwiches for the both of us, which he delivered right to our table. Even though it was very hot, he looked cool and dry in his uniform.

"We better be careful. By the end of this," Mable said, wagging a finger in the air, "we may become Republicans. Or moderate Democrats."

For the first time since we landed, I checked my work phone to find twenty-eight new emails addressed just to me. I wasn't surprised. Even though I was only part-time, a reduced schedule at a law firm meant a regular nine-to-five one. Rather than bill forty hours or more a week, I was expected to bill at least twenty-five to thirty hours; I still had work to make sitting by the pool all day impossible. I sent back a few cursory responses that were vague enough to make it seem like I had opened whatever attachment they'd sent me, and tossed my work phone back into my bag.

Mable was looking at me and I said, "Whatever, I'll start tomorrow."

I told her I wanted to head to the beach, and she said she'd come with me. It was an easy trip, just down a set of steps from the pool, and then down a ladder that reached directly into the mouth of the sea. There wasn't much of a beach, but floating markers with the hotel's name blocked off a large rectangle in the ocean.

Mable easily dived in, bobbing in and out like a seal until she reached the end of the marker. I eased the lower half of my body in, clenching every muscle in it because the water was so cold. When a wave lapped up, I turned my head, getting only a bit of salty spray on the back of my hair.

I could hear her calling me to join her farther out, but I ignored her. I was afraid of the ocean, or really any big swath of natural water. You weren't always like this, my mom had told me. You used to love swimming in the ocean, sometimes even scaring me with how far out you'd go. I remembered loving it then. But for some reason, by puberty, water had started to scare me. Nothing bad had ever happened to me; I had no terrible stories about being swept under. And yet at thirteen and fourteen, I felt like the ocean had sent me a very important and clear message: I can destroy you.

I kicked my legs a few times, all the while holding onto the rocks by the ladder. The water was so dark I couldn't see anything below my waist. Any moment, I imagined, I might be pulled under and swept past the floating markers. I thought of the last time I had accidentally breathed in underwater, the burn that had stayed inside my nostrils afterward. I could hear Mable making friends with someone in her part of the water, and I climbed back up the ladder. I called out to tell her I was leaving and she waved goodbye, still mid-conversation with an older woman in a striped bikini.

Back at the pool I dried myself off with a fresh towel; someone had noticed we had gone to the beach and left fresh ones at our chairs. I lay back down and checked my work phone once again, just out of habit. Even though it was very early in California, Michael, a first-year associate I'd been working with, had responded to my email with a few follow-up questions. *I figured it would be easiest to work with you on your current time zone*, he wrote, *so I've gone ahead and adjusted my schedule accordingly.* Michael had bright red hair, and I imagined him bent over his desk, drafting this message to me. I fiddled awhile with a long message back, only to send something short about how I wouldn't be able to get to his questions today. All of my longer drafts came across as rude, I feared, and I didn't know how to respond to his message, which had made me feel both touched and resentful.

Mable came back soon after, and I forgot about the email. We both fell asleep in the afternoon sun.

• • •

That evening, we decided to get some drinks at the bar inside the main building of the hotel, and spent a while beforehand getting ready. I pretended it was just because I wanted to look nice, but it was more that I didn't want to stick out yet again. I put on a seafoam-green dress with thin straps that fell loose across my body, the hem ending in the middle of my calves. Mable, on the other hand, picked out a sliver of a dress with almost no back; it was obvious she was making some sort of statement, although I wasn't sure what kind of statement she wouldn't have been comfortable saying outright. We spent a long time putting on our makeup in a bathroom in the main suite and telling each other the right things about how the other one looked.

"This feels like college again," I said. "Us getting ready and watching TV." Mable had found a channel that was playing *Titanic* with French subtitles. We kept the bathroom door open so we could have a view of the TV while we got dressed, and Mable had dragged a velvet chair from the sitting room into the bathroom so she could sit while she put on her makeup.

"If we're back in college, then are you going to try to convince me to stay in?" she asked, putting on another coat of mascara.

"No, I want to go out."

Mable slid the wand back into the bottle and closed it. "I'm serious, actually. We don't need to go out tonight."

"I'm serious, too."

"Are you sure? We still have a good amount of time before the iceberg." Mable gestured toward the open bathroom door. Usually we'd turned off *Titanic* by the time the ship started going down.

"We could've stayed home and watched TV in San Francisco."

Mable had paused her makeup and was facing me now, cross-legged on the chair. "I really mean it, Ellie. We don't need to do anything."

"So this is nothing like college at all now," I said. "It's the opposite. Maybe in France I'll be you and you be me."

"Now you've really lost it."

When we finally left our room, we ran into some hotel staff turning down beds. The only time I'd stayed in a place nice enough to have turndown service was in Turks and Caicos, on our honeymoon. My God, I'd said when Ian and I had come back late the first night, someone cleaned our room! I'd walked around as if I was in some sort of daze, running my hands over the bed. Light music was playing on the television, which had been set to some channel that ran through generic images like the ones in a bad karaoke machine. A beach, a sunset, a tropical plant, all on a loop. Ian made fun of my wide-eyed look, and for the rest of the trip it became a joke. Did you like that restaurant? he'd ask. Not as much as I like turndown, I'd say. Should we stay out tonight? No, let's get home in time for turndown. On our last night there, he'd laid me down on top of the covers, unwrapped one of the tiny chocolates on our pillows, and balanced it right on my mouth. It seesawed back and forth as I tried not to smile. But then I gave in, and it fell down onto my clavicle. He bent down and ate it off me, his lips barely grazing my skin. All that remained was a small chocolate smudge in the dip in my collarbone.

"You okay?" Mable asked, looking at me sideways as we walked toward the bar in the main building. I nodded.

The bar was crowded, mostly with couples, but a few people drinking alone, too. They all looked very sleek and shiny, like they had all been waxed and oiled by some sort of collector before they came. As she'd intended, Mable turned the eyes of almost every person there. I felt invisible next to her, and was glad for it. We took two seats and menus at the bar, next to a couple drinking identical cocktails. They looked to be in their sixties.

Mable put her elbows on the bar. "What is that?" she asked the woman, pointing at her drink.

"It's their hotel Negroni," the woman said. She had a British accent.

"It looks good," said Mable, and ordered two from the bartender.

"Oh, it's lovely," said the man next to her, who also sounded British. "It has a decades-old port and some cherry vanilla bitter." Mable introduced us both, and they told us their names were Paul and Bertie.

"I'm obsessed with your name," she said to Bertie, who was wearing a sleeveless violet dress.

"You'd be the first," Bertie said. The bartender handed us our drinks, and Mable sucked hers down fast. I took her cue and drank mine quickly, too. It felt like velvet in my throat.

Another man at the bar, younger than the couple but older than us, leaned into our circle to tell us about a childhood friend he had who was named Bertrand, which, he emphasized repeatedly, is very much like Bertie. "Indeed," said Mable, her hand digging into mine at the bar. I laughed and the man began to laugh, too, thinking something he said was funny, though he was just very drunk. Bertie and Paul joined in the laughter, and Mable passed the menu around to all of us.

"What's next?" she said. "What should we all try next?" I read aloud the ingredients of a gin cocktail—pomegranate liqueur, lemon juice, vanilla syrup, fresh mint, fresh strawberries, fresh cucumber, soda water—and ordered a round for the four of us.

Soon, a small semicircle had formed around Mable at the bar. It was getting louder and louder, and most of us had to lean in, our ears by someone's chest or head while they talked. There was a Frenchman who bought and sold a lot of art by people I'd never heard of, a Russian who kept trying to lead the conversation back to some funny thing that had happened at the hotel a week ago when we weren't there. Mable kept raising her volume, gesturing wildly while I stayed quieter, tipping back one drink and then another.

"You might need some food, dear," Bertie said to me. She looked as drunk as I was. "We can't keep drinking without snacks."

"There's snacks on the menu," said Paul. He wore thick glasses that made his eyes look slightly surprised at all times, and he had a habit of peering straight at you when you spoke, barely blinking. It gave the impression that he'd recently learned an alarming, distressing piece of information.

I scanned the menu and decided on a plate of Iberian ham, another of raw vegetables, and then some ice cream to top it off. When I finished ordering, two men behind me clapped my back, as if I had just won a prize.

"Ham, vegetables, and dessert? A perfectly balanced meal," said Mable.

When the food arrived, we passed around the plates. An American woman in a navy romper had been hanging around the edge of our group, and when she spied an opening, she slipped in. While she was speaking she really looked only at Mable, something that made sense to me. In a way, I would've been surprised if she was paying more attention to anyone else.

"Everything we're doing is pointless, given climate change," Mable was saying. The woman had told us she was on the board of an environmental nonprofit. "Sometimes I think about how most everyone is just going about their lives normally—we're all just re-arranging deck chairs on the *Titanic*."

"We just watched that movie," I said. "In our room."

Mable grinned. "That we did."

"I really love that film," said Paul. "It gets me every time."

"Of course it does," said Mable. "You're not a monster."

The woman kept talking to Mable, and at one point handed her a gold iPhone and asked her to put in her number. Mable switched the phone back and forth between her hands while they talked, then handed it back to her, and the woman didn't seem notice that she hadn't input anything.

When the woman left, Mable put one of her arms around me and the other around Bertie, who was sitting next to me.

"So thin. I used to have arms like that," said Bertie, her hand on Mable's wrist. "Ages ago."

"I think you're trying to give me a compliment," said Mable. "But all it does is make me think about internalized misogyny."

"Of course," said Bertie. "That's absolutely right." She was lean-ing heavily on the bar, her head slouched forward so that a few strands of her hair were in her half-finished cocktail.

"Bertie and I came here for our honeymoon decades ago," Paul said, his eyes shining behind his glasses. "We still have warm memories."

"In twenty years," said Mable, "it'll be me and you, Paul, sitting at this bar." We all laughed at that, and Paul turned a shade of salmon.

"You should be so lucky," said Bertie to her husband.

Before we headed off to dinner I went to the bathroom. As I

walked there, I had to hold the sides of my body because I was still laughing so hard at a joke someone had made, although I was having trouble recalling exactly what was said or who said it. I turned the water faucet to very hot to wash my hands, taking great pains not to look at myself in the mirror. Mable had once said that no one should ever look at their reflection after three drinks or more. You'll never like what you find, she told me.

Back at the bar, Mable was finishing up a conversation with the bartender, though we didn't have a tab to pay, since everything had been charged to the room. I was waiting for her to wrap it up for good when a middle-aged white man in a navy suit sat down next to me. He was wearing a T-shirt under an open blazer, and I wondered if he'd thought he looked young when he chose the outfit.

"Your friend," he said. "What does she do?" He had an accent I couldn't quite place.

This question felt funny to me, and I said, "She exists."

He shook his head. "For a living."

"She does everything," I said, trying to catch her attention, but she wasn't looking in my direction.

"A Renaissance woman."

"Exactly." I paused then said: "She also is a writer. She writes."

"Anything I would know?"

Mable was in my periphery now, I thought, but I couldn't be sure. "No." I put my face in my hands. The bar was starting to feel very bright, and I wished they would turn down the lights. "Shit Stories."

"Excuse me?" He was leaning in close to me, his right ear by my mouth.

"She writes Shit Stories."

He asked again, and I repeated the same answer. On the third try I confirmed Mable was standing behind him. We looked at each other, and though we could both hear the man drunkenly asking the same question, a quiet moment was happening only between Mable and me, like a nasty secret.

"Hey," he said, now seeing her there. "What are these 'Shit Stories'? Are they published?"

She had her arm around me now, and I let her lead me away from the bar. She lolled her head back at him and showed all her teeth. "Yes. Available at your local, independent bookstore."

We walked down the gravel path, back to the same building where we'd had breakfast. The restaurant was crowded for dinner, and we were seated on the patio again. It was dark now and you couldn't see the ocean, only hear the waves, loud and rhythmic. They beat on, over and over, and I felt the cheer I had earned at the bar disappearing. I hated the sound of the waves; they made me feel panicked, reminding me of the bass beat that had been playing on the car stereo when we were following Cat. Mable was still staring at me, too, the way she did at the bar. I wasn't quite sure what she was thinking.

The unforgiving pulse of the ocean went on and on and on, relentless. I no longer cared about anything except escaping it. I could feel it in my blood. I must've looked horrible because Mable took my hand in hers as she began to read the menu.

"Do you need me to talk to you again? About anything?" she asked.

"Yes. Please."

She told me that Paul and Bertie had told her that the restaurant had special menus without prices, given only to the women. "What do you think they'll bring us? Since there's no man with us, we would need to know the prices."

"They'll have to bring us the prices. So we can pay," I said.

"Capitalism would seem to indicate that. But you forget that they have our room number. They could just charge us that way."

"Charge Ian, you mean."

She laughed a bit too loudly, but this time I didn't care. We were already drunk and going to get drunker.

We skipped any starters and went straight to the mains. "We already ate at the bar," Mable said to the waiter. "We had ice cream." She ordered lobster for two, which came with sautéed squid, aioli, and basil-flavored potato crisps. We asked for wine recommendations, and by the time they finished their speech about what would make for the best pairing, neither of us could remember one word of it. "That last one sounded good," Mable eventually managed.

We finished the lobster and got to dessert, sharing a hazelnut soufflé with praline and gianduja ice cream. "We can't get enough," Mable said. "Never enough ice cream." When dinner was over, she wanted to hang out at a bar by the restaurant, where someone was playing piano, but I knew if I drank any more I would be sick. I dropped her off and left her among her fans. Before I could go, she insisted on a proper French goodbye, kissing me on both cheeks.

I had made it halfway through the main building on the way

to our rooms when I noticed the man at the bar who'd asked me about Mable. He was standing at the glass elevator in his white tee, his blazer draped over his arm.

He noticed me, too, and he said, "Going up?" The call button was lit up.

"You liked my friend," I said.

"I did."

"Her name is Mable. She's in the bar by the restaurant." I tried my best to gesture toward the back of the hotel, at the gravel.

The elevator door opened, and he put one hand on it to keep it open. His T-shirt was tight against his body.

"You have to go outside to see her," I said. "She's in the other building."

"I don't want to go see her."

"Why not?"

"You're right here."

He had an easy, casual way about him. His movements all conveyed an enthusiasm for living that felt important for me to try to understand. "Okay," I said. I got in the elevator with him and he pressed the button for the door to close. I found myself leaning against the glass side of the elevator, which was cold against my skin. He pressed another button for his floor.

"So your friend is named Mable," he said. "Who are you?"

"Ellie."

"Jasper," he said.

"Who?"

"Me. I'm Jasper." He was laughing, and I started laughing, too. The elevator was moving, and it took a lot of concentration for me to stay upright. At one point I thought I felt the elevator going down instead of up.

"Easy there." He had a goatee that reminded me of the manicured greenery at the hotel. Then he said, "I'm going out on my boat tomorrow, and I want you to come."

"You have a boat," I said.

He laughed again, and so did I. The elevator stopped and the doors opened. I said, "Are we here?"

He exited the elevator and started down the hallway, and I followed him. When he walked, he somehow transmitted a great deal of energy and power.

"You are very beautiful," he said, slowing down to walk next to me.

"I'm sorry," I said.

"Why are you apologizing?"

"I don't know," I said. I started laughing again. Then I said, "Thank you."

It was too hard to talk and walk at the same time, so I concentrated on staring straight ahead. The pattern on the carpet was making me dizzy.

He said, "Your friend is fascinating to me."

"Me too."

"'Fascinating' is the wrong word, actually," he said. "I like you. You're quiet. Softer."

"I am."

"I like that about you guys."

"Me and Mable?" I said. "She's not quiet at all."

"Asian girls. That's why Mable was so surprising to me."

I started to shake my head, but I felt like I would lose my bal-
ance so I stopped. "What?"

He didn't answer, getting out his room key to open the door.

There were a number of things I felt I could say, and I thought
of the elevator buttons, each waiting to be pressed. Instead, I said,
"I'm not supposed to be here. This isn't my room."

He unlocked his door and held it open for me.

I repeated myself and he said, "You're the one who got in the
elevator with me."

"I know," I finally said. I walked back to the elevator, and for
a moment I was afraid he would follow, but then I heard his door
close behind me. On the way back down, the elevator stopped and
two older women got in. They both wore heavy perfume and were
speaking rapidly in French, clearly enjoying their conversation.
When we got to the lobby and the door opened, I said to them, "I
don't know why I always do that. I realize now that I always do that.
But I don't know why."

"*Pardon?*" one of the woman said to me. The other woman
reached out a hand to me, as if I was going to fall over. But I ignored
her hand and stayed in the elevator when they exited at the lobby. I
somehow managed to press the button for the third floor and made
my way to our rooms. I lay in my bed with all the lights on until
Mable came in, and I started talking to her about nothing so I could
forget what just happened. I talked to her about the color of the
ocean, the seemingly endless supply of fluffed towels, our favorite
drink at the bar. Neither of us could remember if the menus we'd
gotten had prices or not.

Chapter Twelve

Mable and I woke up to the sounds of my two phones buzzing repeatedly. Mable hadn't made it to her bedroom the evening before, and we had both passed out on my bed, on top of the covers. My mom had called and texted me multiple times. The small blue dots that lined the left-hand side of my inbox to indicate unread emails looked angry.

"God, just take the leave they offered you," said Mable.

I put down my work phone and looked at my personal one. "It's not just work stalking me, it's also Mary. She wants to know where I am."

"You didn't tell her we were coming here?"

"No."

She let out a laugh. "Good luck."

When Mable went to take a shower in her own room, I looked for the small black bag I'd packed that contained everything I needed from the firm. I found it resting on the floor of my closet underneath a robe that had fallen off its hanger. I took out my work laptop and logged on to see that the blue dots in my inbox looked larger and more threatening.

I was on a case team, led by Marcus, that was preparing for trial. Before Ian died, Marcus had asked me to research someone our opposing counsel was attempting to qualify as an expert, and then turn that research into a motion to strike, which, if granted by the court, meant the opposing side would be unable to use the witness as an expert. Michael, the first-year who'd shifted his work schedule to match mine, had been assigned by Marcus to help me. I had roughly outlined a draft of the motion the day before Ian's death, but I had yet to do any good work on it since the funeral. It would take me dozens of hours to draft and finalize the brief for filing, and it was due in just a few days.

The right thing, of course, would've been to email Marcus immediately and say that I had made a mistake and that I needed to take leave after all. That this was the right thing made me very angry. I was no star at the firm, but I pulled my weight. My work should be unrelated to Ian and Cat, I imagined myself saying to Mable, her head nodding along. Imaginary Mable had no argument to the contrary.

"Coming to breakfast?" Mable asked. She was standing in the doorway connecting the suite to the adjoining room, wearing a black cover-up over a neon bikini.

"You go ahead. I'm going to do some work, but I'll catch up."

She pressed her lips together tightly but said nothing.

"It'll be fine," I called after her as she left.

I opened each unread email so that there were no more blue dots in my inbox. Some of them I immediately filed away in a subfolder of my inbox and others I read multiple times, hoping the dread would dissipate. It didn't. I pulled up the outline I had drafted for the brief and started formatting and creating stand-ins for my eventual work: "I. Argument Header Here." I looked at the clock on the bottom of my laptop screen. Even though I had been sitting at my computer for close to an hour, I had managed to bill only fourteen minutes of work.

I attached the draft to an email and sent it to Michael. *Take the first pass at this and then send to me for edits.* Almost immediately he responded, asking if we could speak on the phone. *I've never written a motion to strike before, and I'd appreciate any guidance.*

Michael was hardworking and intelligent, but I had seen enough of his work product to know anything he drafted would need to be heavily edited by me. He'd also joined the case team only recently, after I had done most of the research on the witness, and Marcus had asked him to assist me on this motion just a few days ago. He had my notes, of course, but I doubted he even knew what to say.

Rather than respond, I closed my computer and sat for a while on the floor with my arms wrapped around my legs. My other phone vibrated with another text from my mother, this one asking me where I was. It was close to five in the morning in Ohio, and I knew she must've been worried. I used Wi-Fi Calling to dial her.

"Hello? Mom?" My voice was very small.

"Ellie? What's going on? I've been trying to reach you for days."

I said I was traveling internationally. She asked multiple follow-up questions, and eventually much of the story of how I got there began to reveal itself. I even told her that I was paying for it with Ian's life insurance money, too tired to come up with a lie. She paused for a long time, and I could hear the faded sound of someone talking and then an audience clapping. She must've had the television on. Finally, she said: "Well, I'm glad Mable is with you."

"Really? You would worry if it was just me?"

"Come on, Ellie."

"No, tell me."

"I'm not doing this."

"Doing what? I'm just asking you to explain what you said."

"I hope you're feeling better."

"I'm not. And you're only making it worse. Calling me nonstop and then not answering my questions." My voice was louder now.

"Is Mable there with you in the room?"

"No, she's at breakfast. Why? Do I need your permission to be alone?"

I heard a commercial on the other end of the phone. I could see her sitting in her bed, facing the TV, her white Frette comforter with the blue stitching pulled up to her elbows. When I was in high school, she had spent weeks picking out that bedding from a high-end department store. It was way out of our budget, but she had saved for months to buy it for herself, as well as a matching set for me. She had treated hers with utmost care, never once letting me lie on top of it. Even now, it still looked almost new.

Growing up, I was embarrassed by my mom's desire to be part of a group that would look down on her. Her admiration of WASPs seemed somehow both a cliché and a personal affront. Around the time she bought the bedding, I began to wage a silent war against her, unaware that I was only fulfilling another stereotype, the teenager rebelling against an immigrant parent. I would make a point to ridicule her whenever she referred to our home as a two-story house rather than a ranch. Putting on airs, are we? I'd say. You know we have only four steps in our staircase. I'd say this kind of thing to her even—or especially—in front of her friends. I would tell her, You would think after all you went through, you would be telling me how I can do it all on my own. I gave her *The Second Sex* for Christmas my senior year of high school. Her reactions to my attempts to shock her vacillated between ignoring me and offending me. Feminism, she said, this is an American thing. I invited over anyone in high school I could find who would make her uneasy, women with shaved heads and men with brightly dyed hair who thought not showering added to their mystique. Only a few of them were actual friends of mine; the rest were for show.

During the worst times, I would lob my most stinging blow: that she was a self-loathing Asian. I would say it matter-of-factly, like David Attenborough narrating a polar bear's mauling of a baby seal. This neutral tone made it clear that I was being observational and not emotional. When I told Mable about this a couple of years later, I felt it was a sin I needed to confess. She was as horrified as I'd expected her to be. That's so cruel, she had said. Do you really want to punish her for picking up a framework that society has programmed her to desire, when she was alone and vulnerable? Twelve Hail Marys a day, Mable said, crossing herself in a sarcastic way. No lashings? I asked. You had your reasons, she said. She waved her hands as if giving a sermon. God is forgiving.

Mable also pointed out many things in my mom's defense, things I'd told her but had otherwise ignored. For example, for all my mom's obsession with healthy eating, she never had an issue with white rice, which she'd had at almost every meal growing up in Taiwan. Then there were the points that were so excruciating I'd had to hold them at arm's length: that even though my mom was a well-respected engineer, her company hadn't promoted her once in the decades she loyally worked there, never gave her a raise beyond the minimum annual increase that everyone got; that she spoke about almost no one she worked with because they looked down on her, spoke down to her.

"Tell me about how you're doing," my mother said after a moment.

"I'm sorry, Mom. I shouldn't have snapped at you just now. I'm tired. I'm still getting used to the time change."

"It's okay."

I began to tell her about the hotel, how much she would like it. I described the food, the towels and bedding, the pool and the ocean. I knew it was an effort for her not to mention the use of Ian's life insurance money, and I felt grateful for that. After I hung up, promising to call her soon, I got dressed and went to go find Mable.

When I arrived at breakfast, I had trouble spotting her until I heard her voice. She was sitting with her back to the entrance, at a table with two other people. For a moment I thought they were Paul and Bertie, but when I got closer I realized that it was the American couple I'd seen the two previous days.

Mable patted the seat next to her, and I took it, expecting her to introduce me, but she was too caught up in her conversation with the woman. The man, who was sitting directly opposite me, was wearing the same Panama hat he'd been wearing when I first saw him, and he tipped up the brim to get a better look at me. I also got a better look at him. He was very attractive, but there was also a distinct way he held his face that emitted a sense of gentleness that was almost unnerving. He introduced himself as Robbie, short for Robert, and then nudged the woman, who was laughing at something Mable had said.

"Ellie," I said, reaching out my hand to her.

Her hand was somehow cold, even though it was already hot outside. She only said, "Ellie."

"I've only told her the good, Ellie, I promise," said Mable.

I kept my hand in the woman's. "And you are?"

"Fauna." She pronounced both syllables very hard, like she was saying it for the first time and was having trouble pronouncing the word. Faw-na. It was a name I thought Mable would've made fun of in any other situation, but I already knew she wouldn't. She'd barely looked at me since I sat down, the entire top half of her body leaning toward the woman.

The waiter came over, and I ordered something off the menu. All of them were in the middle of their meals, and Mable had clearly loaded up at the buffet again. She began to break apart a pastry, handing bits of it to each of us.

Fauna was giving us her recommendations for restaurants and tourist spots in the area. She made big gestures, and kept pausing to tell us an anecdote from the last time they were there, a waiter who had been rude to them, or how it took them too long to find parking. None of the stories were interesting—in fact, they were quite boring—but I found myself listening with great interest, as did Mable and Robbie. Everything Fauna said seemed remarkable and worthy of great attention, but for no actual reason. Mable butted in from time to time and asked for clarification. What color was it again? Did you ever go back after that? Did the waiter apologize? And so on.

My food arrived, and I realized I'd said almost nothing since I'd sat down. Indeed, to anyone else, this would've seemed like a conversation between the two of them, or really a monologue by Fauna, supported by Mable.

Finally, something Fauna said triggered an interruption from Robbie, and he told us about a time last year when he had gotten lost driving around this area and didn't have his phone. As he narrated the story, Robbie's voice was steady and firm, reliable.

"Sounds like you two have been here before," I said. It was the first full sentence I'd said since ordering.

"We have," said Fauna. "Although this is the first time I've been here in September."

"A bit later than last year," said Robbie. "We were here in July."

"That's high season," Fauna said.

"Ellie and I are strictly low-season people," said Mable. "Peasants." She explained that we had bought these tickets last-minute.

"I can't believe anything was even available," said Fauna. "There must've been a cancellation." She went on to tell us how you could book a stay at this hotel during high season only if you were a repeat guest.

"Well, I guess we're lucky you deigned to come in September," I said, trying for a light tone, but it came out more harshly than I intended. "Kidding," I quickly added.

Mable laughed, and Fauna gave me an amused half smile. She had put on sunglasses while we were talking, and it was hard to tell what she was thinking.

Robbie gave me a warm, gracious smile and a half shrug, then took out a pack of cigarettes from his pants pocket and pulled one out. He gestured to me, but I shook my head. He lit it and took a long drag.

"Damn it, Robbie. You know I hate that." Fauna plucked the cigarette straight from his lips, and I noticed that her nails were painted a maroon red. She motioned for the waiter to bring her an ashtray and took a drag herself, then smiled at me.

"I'm trying to keep him alive. Just a bit longer." When the ashtray arrived, she put out the cigarette.

"Keeping me alive against my will," said Robbie. He was smiling at her, and I wondered if they'd done this routine before, him lighting a cigarette and her extinguishing it.

"Are you two married?" I asked, then realized right away it was the wrong question to ask. I felt very uncool.

"No," said Fauna. "Although I keep begging him to propose."

Robbie laughed, and it was obvious that she'd been joking. But I couldn't tell if he felt in on the joke.

"I used to feel very against marriage in general," said Mable. "But now I'm not sure. Nothing has actually changed in my abstract thought. It's more that, as a woman, I wonder if I could reclaim it for myself." She was breaking apart another pastry but not eating it. "But maybe this is just the patriarchy grinding me down. Stockholm syndrome."

"Marriage," said Fauna, "doesn't bother me one bit."

"Fauna's been married three times," Robbie said. "Never to me, though."

"Thrice," she said, and held up three fingers. "I'm Thrice-Married Fauna."

"What happened?" I asked. This also felt like the wrong thing to ask, and Mable gave me a look that said she was embarrassed for me.

Fauna shrugged. "They ended." She took off her sunglasses and looked at me closely now. She had light green eyes. "I have a lot of thoughts about why each relationship ended, but they're actually not that interesting."

I was very much interested, but I felt like I shouldn't ask for more in front of Robbie. I studied her face again.

Mable said, "All fascinating people are divorced multiple times."

When I was done with my food, we made our way out of the restaurant as a foursome. Just before we reached the door, someone opened it for us; I realized then that the only door I'd opened for myself during the last two days was the one to our own rooms.

The three of them headed toward the pool, and because I hadn't brought a swimsuit to breakfast, I ran back to our room to change. As I pulled on my suit, I realized that I had a strong sense of anticipatory social anxiety. It was the kind I'd had on the first day of college, after everyone's parents had left and we sheepishly wandered from dorm room to dorm room, trying to be coolly casual but still friendly enough. Something about both Robbie and Fauna, but specifically Fauna, made me feel very young and naive. I tried to work up my confidence on the short walk from our room to the pool, blaring loud pop music into my headphones.

I found them clustered around a shaded area at the pool, an empty lounge chair at the end next to Mable. Robbie was sitting behind Fauna, sharing a chair. Fauna had on an expensive-looking black one-piece with large cutouts that revealed a toned, slim body. Her tan skin glowed against her blond hair. Robbie was wearing navy trunks and must've just gotten out of the pool because his skin was glistening under the sun. I confirmed why his clothes were always tight against his arms and legs in the right places. He had thick, easy muscles that looked like they would live on him forever.

While they talked, I was painfully aware of the fact that I would now have to take off my dress and reveal my body in my bathing suit while they were all already positioned atop their towels in their suits. I turned my back to them and slipped off my clothes and then immediately grabbed a towel to wrap around myself. I kept my sunglasses on so that when I faced them, they wouldn't see my eyes, which I knew transmitted exactly how I was feeling.

They were talking about social media. "I have so much second-hand embarrassment whenever I see people who post pictures of themselves multiple times a day," said Fauna. "Not that I never do it myself or that I don't enjoy it. I hope I'm not dating myself here."

Without turning, she reached behind her and patted Robbie's cheek. "Actually, you want to know the best way to feel old? Dating someone younger. But I actually use social media more than he does."

"I don't really post, but I do look at it all the time," he said.

"Oh, you're a lurker, like Ellie," said Mable. "She has all the apps, but really just uses it to look at other people's lives."

"Do you like social media?" Fauna asked me.

I sat down on the edge of my pool chair and hugged the towel around myself. "I don't like it, but I guess I don't dislike it either. It just feels like it's part of our lives now, and there's no point in even questioning it." I thought for another moment. "I have a lot of anxiety if I ever post anything, though."

"Because you feel like others are judging you?" Robbie said.

"I guess," I said. I wanted to say more, but I felt too vulnerable. The truth was that I spent an inordinate amount of time looking at other people's lives. And almost as much time debating what to post, even though I usually ended up talking myself out of posting anything at all. I knew that all of my posts came off as obviously curated. But anytime I tried to put up something that was sincere or in that vibe of ironic humor that I had seen others pull off, it always seemed contrived. The amount of intellectual energy I put into social media was embarrassing in and of itself, but the most monstrous part was the fact that I knew no one looked at my profiles closely enough to notice or care. Everything I ended up posting was straightforward: a picture of Ian and me over the holidays, a group of us at a dinner party. I almost felt like because I had posted for years with a serious sort of brand, it would be jarring to post something different now; I no longer could change the way I wanted others to perceive me, even if the older version of myself felt wrong. I found all these thoughts to be shallow and self-pitying, and felt that they said something terrible about who I was as a person.

Since Ian died, I had even more reason to avoid social media. I'd opened it a few days ago, only to be greeted by a barrage of posts tagging me below pictures of Ian, and comments from people sending me their condolences. A few of them just posted emojis of a broken red heart; these tended to be people in my extended friend group whom I secretly loathed, and now I felt morally superior in my opinion of them. One law school classmate had gone back through all my old pictures and liked each one, as if this was some sort of gift. A couple of days before that, I'd also gotten a notification that Susan, my old law school classmate, had commented on one of my old posts, only to find that her comment had disappeared when I got around to opening my app. I imagined her translucent thumb hovering over her phone screen before hitting the delete button. I scrolled through her pictures for the first time in a long while. She had finally found some shoes that weren't white Keds.

"Let me guess," said Fauna, looking at Mable, "you use it all the time?"

"Not really. I mean, I used to be on it a lot, but now really never."

"She used to have a huge following," I said. For a while last year, Mable had been posting prolifically on social media. And then, after a few months, she had stopped altogether. I wasn't sure she even had any of the apps on her phone anymore.

"Not huge," said Mable.

"Fine, not huge. But bigger than that of most people I know," I said. "You had lots of strangers following you."

"You're only saying that because you have a private profile, obviously," said Mable. "I had some randoms, but I'd rather die than be considered some sort of social media celebrity. Jesus."

"What's your handle?" asked Robbie, pulling out his phone.

"God, I can't even really remember. I might have deleted my account, actually. Like I said, I really don't use it anymore," she told him.

"She's too good for us now," I said to Robbie. Mable took a napkin from a nearby table and flicked it at me while Robbie and Fauna laughed.

"Show me yours," said Robbie. Fauna swung her legs around so she was facing me, and her legs were so long that she could've put her feet in my lap if she'd wanted to. I took out my phone and pulled up my profile, then handed it to them so they could look at my feed.

"Why don't you post any pictures of your face?" Fauna asked. I saw them scroll past a few photos of Ian and me at Ocean Beach, and then Mable and me at a bar a few weeks before Ian died. In all of them I was barely in the frame, or turned so I wasn't facing the camera. "I know I just said that some people post too many pictures of themselves, but you don't do any."

"A lot of my colleagues follow me here. It just feels weird, I don't know." I hated my answer, but I didn't know what excuse would feel less embarrassing.

I wanted to ask Robbie and Fauna to show me their social media profiles, but the idea of it felt impossible, especially asking Fauna. Instead, I imagined what her handle would be, the kind of photos she would post.

"Ellie's got too much to lose if she posts something stupid or dumb, unlike most of us," said Mable, who was now standing behind me, and pulling up my hair into a bun.

I said, "I don't know if it's about having too much to lose."

"Mable told us all about how smart and impressive you are," said Robbie. "Quite intimidating, really."

"Please," I said. "Not true."

"Ellie likes to be modest," said Mable. She was finishing up with my hair and gave the bun a pat. "It's one of her worst qualities."

"Your worst quality is finding yourself more amusing than you actually are," I said. Fauna and Robbie laughed, but Mable was still behind me, and I couldn't see her expression.

For the rest of our morning at the pool, I felt like I was trying to keep up with Mable and Fauna.

"We seem boring next to them, don't we?" Robbie said at one point as they were engaged in a debate about some movie they'd both seen, which Mable hated but Fauna loved.

"Yes," I said, "although I'm not in a place to be talkative, not really."

His face told me that Mable must have told them about Ian's death, and he held up his right hand as if he were a traffic guard telling me to stop. He had the large, broad hands of a farmer, except his fingers were long and elegant, like a pianist's. His other hand was on his thigh, relaxed in a half fist. "Yes, of course. Sorry."

"It's okay," I said.

When Fauna and Robbie finally said goodbye, late for a spa appointment, it became evident that before I arrived at the pool, the two of them and Mable had made plans to go into Antibes the next day. I wasn't sure if I actually wanted to go off the hotel grounds, but I knew I didn't want to stay here alone, so I began to nod along, as if I was also looking forward to it.

As soon as they were out of sight, I turned to Mable. "Why did you promise them that we'd do something with them tomorrow?"

She shrugged. "I only said I was going. You don't have to."

"Yeah, but you know that I have to go with you."

She looked up from her book. "Have to? You don't have to do anything."

I didn't want to admit that I didn't want to be alone. "We don't know them at all, I'm just saying. It may not be any fun."

"I like them. Especially Fauna. She's great."

"I pointed her out to you the first day we were here. At breakfast."

"Did you?" She went back to reading. Whenever she was concentrating hard, she would pull her lips over to the side of her face. It was one of the only times I felt she didn't look very attractive.

The umbrellas next to us had been set up earlier in the morning, and now the sun's rays were hitting our calves and spreading up our thighs with each passing minute.

"Did they say anything before I got to breakfast about what they did? They must have a ton of money if they're regulars here."

"Robbie was a big deal at some consulting firm for a while. I can't remember where. He has an MBA," said Mable. "Obviously I can't roll my eyes hard enough at that."

"'Was'? What does he do now?"

"He said he got sick of it and quit a year or so back. He's trying to figure out his next move."

"And what about Fauna?"

"I have no idea." She closed her book now. "I don't even know where she lives. Robbie mentioned Manhattan, but in the past tense. I don't know where he is now, either, but I imagine they live in the same city."

"They're mysterious," I said. "Especially Fauna. I couldn't tell what she was thinking."

Mable nodded. "She's a tough one, and usually it's not hard for me to read people."

"I think she does it on purpose, to make herself more alluring."

"I don't know if that's true." Mable shrugged. "That might just be the way she is. But it does make you really want to figure her out."

I lay back onto the lounge chair and curled my legs up so that most of my body was in the shade. "I don't like her."

"You just said you barely know them."

"I know. But I still don't like her."

"Why?" She picked up her sweating glass of ice water and held it up to her forehead. Her neon bikini and the sheen of her sweat made her look almost fluorescent.

"She doesn't seem nice to her boyfriend. Or whatever he is."

"Oh, so now you're looking out for Robbie?"

"Did you hear what he said when I asked if they were married?"

"Her not wanting to be married doesn't make him some kind of victim."

"Of course not. I didn't say that. But she didn't seem very nice about it."

She tipped her head to the side. "He's pretty hot. And your type, too. Traditionally handsome. Fresh off some fancy, prestigious job."

"Please."

She sat up, folding her legs so they were no longer in the sun either. "She isn't not nice. She just isn't deferential to him, that's all." She began to place the bottom of the cold glass on the soles of her feet so she wasn't looking at me. "You could take a page from her."

I knew that she wanted me to ask her more about what she just said, that it was meant to relate to me and Ian. Instead, I said, "She was wearing lipstick at breakfast."

Mable let out a loud laugh. "Everyone here is made up." She took off her sunglasses and looked straight at me. "God, you are such a snob, Ellie."

I began to pack up my things. "The ocean is bothering me again. I'm going up to the room." The sea had been unsettling me since we'd arrived, but I hadn't said anything to Mable.

"Ellie, come on." She stood up and threw her arms around me. "Come on. Let's not do this."

I let her hug me for a few seconds and then said: "You've never said those things about marriage before. The stuff you said at breakfast."

She released me. "What? About the patriarchy? I've told you that a million times."

"No, about maybe changing your mind. You've never told me that."

This time it was Mable who looked self-conscious. "I guess it just hasn't come up recently."

"The subject of marriage hasn't come up in our conversations? That's impossible."

"Maybe I didn't want to talk about it with you."

I sat back down on my lounge chair. "Fuck, Mable. That hurts."

She was standing over me. "I'm sorry. I don't mean to be mean. I just wasn't sure if you'd get it."

"You thought I wouldn't understand being okay with marriage?"

"No, you obviously believe in marriage. I mean, I didn't know if you'd understand the change in my thinking."

"But you didn't even try."

"Fair. That's fair." The sun's rays were directly in her vision, and she shaded her eyes with one hand. She looked like she wanted to say something but wasn't sure how to word it. Finally, she said: "You know, you have more power over people than you think."

"If you're trying to do some psychological read on me, don't, Mable. Just don't."

"I'll drop it." She held out her hand to me. "Truce?"

"Truce." We shook hands.

"Indeed," she said. "Actually, I was wrong. Robbie isn't your type."

"Why isn't he my type?"

"He's not white." She gave me a big grin, like a Cheshire cat.

"You know full well that most guys I've dated haven't been white. Only Jeremy and Ian were." Even though my words sounded defensive, I was relaxed now. It was clear that whatever had happened between Mable and me had passed. This topic was safe and well trodden; we'd spent countless hours discussing non-Asian men and, specifically, Asian women dating white men. Mable usually divided her fury equally between the demasculinization, marginalization, and erasure of Asian men, and the ideas that anyone felt entitled to Asian women's bodies, that the measure of anything about Asian women was related to whom we slept with, and that it was assumed Asian women had no agency. Her rants usually ended with no answer. Instead, they'd end on an emotional note: she would say she hated all men, and then all of society. I didn't ask to be born, she'd say.

She was still smiling now, so I said, "What moral high ground are you on? What about all the white guys you've slept with?"

"First of all, you know I fuck a lot of guys," she said. "Of all different races. Are you trying to slut-shame me, Ellie? How dare you!" We both started laughing, and I felt more relief cascading into my body.

"Second of all?"

"Second of all, I obviously knew that. You think I'm *proud* of myself, Ellie? You think I'm happy with myself and my choices?"

"Yeah, but what is it you always say? Being aware of a problem isn't the same as, you know, something about—"

"People think being aware of a problem means you are part of the solution. But it's not. Self-awareness is not profound."

"I seem to remember you saying that a few weeks ago when Martha told us she was going to work in private equity." Martha was a friend we'd met sophomore year of college who was on a group email thread that we had maintained since graduation. A few weeks ago, Martha had made this job announcement and said that she wanted to "make changes on the inside." Mable had been livid.

"I say a lot of things," said Mable. "And Martha has a lot of problems. That's the least of them."

Now onto the scent of another victim, Mable turned to the topic of Martha, specifically how she had spent one quarter studying abroad in Tokyo and then the next quarter telling all of us how everything, regardless of what it was, was cooler, better, more authentic, "real-er" in Japan, her green eyes shining like, in Mable's words, a lobotomized Bambi. Martha also thought she was being interesting and intellectual by not owning a TV or watching any TV, Mable now remembered, a detail that I knew would fuel her fire for the rest of the afternoon.

We spent the rest of the day making sure we didn't talk about anything personal.

Chapter Thirteen

The next morning when we met Fauna and Robbie at the front of the hotel, he had already pulled their car around. Mable was wearing a short, dark green romper, and I had chosen a knee-length, oatmeal-colored linen dress, thinking that it was an outfit a local might wear. But seeing Fauna, who was wearing a white dress with a high slit on one side, making her legs look even longer, I felt prudish. Mable and I crawled into the back of their rental, a two-seater, exotic car that I'd never once seen in America. While Robbie drove, Fauna picked the music, playing various early '00s hits from her phone through the car's speakers.

We all sang along, and because I was seated right behind Fauna, I could see her face in the side mirror. Sometimes, during a certain lyric, she would close her eyes and smile to herself about something. It felt like I was watching something very intimate, even though she was in the car with all of us. Last night before bed, I'd started to wonder if I'd judged Fauna too harshly. Watching her sing now made me think I might have. When a certain pop hit came on, I saw her look over at Robbie, who was concentrating on the road, and her face was soft and tender. It made me question whether I'd misjudged her affection for him, too.

At a stoplight, Fauna turned down the music for a moment and said, "I feel like I'm in my twenties again."

"And how is that a bad thing?" asked Mable.

"I'm thirty-one," said Robbie.

"So the wound's still fresh," said Mable.

"Mable." I laughed. "We're both turning thirty in December."

Robbie said, "I remember thinking that thirty meant something big. It felt so far from twenty-eight and twenty-nine somehow. The great barrier of your thirties."

"Speak for yourself, Ellie. I'm never getting old," said Mable. "I'm going to be young forever." She reached into the front of the car and turned the volume back up.

We parked by the ocean, where rows of boats and yachts were docked. Fauna and Robbie, who had been to Antibes many times, led us into town, where a large, crowded farmer's market was going on. It was very loud, and soon Robbie and Mable split off together to try out different jams, while I joined Fauna at a table of colorful soaps. She held a series of them up to her nose and then to mine, murmuring whether or not she liked each one. We moved to a table piled with produce, where she picked up a bunch of green onions and inhaled their scent. Without asking permission, she split off a piece of one and took a bite, then held it up to me, gesturing for me to try it, too.

"I'm not sure we're supposed to," I said, though the woman selling the produce wasn't paying attention to us.

"No one's going to care." She put it up to my face again. I knew that I had come off as very uptight yesterday. It was a role I often fell into with Mable, but I didn't want Fauna to think of me that way, and I saw an opportunity to change her image of me. I took a bite and the sharp sting of the onion filled my mouth.

"It's good," I said. I searched for other adjectives to describe the taste but came up with nothing.

Next, we came across a table filled with bowls of olives, shiny and wet. They looked like small green eyeballs with red pupils. This table was less busy and the seller noticed us browsing.

"*Vous voulez les essayer?*" he said.

Fauna responded, and even though I knew only a little French, I could tell she had an almost perfect accent. We both took an olive.

I felt very self-conscious as I ate it, and then I didn't know what to do with the pit that still had little tufts of meat on it, until Fauna took it wordlessly from my hand and tossed it onto the ground with hers.

We repeated the same movements at a fruit stand and then a table piled high with sausages and other encased meats. As we went along through the market, I only became more self-conscious.

"You're quiet," she said eventually.

"Compared to Mable, everyone is quiet."

She laughed. "How long have you two been friends?"

"Since college," I said, and I told her a bit about how we met and that we now lived in the same city. When Mable first texted me that she was considering leaving New York for San Francisco, I was out to lunch with colleagues and had been so excited I'd spilled water across the entire table. Mable explained she was sick of New York, that she wanted to be closer to Saratoga and her family. None of the

jobs she'd tried had panned out, and she had heard that it was easy
to get a perk-filled entry-level job at a big tech company.

What I didn't tell Fauna was that Mable had also said she
thought a tech job would leave time for her to pursue other things,
which I assumed to be her writing.

"You're lucky to have your best friend in the same city," she said
when I finished.

"My mom just said the same thing to me."

"Do you not feel lucky?"

"Of course I do," I said. I felt like she had somehow trapped me.
But then she said: "Robbie thinks you two are very different, but I
have a theory that you are actually really similar."

"You and Robbie talked about us?"

"Yes, we're fascinated by you two."

I wanted to admit I felt the same about her and Robbie, but this
would mean giving up something I didn't want to, not yet. "People
always find Mable to be the interesting one. I don't mean that in a
bitter way, just descriptively, if that makes sense. In college we had
this long-standing debate about who was whose sidekick." This was
usually carried on late at night, lying next to each other in one of
our twin beds. She was the lead actress and I was supporting, I was
sure of it. I'm the quiet, compliant Asian girl, I'd say. I'm smart and
I'll never make any trouble. So I guess I have to be the sidekick. To
this, Mable would say: Does that make me a dragon lady? Untrust-
worthy, aggressive, dangerous? No, I'd say, you're the one who's fascinating, the smart one, the popular one. Why would the camera
follow me when it could follow you? Either way, all roads lead to
Rome, said Mable, and we'll both be sexualized and exoticized.

Then she would launch into the insidious power of the patriarchy and white supremacy, and how one of their greatest legacies was that we had internalized racism and sexism so much so that even as close friends, we could see each other only through these offensive, problematic lenses. By this point in the conversation both of us were so affected—me depressed and her furious—that we would have to change the subject altogether.

"What was the verdict?" said Fauna.

"I think it's obvious: I'm her sidekick." This must've been immediately apparent to Fauna or anyone we met. The alternative was impossible. Saying I was the main character was like saying *The Great Gatsby* was about Nick Carraway. I never said this to her, though, because I knew she'd laugh at my referencing a book everyone had to read in tenth grade.

"I don't know about that," Fauna said. "Although I think I understand why you think you'd be her sidekick, and why Robbie thinks you two are so different."

I imagined Robbie thinking about me, talking about me. It felt delicious.

"I didn't realize how much I revealed of myself yesterday."

She laughed. "See? This is what I mean."

"That I can be funny like her?"

"No, that you can be just as biting." She bought a handful of strawberries from a table and took a bite of one. She wiped her mouth clean of red before continuing. "Your questions about whether Robbie and I were married, and about my previous relationships, were pretty obvious."

I started to apologize, but she cut me off. "No, I'm not offended.

I'm flattered, actually. It's obvious that that's what you find inter-esting."

"I don't want you to think I'm this boring person who only evaluates people by their marital status."

Fauna seemed to contemplate my answer as she picked up a few blueberries from a table and handed them to me. "Why did you ask me, then?"

"Because of Ian. Who I'm sure Mable told you about." The blue-berries were ripe, and when I took a bite, some of the juice dribbled down my lips.

She nodded, and began to wipe the blueberry juice that had stained the corners of my mouth with a napkin, in a way that felt maternal. I began to think of my mom, of her alone at home in Ohio, calling me in the middle of the night. I thought of how I'd been short with her the last time we talked, and I turned away, not wanting Fauna to see me cry.

Maybe because she'd noticed, she engaged in a conversation with the cheesemonger at the next table about what he had on offer.

I gathered myself and waited until she was done chatting with the seller, then said, "You must have friendships like ours."

"Sure."

"You know, since you're so interested in us."

"Here we go." She had a small smile on her face.

"I just mean if you and Robbie talk about us and you have a theory about us, you must have some interest in friendships in general. And maybe that has to do with your own."

"Of course I have close friends. Who doesn't?" She picked up an orange block of cheese, then set it down on the table. I thought this was all she was going to say when she added, "I'm actually not in touch with some of them anymore."

"Did you have a falling-out?"

"You could say that."

"Would you say that?"

She openly laughed now. "Yes."

"I couldn't imagine us not talking. Mable and me, I mean."

"It's not like I'm proud of this," she said.

I wanted to ask why, then, had she shared this fact about herself, especially when it was clear she wanted to say as little as she could about her own life. But instead, I followed her to another table, this one piled with tomatoes and figs. Finally, I said, "What do you do?"

"You mean, what's my job?" She barely looked at me, but I knew it wasn't out of embarrassment. That small smile was still on her face; this time, it felt mocking.

"Yes."

"I'm in between things at the moment."

It was clear she wasn't going to elaborate, but she linked her arm around mine and we walked toward the market entrance, where Mable and Robbie were waiting for us. It was close to the lunch hour, and the aisles were starting to get even more packed. Before we reached them, a man passed us wearing a tank top and swim trunks, and eating an ice cream cone that was dripping onto his hand. He was very attractive, someone who looked like he belonged at our hotel, but he might've been a local. He was speaking French and was my age, if not a few years younger. Fauna was also looking at him.

We were only a few feet away from Mable and Robbie, and I saw that Robbie was watching Fauna. His left hand was in the pocket of his pants, his right arm loose against his side. It seemed he was trying hard to look casual, but I could see the outline of a fist in his pocket, and he was shifting his weight back and forth on his feet.

It was the first time I'd seen Robbie when he wasn't smiling or talking, or otherwise aware that he was being observed, and his face had a contemplative quality as he watched Fauna watch the stranger.

I unlinked my arm, suddenly feeling like I didn't want to be associated with her, and went up to Mable, who enthusiastically showed me everything they'd bought to take back to the hotel. I pretended to be interested in her purchases, although all the while I was very aware of Robbie and Fauna in my peripheral vision. They seemed to be having some sort of silent conversation, one in which Fauna was comforting him somehow.

By the time Mable finished her show-and-tell, Fauna and Robbie had resumed their smooth and impassive expressions.

• • •

We had lunch outside at a nearby restaurant Robbie and Fauna picked out. Both Jean-Michel and Marcus had also recommended it. I ate greedily; my conversation with Fauna had drained me of energy, and again I found myself second-guessing everything I was saying, then falling quiet in the foursome. It was probably because of Ian and Cat that I was feeling loyal to Robbie after that moment in the farmer's market, and whenever Fauna told a story that made everyone laugh, I felt somehow guilty about participating, even though Robbie was laughing, too.

I was also consumed by how little information I had gleaned about her. I wanted to know where she lived and how she could afford to vacation here every year. And yet she had no problem being so familiar with me, my friendship with Mable. She had already learned quite a bit of information about me, much of it too personal to share with someone I barely knew. Close to the end of our meal, I remembered that she had called me "biting." When I replayed it in my mind, it came across as cruel.

As we left the restaurant, Mable expressed interest in going to the Picasso Museum, which was just a short walk away. Robbie and Fauna had been there multiple times but were happy to go again, they told us. I was nervous after my experience at the de Young the day we left San Francisco, and by the time we reached the doors of the museum, I knew I didn't want to go inside. I made an excuse about wanting to walk around town, and no one pushed back, not even Mable.

I headed away from the farmer's market and the museum, and quickly found myself in a series of alleyways and small streets, surrounded by yellow and brown stucco houses with iron grating. Almost all the houses had window boxes filled with white and pink flowers, and the ground was covered in bricks or cobblestone, depending on the street. It was quaint and beautiful in a sentimental way. After close to an hour of wandering, I found myself in an area that felt devoid of tourists. A woman walking ahead of me unlocked the front door of her house, and for a split second, I caught a glimpse of the tiled floor of her living room.

I turned a corner and saw Robbie standing there, looking up at a house with green shutters. He looked a bit embarrassed that I'd found him.

"I'm not an art person, I guess," he said. "I always feel stir-crazy in museums."

I told him I was the same. I found myself sharing with him what had happened at the de Young. We were walking together now, working our way even farther from the tourists. I no longer had any idea where we were in relation to the museum.

"I've felt that way, too," he said. "But it's not with art. It's with music. I feel it deeply, sometimes I think more than other people do." He looked sheepish. "I realize how stupid that sounds. Like I'm in college."

"It was the first time it's happened to me. I mean, I've been affected by art before, that's not what I'm saying. But it's never made me so profoundly sad."

"You were probably thinking of your husband."

There was a pause, and the only sound was the murmurs of music from the open window of a nearby house. "How much do you and Fauna know about what happened?" I asked.

"More or less everything," he said. "Mable told us about Ian and the other woman with that odd name."

"Cat."

"That's right."

"Does it bother you that Fauna and I know?" he asked. "When Mable was telling us, I did feel a bit uncomfortable, even though I didn't know you then."

A man was behind us on the narrow street, his arms full of grocery bags, so we stopped, making room for him to pass. He looked like a local, and I had no idea how much English he knew, but I waited until he was out of earshot to say, "I'm not surprised that she told you all of it. That's Mable." Then I asked, "Did she talk about Ian only in the context of Cat?"

"What do you mean?"

"I'm wondering if she shared her opinion on Ian otherwise. How she felt about him as a person, I mean."

He rubbed his right hand on the side of his face. "There was some of that, yes."

"Well, I don't know how she described him to you and Fauna, but it's possible it wasn't a fair portrayal. I don't know how she ever felt about him."

"I'll take what she said with a grain of salt."

"That's right," I said. "They never really quite hit it off. But I guess it wouldn't be fair to say they disliked each other either. Actually, I don't even know how he ever felt about her." Robbie was so unlike Fauna, and it felt easy and natural to talk about myself. I told him about the first time Mable and Ian met, at the wedding of an old college friend. Ian was my plus-one, and I was nervous about introducing them. Ian was closer on the political spectrum to Mable than other boyfriends I'd had, so in that sense I didn't anticipate any trouble. But everything else, I wasn't sure of at all.

"The night went fine," I said. "I don't really have another word to describe it. They both talked enough so it wasn't awkward, but they kept it light. I think I heard Mable discuss the weather for the first time in her life."

It was as if each of them had decided to put forth the blandest version of themself, which I guess I could've found flattering since it was so clearly done for my sake. That night, I'd gone to bed wondering how it could be possible that I could love both Ian and

Mable so much, but have them feel tepidly about each other. There must've been a version of me that Ian loved and a version of me that Mable loved. Wouldn't those two versions have some sort of overlap? I wondered. I imagined a Venn diagram with me in the middle, my arms and legs spread out like the Leonardo da Vinci drawings. What exactly was in the middle? I worried that I couldn't figure that out, and I was pretty sure both Ian and Mable knew exactly what lay at their own cores and that it was unchanged no matter what situation they were in.

It was starting to get really hot out, and Robbie's thick, dark hair was beginning to loosen. Strands fell against his forehead. I said, "What was it like when you and Fauna met?"

He shrugged. "That was about a year ago, right around when I left my job. It wasn't an easy time. She made it much better. Lighter." He put his hands into his pockets. "I had just moved."

"You were in Manhattan before."

"That's right," he said.

"As a consultant."

He gave me a wide smile and said, "I guess it's only fair that what I told Mable gets back to you. Since I just told you what Mable said about Ian."

I laughed. "Mable said you left your consulting job."

Robbie nodded. "I'd had the same job since business school. It was fine, don't get me wrong, but I hated the feeling that my life was decided. I'd just turned thirty, and the idea that this was all that was ahead of me was terrifying." He took his hands out of his pockets, crossed them in front of his chest, and then uncrossed them. "So I quit and drove across the country. That's when I met Fauna."

When Robbie had driven us into town that morning, he had left his window open, his left arm tapping against the side of the car to the beat of the music. I imagined him doing the same but on a deserted highway in the middle of the States, his life packed into the back seat and his trunk.

He went on. "I know this makes me sound terribly indulgent. I'm lucky to be able to do this. I had a lot saved up from my job. And also, my parents, they have a good business. Real estate development." Up until this point, Robbie had been looking at me out of the corner of his eye, but when he mentioned his parents' business, he stared straight ahead.

I thought about telling him about Ian's life insurance money, but instead I said, "It was brave of you to quit. I admire that. I don't know if I could do the same."

"I couldn't recommend it to everyone. But I'm glad I did."

I pulled out my phone as if I had gotten a message, even though I knew I hadn't, then put it back in my bag. "You know, Ian was white. I don't know if Mable mentioned it," I said.

"She did." There was a silence and then he said, "You know, Fauna is white."

"Really?" We both laughed. "You're not going to make some crack about how I married a white guy?" I asked.

"I could," he said. "I definitely could." Then he said, "It's not always easy. To be with someone white."

"No, it's not."

"I don't know about you, but when I'm dating someone white, there are periods where I question so much. I find myself having imaginary debates about myself, about her, about our relationship.

But this debate is in my head, so I'm obviously the one arguing both sides. I understand the other side, I'm sympathetic to it, and I want it to win a lot of the time." He shook his head. "And yet that debate framework isn't quite right either. I don't think relationships are supposed to be set up like that, zero-sum. I guess what I'm trying to say is that it can be exhausting."

I said, "I can feel that way even when I'm not dating someone white. It's just the world we live in. Always having to engage with whiteness, at a minimum."

He nodded, and we were silent for a few paces. Then he said, "Mable didn't describe Ian as a terrible person, if that's what you're worried about."

"No, she would've saved that kind of vitriol for Jeremy."

"Jeremy?"

"My serious college boyfriend. She hated him. They got in a horrible fight the first and last time they ever really talked." A door swung open onto the street, only narrowly missing us, and Robbie instinctively put his right arm around me. His hand was warm and firm against my skin, and I could feel the pads of each of his fingers. He kept it on me for a few more paces after we sidestepped the door. After he let go, I touched my right shoulder, the place where his hand had just been.

I continued. "We had this college professor who was super famous. He had just gotten the MacArthur grant. Anyway, there was a rumor at school that he slept with all his female grad students."

"What a guy."

"Jeremy and I met when Mable was studying abroad in Amsterdam, and when she was back, I set up this dinner for both of them to meet each other. Jeremy spent the whole night defending the professor. He said something I'll never forget: 'That comes with the territory with geniuses.' I'm sure you can guess how Mable took that." Jeremy had also given us a hypothetical about someone who made a great invention that saved millions of lives but was abusive to his children. He came to the conclusion that it didn't matter. There's nothing more boring than a tortured genius, Mable had said. Artist, CEO, whatever. Who gives a fuck, she said. Later that night, Jeremy had stood over the foot of my dorm room twin bed, giving me a list of reasons why he found her annoying, a killjoy, not nearly as funny or smart as she thought she was.

"I'm not sure this is the reaction you're looking for, but he does sound like an ass," said Robbie.

I nodded. "He was my first serious boyfriend, and he felt so important back then," I said. "That's embarrassing to admit, but it's the truth."

My relationship with Jeremy marked the beginning of the period when I began to question whether I had become just like my mother. She might as well have picked him out for me. His family was from Manhattan; he'd gone to a private school that had a long list of "Notable Alumni" on its Wikipedia page. He went on about his dad's job, pronouncing "finance" unlike I'd ever heard it. It was a short "i" sound with an emphasis on the last syllable. Fi-*nance*. His whole family pronounced it the same way. These were things that, although I would've rather died than admit it, made me faintly proud of dating him, like he was some sort of sought-after bird I'd coaxed into the view of my binoculars.

"I'm talking so much about myself," I said now, letting out a small laugh. The road narrowed farther and I paused, thinking that Robbie would want to walk ahead of or behind me. But he moved closer, walking up right next to me so our bodies were pressed up against each other, his right arm hard and steady against mine. He was more than a head taller than me, and I could feel his breath against my neck, moving a few strands of hair around.

"I like hearing about you," he said.

As soon as the road widened I took a step to the side to maintain our original distance. I wondered if he would've moved to the side if I hadn't. I wouldn't have done it if it had been possible for me to form words, continue the conversation in any way, when I could feel him that close to me.

"So this is interesting to you, then," I said. I let out another short laugh and looked right above his head to a window box with white flowers.

"It is," he said. "Don't stop."

I looked straight ahead rather than at him. "By junior year," I continued, "Mable and I had made a deal that she could complain about Jeremy all she wanted for one day each quarter, but she couldn't say anything bad on any other day." This compromise had satisfied both of us, since I could steel myself for it, and she could prepare all her remarks, like it was a TED Talk. During the rest of the year, whenever he did something I knew would upset her (like dismiss the shuttering of a beloved local bookstore as nothing more than capitalism working correctly), I was nervous because I knew she'd be adding it to her running list.

"What reasons did she give?" asked Robbie. "Besides the obvious."

I tried my best to recount them. Mable's list always contained at least some things that I could've written myself. He was not only in a fraternity, but he was the president, and he had the paper version of the *Financial Times* delivered and would read it in the cafeteria, laying the salmon pink papers on the side of his tray, next to his food. He chose it because it's not the *Wall Street Journal* or the *New York Times*, she said. He never reads it when he's alone. But Mable's list also contained things that slammed against my body. Things that even I had to admit were serious: he was only interested in my opinions when they lined up with his; he didn't take my anger seriously. That I was afraid to take him home for the holidays, to show him where I had grown up, and that when I would broach the topic of this fear to him he'd shrug and say, To be honest, it's just easier if we visit my parents anyway. I'd rather fly than drive through snow, he'd elaborate, and we can make it actually fun. This phrase was something Mable had harped on: we can make it actually fun. He really said that, "make it actually fun."

While I was telling him about Jeremy, Robbie made sympathetic comments, but it didn't lead him to share any more personal information about himself. Robbie and Fauna were both deliberate in what they divulged. While I'd found Fauna's deflections explicit, however, Robbie's were more subtle. He conveyed a genuine warmth that invited vulnerability. I imagined I might feel similarly talking to a therapist. When he listened, he would do so with his whole body, leaning in as if I had some sort of magnetic pull.

When we finally took out our phones to figure out the way back to the museum, and started to retrace our steps, I said, "Isn't it odd that I'm telling you so many intimate things, and I only met you yesterday?"

"I'm part of your story now," he said.

"I guess so," I said. "But I'm part of yours, too. All of us are." After a moment I said, "Actually, I think you and I are a part of Fauna and Mable's story."

He let out a short laugh.

I thought of the silent exchange Robbie and Fauna had had earlier, but I wasn't sure how to bring this up without making him uncomfortable. I knew, however, that whatever kinship I had felt with him during lunch was stronger now. It felt like both of us were defined primarily by our feelings toward those we were closest with, the kind of people who were defined in contrast to those around us. This only struck me more deeply when we finally met up with Fauna and Mable, neither of whom acted like they'd registered our absence. They were deep in conversation about some piece they'd seen at the museum.

When Mable and I got back to our rooms, I made some comment about hoping that Fauna didn't think it was odd that Robbie and I ended up spending the afternoon together.

She looked surprised. "But you would never cross a line with someone else's partner. And Robbie is the same, I think."

"So there was nothing weird about it?"

"Not at all."

I knew she meant it as a compliment to my integrity, but for some reason, I was disappointed that Fauna found me so unthreatening.

Chapter Fourteen

The next day, the four of us met for lunch at the pool. When we arrived, Paul and Bertie were just leaving. Bertie was wearing a white cover-up over a lavender one-piece, and Paul had on a pair of cerulean swim trunks. Both of them smelled strongly of coconut sunscreen. Mable and I said a quick hello to them while Fauna and Robbie went ahead and got us four lounge seats together.

It had been an unusually hot morning, and after eating we had all lain on our chairs, watching the sky. Robbie fell asleep next to me as I finished one of the magazines I had borrowed from Mable, who was chatting with Fauna. I had my headphones in since I'd been listening to music while reading, but I hit Pause. I was about to take the headphones off and join the conversation when I heard Mable say, "What about them? Do them."

Out of the corner of my eye I could see her nod toward a family near us: a man reading to a young boy sitting in his lap; a woman next to them putting tanning oil on her arms and legs. They had taken up an inordinate amount of room, almost six chairs, despite being a group of only three, and they had multiple beach bags with them.

"Not her kid," Fauna said. "Strictly a stepmother situation. I'm going to say third wife."

"How do you know that?"

"The kid isn't remotely interested in her. And look at her, she's way too young for the husband." We couldn't see her face, but it was true that from the back, the man and woman looked to have at least fifteen years' difference in age.

"And them?" said Mable.

A group of three American women who looked to be in their late thirties were talking and laughing loudly. There was a tipped-over wineglass under one of their chairs, a plate of half-eaten fries resting on another. One of them, clearly drunk, was talking loudly about how she wished they could change the music playing over the speakers.

"Jesus," said Fauna. "Even I believe in mercy."

The conversation felt cruel to me, and yet I couldn't help being fascinated. I knew I wasn't much better than them. I also knew that Mable wasn't actually interested in who these other guests were; she was doing this strictly to understand what was in Fauna's head, to get a better sense of the cast of her mind. Fauna already had great power over Mable, that was clear.

She seemed poised for Mable to pick another victim when Mable said, "Where do you live?" Mable and I had spent the previous evening parsing through the few morsels Fauna had given me at the farmer's market about her life, and wondering why she was so elusive. The little information we had received had given us a great deal of energy, making it difficult for us to fall asleep.

She laughed and said, "You already know. The U.S."

"Well, sure. But where?"

"California."

"Oh, Bay Area, too?"

"No."

Even from my chair, I could tell Mable was nervous, something she rarely was. She drew her knees to her chin and hugged them closer to her. "Southern California, then?"

"Yes."

"Where?"

Fauna took a long drink of water and then said, "Los Angeles."

"Were you there for work? Your last job, I mean. I know you aren't working right now."

At this, Fauna put down her glass. "Clearly you and Ellie have been talking about me."

"She mentioned you were between things, yes."

"Yes, I came back to the West Coast for work."

I noted that she used the word "back," and felt sure Mable did, too. So Fauna was originally from the West Coast.

"Robbie is from all over. He spent the majority of his childhood in the States, but he traveled a lot when he was young," said Fauna. "He's more worldly than most."

I had no doubt that later Mable and I would find this to be another skilled deflection from Fauna, but this detail would feed us. Robbie was with Fauna, which meant that any information about him fed our obsessive curiosity about her. In fact, earlier in the morning, Mable and I had discussed what Robbie had told me the day before. All this time, I'd wondered about Robbie being with Fauna, I had said, instead of having a more traditional relationship.

I knew he must've had some sort of contrarian side. It's coming out now in his thirties, quitting his good job and wandering around the world, I said. How rebellious of him, said Mable, a sarcastic smile on her face. Using his consulting money, his parents' wealth, to hang out in Europe.

Now Mable lowered her right foot and dragged it back and forth across the ground.

Fauna said, "And you? Where are you from?"

"Northern California. I came back after a few years in New York. It just feels like my parents are getting older and I didn't like that it took a day of travel to see them. My brothers are also finishing high school next year, and I wanted to spend time with them before they leave."

Mable waited, as did I, to see if Fauna would mention anything about her own family. But instead she said, "Did your company transfer you out to California?"

Mable let out a laugh. "Not at all." She talked a bit about her string of jobs in New York City, and what she had done in San Francisco since moving back.

When she'd finished, Fauna said, "Must give you good time to write, though. To have those breaks between jobs."

I hadn't realized Mable had told Fauna that she was a writer. This struck me as odd, since very few people knew about it.

"Yes," Mable said. "I mean, that's what I tell myself, I guess."

"Would you like something longer term, then? It doesn't seem like you do."

"I want to want something long term."

"Does that go for relationships, too?"

"Sure, I guess. I mean, when it comes to romantic relationships, I feel less of a desire for a serious thing. I don't necessarily mean it would be something bad to have, just that it isn't something I'm particularly interested in."

Fauna was quiet and then said, "You have time."

"I have time," Mable repeated.

From my angle, I could see that Mable had picked off almost all of her nail polish during this exchange and had taken her hair out of her bun, running her hands through it a few times. She did things like this only when she was uncomfortable, and I found myself feeling suspicious of Fauna again. I removed my headphones and asked them about the weather forecast for the evening, making sure to be loud enough to wake Robbie. When Mable and Fauna turned to answer me, I could sense relief in Mable's face.

We decided to order a round of drinks, and Mable floated the idea of our sharing a pitcher of cocktails. We settled on a gin concoction made from a French apéritif, grapefruit juice, lime juice, grapefruit syrup, and tonic pink pepper.

When the pitcher arrived, we downed our drinks as if they were water, as if rehydrating from the afternoon in the sun.

I went to the bathroom, and when I came back, Robbie and Fauna were laughing at something Mable was saying. "What's so funny?" I asked, holding a cold glass against my forehead.

"Oh, nothing," said Mable. "Just drawing from my catalog of dating horror stories."

"College or after?" I asked.

"After," said Mable. "My prime."

"No, that's not right," said Fauna. "Women don't really reach their sexual prime until their thirties or later."

"So I do have something to look forward to after thirty," said Mable.

"The older I get, the better sex I have," said Fauna.

Mable turned to Robbie and held up her drink. "Here's to you," she said.

Robbie laughed and thanked her. He and Fauna were sharing a lounge chair again, and she leaned against him, nuzzling her face into his neck.

"I don't think the sex in our twenties is too bad," I said. I took off my sunglasses and wiped off the sweat that had gathered on the bridge of my nose, then put them back on.

"I'm not saying it's bad in your twenties," said Fauna. "I'm just saying it gets better."

"Maybe," I said. Robbie was now caressing her arm. I thought about his hand, the way it had felt against my skin when we had been walking in Antibes.

Mable nodded at Fauna. "I think she's right. It's only going to get better."

"God, I remember casual sex in my twenties," said Fauna, now half lying on Robbie, her head on his chest. Robbie leaned down and kissed the top of her head.

"I guess," I said. I refilled everyone's drinks and put the now-empty pitcher on a nearby table.

"What do you two think about open relationships?" asked Fauna, sitting up so that her legs hung over the sides of the lounge chair. "I tried it out before, a few years ago."

Mable said, "It certainly makes more sense as a concept than monogamy."

I said, "Was it with one of your husbands that you tried it?"

She gave me the same smile she'd given me at the farmer's market when I asked her about herself, and shook her head. "In between."

"It's not you, is it?" Mable said to Robbie, clearly teasing. "What a twist that would be."

He let out a snort. "No."

"You seem to find the idea funny that it would be you," I said.

"I just don't find that lifestyle alluring at all," he said. "I don't think I'd get anything out of it." He held out his right hand, as if he was giving me something that was in his palm. "This might sound stupid to say aloud, but I enjoy monogamy. I admire that type of singular devotion."

"I'm the same," I said.

"Ah," said Fauna. "So now Ellie answers my question."

"You know how some people are strict constructionists about the Constitution?" Mable said. "That's Ellie with monogamy. Strict adherence."

I placed my glass down on the nearby table, harder than I'd anticipated. I'd finished my second cocktail by this point. "The thing is, strict monogamy requires both members of the couple to be adherents."

It was the first time I had mentioned Ian's infidelity to all of them at once, and I could tell no one knew quite what to say. And then Mable said, "Fucking piece of shit."

"What was he like?" asked Fauna. She leaned toward me so she was no longer touching Robbie. I wondered if she had waited for an opening from me to ask about Ian.

"He got along with everyone," I said. "Funny and nice. Very sociable." It felt like such a flat description for him, and I added, "He made me laugh a lot."

"He sounds charming," Fauna said.

"He was," I said.

And then Mable said: "Not everyone has the same definition of 'charm.'" This was the first time she'd said something derogatory about Ian since he died. Coupled with her saying it in front of Fauna and Robbie, it felt like a direct affront.

Fauna said, "Charm can be hard to resist, that's for sure." I knew she was trying to defuse what Mable had said, and that only made me angrier.

"He was a lot more than that, too," I said. "You know, it's not that easy to sum someone up like this." I began to gather some of the magazines I'd been reading into my bag. It was getting closer to dinnertime, and we'd been at the pool for hours.

Robbie had finished his second drink and placed his glass on the ground next to his chair. He sat back in the chair and was quiet. But Fauna said, "You're still pretty loyal to Ian."

"What's wrong with that?" I asked.

"Well, he cheated on you, didn't he?"

"I'm very aware of that. I think there is no one else in the world who is more aware of that fact."

"It's just interesting, that's all. That you're still loyal to him," she said.

"Well, maybe it's because you've never had a husband die. You've only left them." I picked up my bag and walked toward the restaurant adjoining the pool.

Inside, I sped past a maître d' who nodded at me when I took a seat at an empty table. The air conditioning was very strong, and soon I was shivering. After a moment, Robbie came in and sat down next to me.

"That was bad," he said. "Fauna feels pretty guilty about what she said."

I waved my hand at him. "It's not really her. It was Mable I was annoyed at."

"I see."

"I keep doing this. Being mad at the wrong person. I did it with my mom a couple days ago."

"You seem to be really angry," he said, then added quickly, "which makes sense. You have the right to be angry."

"It comes on really quick in me. But mainly I just feel sad."

There was a moment of silence between us, and I caught my reflection in a shiny spoon that was laid out on a place mat. My head looked like that of an alien, and my throat resembled a straw. "How do you know Fauna felt bad? Did she say that?"

He spoke very slowly. "No. But I can tell. I know her. I know she likes you and wants to be gentle around you."

"That feels patronizing."

"I don't mean it to be, and she doesn't either. I think she just cares about how you feel." I think Robbie could read the surprise on my face.

"So she sent you over to apologize? Like some kind of messenger?" I said, then immediately backtracked. "Sorry, that came off wrong."

He fiddled with the spoon on his place mat. "I know how we come across to others. Like I'm the one who wants commitment, and she won't be pinned down. I've made peace with that."

"Have you, though?"

He smiled at me. "Maybe I'm just kidding myself."

"Do you ever wonder why we like who we like? Why did I like Ian? And Mable and me, too—why are we best friends?"

"I think that's something you'll never really understand. And it's pointless to try."

A waiter came over to us to take our order. We told him we weren't eating and got up. "Should we head back?" he asked. "Are you feeling up for that?"

I said I was and we went back to the pool, where Mable's and Fauna's heads were close in conversation. As soon as they saw me, they stopped talking abruptly and broke apart.

Fauna reached out and grabbed my hand. "I shouldn't have said that, Ellie."

"Same," said Mable, leaning back in her chair and not looking at me. All of the feelings of forgiveness I had worked up just a few moments ago had evaporated.

"Can we talk?" I said to Mable. "Alone?"

She shrugged but walked with me to the far side of the pool, where the bathrooms were. The only person around was a woman on her phone.

"'Not everyone has the same definition of "charm"'? Really?"

"I didn't mean to hurt your feelings. But it feels so fake that we still sit around and talk about how great Ian was. He was horrible to you, and I don't mind saying it."

"He was *my* husband, Mable. I get to decide when and where we shit on him."

"Well, then we'll be waiting until we die," she said. "I'm sorry, but you really haven't processed your anger, and it shows."

"You don't understand. You've never been married."

She put her left hand on her forehead so her thumb and middle finger were pressed on her temples. "Really, Ellie? You're going to use that to ignore my point?"

"It's a fact."

"Well, another fact is this right here?" She pointed to herself and then to me. "You were never direct like this with him, and that was a problem. And why shouldn't someone point this out to you? Overlooking his faults doesn't come from a place of kindness, it comes from one of fear."

"So because my husband is dead and was fucking someone else and I don't want to talk about it with you all day long, I'm a coward?" I was very loud at this point, and the woman on the phone glared at us. "Is this what you want, Mable? For me to be angry like this? Is this anger *good* enough for you?"

I left her there and walked around the side of the pool farthest from Robbie and Fauna, then made my way back to our rooms. Inside, I opened my laptop, and pulled up the motion I was working on, and drafted a few introductory sentences with little substance; they'd no doubt have to be rewritten. I billed half an hour of work before feeling overwhelmed again. Marcus had written me a very sweet email, gently noting that Michael was looking for more guidance from me. His kindness made me only feel worse, and I called down to the lobby for a drink. When the knock came at the door, it was Jean-Michel outside.

"Ms. Huang," he said. He handed me the cocktail, which was in a cold glass.

"Thank you."

He studied my face for a moment and then shifted his weight from right to left. "I believe the rest of your friends are still at the pool."

"Mable is here," I said. "She's just in the bathroom." I closed the door.

I drank the cocktail quickly. It tasted like flowers. I wanted to order another one, but I didn't want Jean-Michel to come back. Instead, I closed all the shutters and turned off all the lights. It was very dark, and I could pretend that it was night.

The day after the disastrous Mable and Jeremy dinner, I had met Mable on the lawn by Deering Library. It was in the afternoon and summer was a few weeks away.

What do you like about him? she'd asked before I could say anything. I remembered she was wearing a bright orange dress she had bought in Amsterdam.

I thought about it for a minute, knowing I would have only one chance with her. I said, He's really supportive about my career ambitions, law school and everything. I mentioned that he got along well with my mom, and that this past Valentine's Day he'd arranged for three big flower arrangements to be delivered to me in a seminar class.

Mable said, Look, I wouldn't date him, not like that matters. We're not interested in the same kind of people. I braced myself as I knew she was just beginning. She went on: But the qualities you're giving me are so baseline. He supports your career plans, as he should. He likes your mom, as he should. And the flowers? I'm not sure that was about you. Having them arrive in the middle of class, in front of everyone—that was about him, I think, Ellie.

I'd found her feedback cruel. She could make anything look stupid, and she was doing it here. Besides, Mable had never held a relationship for longer than a quarter. On the long-term relationship front, I was more experienced than Mable; the list of things I knew more about than her was short, but I clung to each item like a buoy.

She wasn't finished. But, really, that's not even all that bothers me, she told me. None of this really matters. Mable had brought an iced tea with her, and she took a long sip, dragging the moment out for effect. She said, I don't get why you don't say anything around him.

What do you mean? I talked plenty at dinner, I said. Well, yeah, said Mable. About things that were easy. She brought up the Mac-Arthur professor, and I cut her off. I genuinely don't know much about him, I said. No, but you didn't say anything, said Mable. It made me nervous that you didn't seem to want to. And Jeremy didn't seem to mind at all.

I protested more. He knew that I didn't want to get in the middle, I explained. Mable shook her head hard. *Jesus*, Ellie.

We sat in silence for a moment. Some students were playing Frisbee nearby, and we could hear them calling back and forth to each other. I studied them, as if they were of interest to me. Finally I told Mable I agreed with her about the professor. But you had no problem holding your own in that debate, you didn't need me, I said.

No, said Mable. It's not about needing you. I cut her off again. Can we change the subject? I asked. It's bad enough that you guys didn't like each other. You can be so self-righteous, you know. Mable grinned at me, all her teeth showing. See? she said. This is what I mean. You have no problem calling me on my shit. You can do it with him, too.

By then I knew we were both going to let it go.

I opened my eyes, forcing myself back to France, to my hotel room. Mable in her orange dress disappeared. I had been sitting on my bed, the empty cocktail glass by my feet on the ground. I picked it up and placed it outside our suite's door. The hallway was empty. Back inside, I lay back down on the bed and I must've fallen asleep, because when I opened my eyes, the small amount of light that had been peeking around the edges of the closed shutters had disappeared. It was now dark outside. As I got up, I noticed a sharp twinge in my neck. I'd slept awkwardly on the middle of the bed without a pillow. I replayed the conversation at the pool in my mind, and the anger and indignation I felt earlier had been replaced by embarrassment. I felt small and childish. I knew that Fauna, Robbie, and Mable would be down at the bar where we'd met Paul and Bertie the first night. I imagined what they'd said about me while I was gone. Perhaps Fauna or Robbie had told Mable to give me some space, which explained why she hadn't come looking for me.

I changed out of my bathing suit and into a dress, and then left my room to find them. They were huddled in a corner at the bar, and I was making my way over when a middle-aged man holding a drink stepped in front of me.

"Ellie, right?" He had on a very crisp white shirt, which only served to highlight his sunburned pink skin.

"Yes. Do I know you?"

"We met a few nights ago. Remember?"

I really couldn't, but I nodded.

"How has your stay been so far?"

"It's been fine."

"Have you tried out this place yet?" He pulled out his phone and showed me a photograph of himself standing in front of a restaurant I didn't recognize. He began to scroll with his thumb, showing me an inordinate number of pictures of his food, all of the images badly lit and composed.

"No," I said.

"We should all go," he said.

"I guess."

"It'll be fun. Just like the first night we met."

I tried to look over his shoulder, to see if Mable and the others were still there, but my neck was so tight that I winced.

"Neck pain?" he asked.

"Yeah, it's just a knot or something from sleeping the wrong way."

Without saying anything, he reached over and put a hand on the base of my scalp and started making circular motions against my neck with his fingers. I thought about shouting or telling him to stop, and was feeling very panicked, when I sensed Mable beside me. Relief swept through me so powerfully I could have cried.

"What are you doing?" she said. It was only her voice that came to me, since I couldn't turn my neck to look at her.

"She said there was a knot in her neck, and I'm massaging it out," he said.

Mable put her hand on his forearm and lifted it away from me. "Stop touching her."

He stepped back and held up both hands in surrender. "Sorry, just trying to do something nice."

"Fuck off," she said.

She put her arm around my shoulders and led me over to a table with velvet chairs, where Fauna and Robbie greeted us with applause. "Hear, hear," said Fauna. "To Mable the savior."

I pulled her close to me into a hug. In her ear I said: "Let's both be good." She nodded and handed me a drink, which they must have ordered for me when they saw me enter the bar.

The rest of the night went fine, and I could tell that they'd promised one another to be nice to me, which somehow didn't really bother me. Later, when Mable and I were back in our rooms getting ready for bed, we shared notes again on Fauna. I told Mable I had overheard her conversation with Fauna by the pool.

Mable said, "I got nothing more from her. Absolutely nothing."

"Well, she's from LA."

"It took a cross-examination to get that little bit out of her."

"And then she deflected. Turned it on you."

"I didn't even realize it had happened until much later."

"You aren't normally so timid when you're curious," I said.

"I've never seen someone hold the power in the conversation with you."

Mable was quiet for a moment, then said, "You're right."

"I looked them both up online the other day, but it wasn't illuminating at all." In bed the night before, I'd spent an embarrassing amount of time trying to find any information about them on my phone.

Mable nodded her head. "Me too. When I looked up 'Fauna, Los Angeles,' all I got were pictures of greenery. I don't know her last name. And 'Chu' is too popular. I couldn't find anything about a 'Robert Chu' either."

Not long after, Mable went to her bedroom and shut the door. I tried to sleep, but the nap before dinner had thrown me off schedule. Finally, I decided I was going to learn to conquer my fear of the ocean. I picked up my phone from the nightstand, pulled up a search window, and typed: "fear of water, how to get over." I read a bit about immersion therapy. I decided I'd try it at some point when the others weren't around. Eventually, I figured, I would stop feeling like I was being eaten alive.

Chapter Fifteen

The next day at breakfast, everyone continued to treat me gently. In the middle of the meal, Robbie suggested going to a restaurant in Saint-Tropez, which was ninety minutes away. It sounded like a long trip to me, but when Mable looked up the restaurant, Le Club 55, and saw that it was frequented by famous actors, models, and pop stars, she immediately agreed. I would've rather stayed at the hotel since it was starting to feel like home, as weird as that was. Luxury comes easily to you, Mable said, smirking, when I told her this. I decided to join them.

We set off soon after breakfast, Fauna in the passenger seat again and Mable and me in the back. We kept the windows down and blasted music like last time, but Mable chose the music this time, and she changed the genre every few songs, so we never quite knew what was coming. When we knew the lyrics, we all sang along.

Because we hadn't hit any traffic, we had time to walk around Saint-Tropez before our lunch reservation. Fauna wanted to go shopping, so Robbie parked and we all followed her as she went from store to store, almost all of them some designer or luxury brand. I felt out of place, even though every salesperson greeted us warmly. I vacillated between picking up objects I would never buy and feeling guilty when a sales associate would talk to me, and just feeling guilty when I walked in and made it obvious I wasn't going to buy anything. Mable, of course, had a lot of fun looking at all the price tags and making cutting remarks. Fauna didn't seem bothered by it and even started to egg her on, pointing out a purse or piece of jewelry she wanted Mable's comments on.

At one designer store, Fauna tried on a series of outfits. Each time she left the dressing room she would look to Robbie, who gave her his seemingly honest opinion, even when it was bad. She took it all very well and seemed to agree with him. Both of them picked out a few new items of clothing to buy. Robbie chose variants of what we'd seen him wear the last few days: expensive T-shirts and linen pants. Fauna purchased a dark red bikini, a black cover-up that swept the floor as she walked, and a lemon-colored dress.

Whenever she stepped out of a dressing room, I noticed her age more than usual. It reminded me of when I first saw her at the hotel and thought she was the same age as Robbie. It took certain lights, and turns of her face and body, but it was there if you wanted to see.

While they were in the dressing room, Mable and I sat on one of two large cream-colored couches. Other shoppers looked at us as they entered and exited the dressing rooms, and I wondered what people thought. Mable was scrolling through her phone, slouching so that most of her thighs were visible under her short black skirt. Her oversize white shirt, partly tucked into the skirt, was see-through under the bright lights of the store, and from time-to-time, she tapped her tennis shoes to the music that was playing. I was on the couch next to her, wearing my nicest leather sandals and the most expensive clothing item I owned, a dusty blue crepe dress for which I'd paid a fraction of the price of anything in this store.

Because I was curious who was paying, I followed them to the cash register while they paid, making small talk with Robbie to disguise what I was doing. The clerk rang up all of their items together, and Fauna pulled out a dark blue credit card from her wallet. I was able to get a good look and finally catch her last name. Although I initially felt pleased that I now knew it was Fauna who was paying, it soon bothered me that I would judge them based on that. Fauna brought out a side of me I didn't like, I saw that now.

There were a few kitschy gift shops for tourists tucked among the luxury boutiques. Mable kept making us stop at them to browse, and at one store there were fake license plates with pictures of dogs on them. As she held up one with a beagle, she turned to Fauna and said: "It's perfect, don't you think? This store?"

"For the setting for the second half?"

"Yes, exactly."

"Are you still in the middle of revising?"

"Yes."

There was no doubt that they were discussing Mable's writing. She'd never gone into this level of detail with me, let alone asked me my opinion. For the rest of our morning wandering, I stuck close to Robbie.

When we got to Le Club 55, there was a long line of expensive cars waiting to be valet-parked. I could spot the parking lot, and I'd never seen so many cars that were red or neon green. There was even an SUV that was somehow black matte, as if it were covered in velvet. When we reached the head of the line, we climbed out and

Robbie dropped off his keys with the valet. The restaurant hadn't been entirely visible from the car, and it wasn't until we walked in that I realized it was located right on the beach. All the tables were covered in blue linen, and there was a thatched roof overhead, the kind of casual look that you know is incredibly expensive. The restaurant tables were mostly full, and above the music playing, the sound of lively conversation permeated everything. The attractiveness of the waitstaff was outdone only by that of the clientele. All the women were tall and thin, it seemed, and the men were tanned and spread their legs wide when they sat down. We were led in and seated at a corner table with a good view of the ocean.

A server stopped by to take our drink order, seeming to pay the most attention to Fauna and Robbie; it was like he'd been trained to know which people at each table were the ones who mattered. We ordered a bottle of wine from him before a blond ponytailed waitress came over. Robbie ordered for all of us in French and even though the waitress could hear him just fine from across the table, she walked around to be closer to him. By the time he was done ordering she was half crouched, her head next to his.

Fauna said nothing while the waitress was there, seemingly taking great care to listen to Mable. Before she left, the waitress turned to Fauna. *"Et pour vous, madame?"*

Fauna shook her head, and when the waitress left, she was looking at Robbie, one side of her mouth turned down.

Even though I hated cigarettes, I found myself taking one from Robbie when he offered them to the table. The only other time I'd seen him smoke was the first day at breakfast, but there seemed to be a permanent outline of a small rectangle in the back right pocket of his pants. I put the cigarette in my mouth and leaned forward so he could light it.

The waitress brought out a large wooden board piled with raw cauliflower florets, tomatoes, and mushrooms and placed it in the middle of the table. Because I was sitting next to Robbie and the restaurant was loud, it was easy to speak only to him and to avoid Mable. I couldn't stop thinking of the conversation she'd had with Fauna about her fiction, how much she'd revealed to this near stranger that she hadn't said to me.

Next to our table was a couple who were both so physically attractive it was painful. The woman was eating a plain salad while the man picked at a large lobster with his hands. They had the air of people who had just gotten in an argument, and I could tell the man was trying his best to make her smile. At one point he picked up a piece of lobster meat and held it to her lips, but she pushed his hand away.

While I watched them, I could only think about how different they were from Ian and me. Whenever I got mad at him, I couldn't hold out for even the length of a meal; soon, he would get me to laugh or smile at something and the spell would break. I'd realize the thing that had angered me was small and unimportant, a sight in my rearview mirror. I remember thinking that this dynamic in our relationship was a good thing because it meant we got over our problems quickly.

I said as much to Robbie, who was also looking at the beautiful couple next to us. He asked me what Ian and I had fought about.

"Oh, you know. The usual things, like our laundry preferences and stuff. Details."

"That's a pretty small disagreement, though. I wouldn't worry about moving past that too quickly."

I took a mushroom and put it on my plate. Even though I could've easily eaten it whole, I began to cut it up into small pieces, as if I were about to feed it to a child. "I lied to you just now. It was more than that."

"I see," he said.

"I'm so used to telling people that that's what we fought over," I said. "But there were some big things I didn't like. It wasn't easy going to law school with him."

"No? He was a partner when he died, right? Was he too intense about school?"

For a while Ian and I had tried to pretend we were on equal footing, but that became impossible when our grades were released. Stanford didn't have traditional grades, doling out only an Honors or a Pass, but the day the Honors and Passes were given out, we sat next to each other, anxiously refreshing our laptop screens at the same time. My "H"s made a ladder down my screen while his "P"s reminded me of a column of cartoon faces, flipped sideways, sticking out their tongues.

"The first time it happened, he said he didn't care. But the second time, it did matter." I took a carrot from the board now and began to cut it up, too, avoiding Robbie's face. "I told him we should look at our grades individually, but he insisted we do it together."

When the grade pattern repeated itself, I acted nonchalant, asking if we should go out to dinner or stay in. You don't need to act weird, Ian had said. Sorry, am I being weird? I don't mean to be, I said. What? he said. Nothing. I'm sorry, I said. I was halfway out of the room when he said, You're so lucky you're good at test-taking. I know, I said, it's ridiculous our entire grade is weighted off just the final. He was standing closer now, and pulled me into a hug. He said, You should think about signing up for more challenging classes next semester. It's nice to be in classes with 2Ls and 3Ls. You'll see.

"He said that?" said Robbie. He had pulled his chair closer to me and put his arm around the back of my seat.

"Yes," I said. When Ian had said it, I'd only been able to think about whether I'd bragged too much the previous quarter when I called my mother and told her about the academic awards I'd won. Ian had been hanging out in the living room of my dorm while I spoke to her, and the walls weren't too thick. I thought that the noise my roommates made in the kitchen, or in their rooms watching TV or listening to music, would have muffled my conversation, but maybe I was mistaken. I debated whether grades really were a measure of intelligence at all. I considered whether I let Ian's strengths shine enough.

I looked up from my plate. Mable and Fauna were staring at me, clearly having overheard the whole story. The waitress arrived now and began to put our main courses on the table. There was filet au poivre, steak tartare, roasted chicken, and grilled prawns. We hadn't finished eating the vegetables, so she left the wooden board and refilled our glasses. At that point, the wine we had ordered was finished, and Robbie asked her to bring out another bottle.

It occurred to me now that my story about Ian had the unintended effect of signaling to Mable that there were also things about me that she didn't know. I hoped that on the drive back, she would think about all the things she didn't know about me, much like her conversation with Fauna had rattled around in my head.

"Remember your twenty-sixth birthday?" Mable asked when the waitress had left.

"Birthday?" asked Robbie.

I explained that, when I was living in DC, my co-clerks had arranged to throw me a small birthday party, making reservations at a nice restaurant and getting together some friends. Mable was going to take the train down from New York, and Ian said he would come from San Francisco as well. But the day before, Ian told me he couldn't take Friday off from work.

"He never said that I needed to go to San Francisco, but he also never said I should celebrate my birthday without him. Then he told me his birthday present for me was a flight to California," I said, then added, "I ended up celebrating on another weekend with Mable and my coworkers in DC."

"Don't forget your outfit that night, too," Mable said. She had seen photos of the dinner Ian had taken me to in San Francisco.

"Yeah, I hated that dress. But he always asked me to wear it. He liked me in it."

"Christ," said Fauna. But she didn't say it in a mean way; it sounded solemn, like we were in church.

"He didn't like to be around me when I wasn't in his sphere," I said. "And that included when I was clerking."

I could tell everyone was trying very hard to keep their expressions impassive. "It's okay," I said. "I won't freak out."

"The other woman," said Fauna. "Cat, right?"

I nodded.

"What does she look like? Right now I can only imagine an actual cat."

I pulled out my phone and opened a social media app. It was easy to find her; I had already gone through many of her pictures, especially the past few nights after Mable was asleep. There were some pictures that I returned to compulsively, and one in particular, where she was standing in Golden Gate Park holding a goldendoodle puppy in her arms and smiling at the camera, her hair blown by the wind. She looked easy and natural and beautiful. I understood why Ian was taken with her.

I usually looked at these pictures after I reread the last text message Ian had sent to me. I found myself repeating these seven words over and over to myself, like an incantation: "Coming home late. Start dinner without me." It was sent the night before he died. Then I would go through Cat's pictures in a defined order, and then reread Ian's text. Sometimes I would go back to her pictures again after reading the text, words that had felt increasingly sinister ever since I arrived in France.

I handed my phone to Fauna, and Robbie and Mable crowded around the screen. With each scroll of Fauna's finger, they would make faces and say mean things I knew were intended to make me laugh. At the same time, I was surprised to feel some guilt about the cruelty they were directing toward Cat.

"She looks so young," said Fauna. "How old is she?"

"A few years younger than Mable and me," I said. "So maybe like twenty-six?"

"I give her a little lenience because she's young, but not much," said Fauna. "This will be defining for her twenties, though."

"And mine?" I asked. "I'm twenty-nine."

"You're so young, too." She said this so quietly that it was difficult to hear her over the music.

"Doesn't feel like it," I said.

"There's nothing more boring than women who lament the process of aging," said Mable.

Fauna handed me back my phone and asked how I was feeling about Cat at the moment.

"I guess I should have a grudge," I said. "But I oddly feel very blank when I think of her. Maybe it's some sort of coping mechanism."

Fauna said, "I love holding grudges. I nurse them and take care of them so they grow. Like babies." She laughed hard, and I couldn't really tell really if she was kidding.

"Are these grudges against your ex-husbands?" I asked. Robbie, who'd gone through a few cigarettes since we sat down, lit a new one.

Mable said, "That's quite an intrusive question."

"I thought you'd be just as interested," I said. I wanted to go on, to reference our late-night discussions of Fauna, but I stopped.

"Yes and no," said Fauna. "It's about my second marriage."

"Ah," I said. "So I finally get a direct answer from you."

Fauna smiled at me again and shook her head. She signaled at the waitress to bring over another menu. "Does anyone want dessert?"

"I'm fine," I said.

"You're no fun," said Fauna. She ordered sorbet for the four us to share. By the time it came out, Robbie had finished his cigarette.

He put the pack back in his pocket but kept the lighter in his hand, tapping it against the table every few seconds.

Mable picked up the bottle of wine and poured some into her glass, then Fauna's, and then Robbie's. When she reached my glass, the bottle was empty.

"Sorry," said Mable, setting it on the table.

I stared at her and she stared back. For the first time since we met them, both of us were more consumed with staring at each other than caring about whatever Fauna and Robbie had started talking about now, which was, of course, nothing at all.

• • •

I split the lunch bill with Robbie. Mable, who had thanked me the other times I paid, was lost in conversation with Fauna and didn't seem to notice. We decided to go down to the beach, which was only a few feet away. Again, everyone else had thought to wear a bathing suit under their clothes except for me, something I had immediately regretted when we set off from the hotel that morning.

The beach had a small area with a few stand-alone changing stalls, though the only free stall had a broken latch. Mable stood guard outside the door while Fauna and Robbie went down to the beach to find us a spot.

Inside the stall I took off my dress and pulled a black bikini out of my bag. There was a mirror on the back of the stall door that was slightly askew, so when I looked at it, I saw only the lower left half of my face and body. I was tan, and with the mix of sweat and SPF on me, my skin was also shiny.

Mable and I barely spoke as I changed, and as each second

passed in the stall, I was more aware of the silence between us. Finally, I said, "Did you see how Fauna paid for everything at the stores but he paid for lunch? Wonder if they're splitting this vacation. Although who are we to comment on splitting things equally?"

There was no response. I finished changing and opened the door.

Mable wasn't standing there. Robbie was. His lips were set in a line and he looked at the ground and then at me and then back to the ground.

"Oh, God. Where's Mable?" I managed to get out.

"She ended up switching duties with me."

We looked at each other for a moment. "I'm so sorry," I finally got out. I added, "I must have drunk too much at lunch."

"It's fine, really," he said. He had taken off his sunglasses, and it was so bright that his dark eyes looked almost all black, like they were only pupils. "And we're splitting the hotel. Neither of us would want to owe the other that much."

This was one of the few pieces of information he had given me about his relationship with Fauna. It felt almost holy.

"I'm really sorry," I said.

"Well, now I know that you're paying for everything here," he said. "Although that was pretty obvious."

"So we're even," I said. "You know something about us and we know something about you."

He smiled, and I found myself returning his smile. "It's good to be even," he said.

A woman was waiting to use my stall, so we left and started

toward Mable and Fauna. Before we reached them, Robbie asked me not to mention what just happened to Fauna. I was surprised since, if anything, I should be the one asking him to keep quiet. But I agreed.

. . .

The next few hours felt very sleepy. Our bellies were full of rich food and wine, and the sun was very hot. We lay on towels while children played in the sand nearby. Soon Mable declared that she was too warm and went down to the ocean. It was clear to both of us that I would not follow her, but Robbie said he would go with her. Before they left, Mable took off her beach wrap and he removed his shirt. Because they were standing next to each other as they did, I could look at him as much as I wanted to. He had gotten tanner in the past few days, and as a result his thick muscles were even more accentuated. Robbie and Mable didn't take towels with them to the water, and I wondered if, when he came back from the ocean, he would do the same thing he did whenever he got out of the pool: use the towel to dry his hair first before anything else so that there seemed to be nothing that existed but the water rolling down and off his body.

After they left, I said to Fauna, "I'm going to take a walk."

She nodded, and I grabbed a towel and my phone and headed in the opposite direction of Robbie and Mable. When I was far away enough from everyone that they looked small and unrecognizable, I laid my towel down on the sand and sat on it. I pulled up and reread the articles on immersion therapy I'd read multiple times, then headed into the ocean.

The waves were cold and loud. It was easy to walk far enough out into the sea so that the water was up to my waist, but every step after that took sheer willpower. By the time I was deep enough to swim I found myself clenching every muscle, my jaws tight with anxiety. There was a family only a few feet away from me and I saw a young girl, not much older than seven or eight, splashing gleefully with her older brother.

I swam a few more strokes and then turned back to the beach. It was difficult to get through the surf, and when it was shallow enough that I could stand, I walked as fast I could through the water, almost losing my footing at one point. When I finally reached my towel I wrapped it around myself and lay down on the sand, not caring that it would stick to my wet hair. Even though I had been in the water for only a few minutes, I was breathing hard. I closed my eyes and listened to the young girl yelp with joy.

When I caught my breath, I walked back to where Fauna was sitting. Robbie and Mable hadn't yet come back.

I stretched out wordlessly, and Fauna didn't say anything. I put on my headphones and pulled up the music app on my phone. It was on a random shuffle of my most-played music, and the first one that came up was the first song Ian and I had played at our wedding. Whenever I heard it, it called back warm air, his tux damp from spilled champagne.

I started to cry. I was wearing dark sunglasses, so I didn't think Fauna could tell, but I wasn't sure. We were so close to each other that I could smell her mix of sunscreen and sweat and upscale laundry detergent. I skipped to a track that meant nothing to me and grabbed my work phone from my bag, scanning the ever-growing stack of emails in my inbox. At the top was a new message from

Colleen, an associate the same year as me at the firm, and who was on my case team.

> Ellie: You obviously didn't review anything that Michael wrote. The draft of the motion to strike was riddled with elementary mistakes (glaring blue booking errors, and even some misstatements of the law). It's also evident he was trying to summarize your research notes, which you apparently never even spoke to him about. I didn't get a chance to review until the final pass before filing, which meant that many of us had to stay up all night to rewrite the motion that you were supposed to be overseeing. Obviously, this is unacceptable. If you are unable to keep up with your work during this time, please tell Marcus and take yourself off this case.

I read it twice before putting my phone down. I had no one to blame but myself, and yet I felt like I'd been wronged. I wanted to write back something savage; I wanted to hurt her for calling me out. At the same time, I knew that I would've written the exact same kind of email she had in her position.

Was I sinking my own career because I was mad at Ian and Cat and too stubborn to change my own circumstances? I started to laugh at the thought, and Fauna looked over at me. I explained it to her, and it started to seem more and more absurd to me, like my actions were being taken by someone else. I was being stupid and irresponsible and ridiculous, I told her, and yet I couldn't stop.

"Self-sabotage," she said when I was done. She took off her sunglasses, and I caught her eyes.

"Yes, I guess so."

"Do you care about your future at the firm?"

"Not really. I wasn't doing badly, but I wasn't excelling. I was doing okay." I paused. "Now, after this trip, I can't even say that."

"And yet you can't stop."

"Yes."

"Why do you think that is?"

"I don't know exactly. But something is happening to me, and I'm not sure if it's grief or something much worse." I explained to her how I found myself detaching from situations, and how I spent a lot of time and energy berating myself.

"Do you enjoy it?" she asked. "Talking to yourself that way?"

"I don't know. I guess so, since I let it happen."

She sat up now. "Maybe there's a part of you that's unhappy. I don't mean about Ian, that's obvious enough. I mean about yourself."

"Yes, but this stuff never happened before I met Ian. So wouldn't it be connected to him?"

"Maybe his death just jostled this part of you loose."

"Maybe," I said. "Mable thinks I should go see someone. A therapist."

"You sound skeptical."

"I'm not against the idea of therapy. I just don't know if I personally want to do it."

"Therapy can be helpful, but it also can do nothing. It depends on a lot of factors."

"I know," I said. "Mable's mentioned how you've got to find a good therapist, which isn't always easy. And that you have to be a willing patient."

She paused for a minute, seeming to debate something, then said: "You don't need to compare yourself to her all the time, you know."

"I don't. I mean, I try not to."

"She has her own issues, too."

"I know she does. She's my best friend."

"She's very interested in the abstract and philosophical side of concepts. But she has trouble finding her footing in the real world."

I'd been alternately repelled and fascinated by Fauna, but I had to admit she impressed me. Here was someone I'd met a few days ago who could say aloud what I'd always known but had been too afraid to articulate, to myself or to Mable. She knew this about Mable days after meeting her, even though it felt like a secret only I was allowed to keep. I said, "It's hard not to compare ourselves, though. She is so many things, and I feel like I am only one thing."

She shrugged. "You aren't fully formed yet."

"You say that like that's a good thing."

"Mable is more formed," she said. "Or at least this is how you read yourselves, which is what ultimately matters here. But as to what you just said, yes, it is a good thing, I think. You're still malleable."

I didn't know how to respond, but said, "Ian was fully formed, too, I think."

"It sounds that way to me from your description. Again, it's the way you read him."

"That really is how he was." I turned to face her directly, my back to the ocean. "Sometimes it feels like they're similar, Ian and Mable. But maybe 'similar' isn't the right word."

"I think, to you, they are similar. And that means something to you."

We hadn't said anything very substantive; the entire conversation had been a bit abstract. But it somehow felt like Fauna had seen right through me. It was at the same time comforting to know that my problems weren't obscure, and terrifying that someone I'd just met could see them more clearly than I could. I knew I would soon feel resentment toward her for this; I could already feel it working through me.

At that point, Mable and Robbie came back from the ocean, shaking off the water and laughing playfully. We joined in their laughter, and I felt relieved that my conversation with Fauna was brought to an end.

By the time we got in the car to drive back to the hotel, the sun was setting and we were all quiet. I saw a text from my mom asking how I was, and I replied with a few pictures of Mable and me from the past couple of days. We looked very happy and relaxed in the pictures, so in a way it felt like a lie, but I didn't want my mother to worry about me.

Mable and I weren't in the mood to talk when we got back to our rooms. We ordered room service, but only picked at it when it arrived. We turned the TV on loud so the silence between us was more muted. When we did speak, we said very little and nothing of importance.

Chapter Sixteen

When I got out of bed close to noon the next morning, Mable wasn't in the suite or in her connecting bedroom. I'd been awakened a few hours earlier by the sound of the shower in her room, but I'd let myself drift back to sleep when I heard the water start to run. It was also the first day she didn't open my bedroom door right when she woke up, sticking her head in to check up on me. Usually she'd then wake me up by turning on the television in my room or getting into bed with me to announce some joke she had thought of the night before. But the visits started to feel more perfunctory as the days went on, and soon it felt like she was doing it out of a sense of obligation. Now, it seemed, she didn't feel the need to do it at all.

I checked my phone and didn't see any messages from her. Out of habit I also checked my work phone and saw an Outlook invite for a phone call from Marcus at the top of my inbox. *Ellie, let's chat about your workload and whether it makes sense for you to continue part-time, or if it's best for you to go back on your leave. Let me know if another time works better, but it's important we touch base.* The call was scheduled for tomorrow evening in France, when Marcus would be starting his day in California. I accepted the invite and then put that phone facedown in my nightstand drawer, not bothering to open the other unread emails in my inbox.

I knew breakfast service was likely almost over, and I contemplated going to the restaurant for lunch but instead called down for room service.

When I was finished eating, I debated texting Mable, but I also hated the idea of reaching out to her before she'd reached out to me. I decided to use this time alone as a second opportunity for my immersion therapy project, changing into a bathing suit and speed walking to the ocean before I could talk myself out of the idea. By the time I got to the hotel's ladder that reached the sea, I was using up the last reserves of my courage. I climbed down into the water so slowly that I could hear the person a few rungs above me sigh in impatience.

Besides a few other guests swimming, there was no one else in the ocean. I'd found a pair of goggles lying by the pool area while walking to the ladder and put them on now, forcing myself to put my head under the water and open my eyes. I tried to tell myself I was just swimming in a pool, but by the time I got to the middle, the lie was starting to crumble. I didn't like that the ocean had its own mind, pulling me deeper inside itself with each wave. I was something alive inside something else that was alive. As soon as I reached the middle, I turned around and swam back to the shore, and by the time I pulled myself onto the rocks, I was nearly having a panic attack. I gasped in and out so loudly that a couple looked over at me. The man asked if I was okay, and I knew if I tried to speak the panic attack would be inevitable; I would be summoning it. I pretended I didn't hear him, pulling myself out and back up the ladder.

I lay by the pool, breathless. My eyes were closed, but the sun immediately formed red shade inside my eyelids. It was in this moment, catching the rhythm of my breath, that I thought of Susan. We had run in different circles at law school and had never become close friends, but whenever she saw me she seemed endlessly friendly. I always attributed this warmth to her embarrassment about naming only Ian on her list. The last time I saw her was during our 3L year when she was dropping off Ian in front of my apartment in Palo Alto. It was fall, and I'd been at the stove making mulled wine. I had been worried about what exactly constituted a "simmer" when I heard a car pull up in the driveway. I walked over to the living room, which was just a few strides away from the kitchen. Through the window, I could see both of them in her Honda. She was clutching the steering wheel hard, her white-pink fingernails betraying a strong emotion. She was staring ahead, but Ian was in the passenger seat facing her, saying something in a deliberate way. The top of his left hand moved in a familiar way, like it did when he was trying to calm someone down: gingerly, just barely skimming the air beneath. It was a week away from finals, and I remembered thinking that I should invite her inside and offer her some of the mulled wine. It would've helped take the edge off.

Then the car lurched forward an inch. Susan had shifted the car into park. Even though it was invisible to me, hidden by the layers of metal in her car and the window between us, I felt I knew exactly what it looked like when she lifted her right foot (one of her dirty white Keds, always) off the brake. At the same time the car staggered forward, her right hand disappeared from the windshield and never came back. One of Ian's hands disappeared, too. Her left hand, now alone, loosened on the wheel. Her fingernails were now back to their pale, ghostly color. I eventually walked back to the kitchen when it was clear the conversation would not end soon. By the time Ian came inside, Susan had needed to turn on her car headlights before backing out of our driveway. I asked Ian about her, something easy, and he had answered just as easily.

This memory was marvelous to me in its power. The nearby beach might as well have been made of cinnamon instead of sand, the smell of that mulled wine was so strong. No one openly discussed grades at Stanford, and we didn't have class rankings, but it was obvious to anyone that Susan was one of the best among us. I couldn't fathom what test, what challenge, could possibly exist that would make her anxious while Ian remained calm. There was another reason that this memory was so astounding: I had done what I had done, which is to say I had done nothing.

• • •

By the late afternoon, I still hadn't heard from Mable, but I spotted Robbie and Fauna walking back from the tennis courts. I'd been reading at the outdoor bar area in the main hotel building, looking up periodically at the view of the ocean and the gravel-lined path, and drinking a glass of white wine. They waved, and Robbie started heading over toward me. Fauna shouted that she was going to go back to the room to shower but would join us soon.

"Am I bothering you?" Robbie asked, pointing to the empty seat across from me.

I told him he wasn't, and he sat down. He had clearly exerted himself at tennis, and there were sweat marks on his shirt. I could smell him from across the table, an animal scent.

He made a motion to the waiter, who came by our table. At this point we had grown familiar with many of the servers at the hotel, but this was someone new. He had meticulously gelled brown hair.

"Mrs. Anderson," the waiter said to me, nodding. I had given him my room number when I sat down, and he'd learned my name.

I ordered another glass of wine and Robbie ordered a cognac drink, to which the waiter said, "Very good, Mr. Anderson."

"We should correct him," said Robbie once he walked away.

"Does it matter?" I asked. "This one can be on me."

When the waiter came over with our drinks, Robbie and I looked at each other, as if each waiting for the other to say something. But we didn't.

"Have you seen Mable today?" I asked.

"Yes, for breakfast. Where were you?"

"I slept in. Needed to, honestly." It was only a half lie. I had indeed let myself sleep in. Every night since we'd been there, I had slept like an animal in the wild, never getting past a doze, and waking up every hour or so to check my surroundings.

"She walked a little around the grounds with us, but Fauna and I split off for tennis. We invited her, but she declined."

"She doesn't know how to play tennis," I said. "And she wouldn't enjoy sitting on the sidelines watching you two. She'd be too far away for you to hear how funny she is." It was the first time I'd said something that revealed the way I was feeling about her, and I could tell Robbie was a bit surprised.

Then I said, "I tried to go swimming in the ocean earlier today. When I couldn't find any of you."

"Tried?"

I told him how the ocean scared me. "But I'm working on overcoming it. Seems really silly, especially here, since it's all walled in with the hotel's buoys."

"Were you successful?"

"A little. I reached the middle of the area, which is something for me."

"Just keep trying to push yourself farther each time. You can do it," Robbie said, smiling. "I'm just trying to be a good, supportive husband to you."

"You're a swim coach, too?"

"A swim coach and a husband. It's an honor," he said. "What are my duties?"

"The normal ones," I said. "You have to save me."

"You need saving?"

"I do." Mable and Fauna suddenly came to my mind, how when Robbie and I had spent the afternoon walking through the town of Antibes, neither of them had thought anything of it.

He had taken off his sunglasses earlier in the conversation, and now his dark brown eyes gleamed. "And after I save you? Then what?"

"Well, then I'll owe you."

"What will I get?"

I shrugged. "Whatever you want. You saved my life, after all. I'll even be brave and swim across the sea to see you if you ask."

"Who says I'll be there when you get there, waiting for you?"

"I'll wait for you, then," I said. "I'll wait on my knees at your doorstep until you come home."

"Ellie," he said. He was clearly enjoying the conversation, but also seemed to be in a great deal of pain. I was certain of this because I was feeling the same way.

He took out his cigarettes but didn't light one, instead flipping the pack backward and forward on the table.

The waiter came back and collected our empty drinks. "Another round, Mr. and Mrs. Anderson?" he asked.

Robbie nodded, and I said, "Sure."

As the waiter was about to leave, we saw Fauna and Mable approaching our table.

"Wait one moment, please," said Robbie to the waiter. "The rest of our party is joining us."

My moment with Robbie had passed, and I was both relieved and infuriated about it.

Before they sat down, I checked my phone. Mable hadn't checked in at all before now. When she greeted me, though, she acted as if nothing had passed between us, giving me a kiss on the top of my head while continuing her conversation with Fauna. She sat next to me on my side of the table, and Fauna took a seat next to Robbie, across from us.

They ordered their own drinks, and when the waiter left I said, "He thinks that we're married, Robbie and me."

Robbie shrugged and Fauna pulled him in for a kiss. "How funny," she said.

"Usually, this would bother me, because they probably thought you two were married because you're both Asian. But what a pair you two are. Made for each other," said Mable. "It's that obvious."

"How was walking around the hotel after breakfast?" I asked. I wanted her to know I had known where she had gone this morning, and that it didn't bother me.

"Really gorgeous," she said, looking at me intently. "I figured you'd want to sleep in."

I didn't say anything. The waiter brought over the drinks, and I asked him if he could recommend a small bite for the table. He told us his favorites were the duck foie gras canapés and caviar. Without asking anyone else, I told him we'd take the caviar.

"*Et pour vous, monsieur?* Anything you'd like to add, Mr. Anderson?" the waiter said to Robbie, who shook his head.

When the waiter walked away, Fauna said, "You'll like the caviar, Mr. Anderson." She smiled at me. The idea of Robbie being with me clearly amused her, unlike yesterday, when she'd seemed affected by the waitress flirting with him. I hated her for this.

I drank most of my drink in one gulp. "Well, you look like you've had a day," said Fauna.

"Ellie went swimming," said Robbie. "In the ocean."

"Were you able to actually make it to the end?" asked Mable.

"Without a problem," I said. "Was really nice to do it alone, actually."

She didn't respond, and I couldn't tell if she believed me. Fauna kicked off her sandals and put her feet in Robbie's lap. He began to massage them and she leaned her head back in the chair and said to me, "Sorry, I know he's your husband."

The drinks were working their way through me, and it felt like one of the funniest things I'd ever heard. I started laughing and couldn't stop.

"I never knew I was so funny," said Fauna.

"You're hilarious," I told her.

"I thought the topic of your husband was off limits, Ellie," said Mable.

I finished my drink and said, "Well, that was when my husband was Ian. But now I'm married to Robbie." I put down the empty glass, and saw that everyone else was still only halfway into their drinks. "Okay if I get another?"

"You don't need to ask us," said Fauna.

"She'll be more fun now," said Mable.

"Maybe you will, too," I said. I motioned to the waiter and ordered another round for everyone.

Before the drinks arrived, Robbie and Fauna went to take pictures of the view from the gravel-lined path. Now that it was just Mable and me, I wasn't sure what to say. There was a moment of silence before she said, "You're being very passive-aggressive, you know."

"I am?"

"Yes. If you're upset, you can just tell me."

"Well, you can, too."

"Jesus, Ellie." She pulled her feet up onto the chair and hugged her knees. "Are we in a fight?"

"Fight? About what?"

She waved her hand in front of her. "We've got loads to pick from. But the conversation about Ian the other day by the pool, I'm guessing. We never resolved that."

"What about you telling Fauna all about your writing? Sharing something you're apparently in the middle of revising with her? Asking for her input, even?" I took a great deal of effort to look right at her when I said that, holding her gaze even though it was difficult because I was already drunk. I blinked many times.

"Are you jealous?"

"No."

"So I'm not allowed to tell anyone else about my writing?"

"I never said that."

"But you brought it up. It obviously bothers you."

"You know, you always seem to have an opinion of how I deal with things. Like, just now, saying that I'm passive-aggressive," I said.

"One of us has to have an opinion," she said. "Or else what? We'll both just be nice to each other all the time?"

"Now who's being passive-aggressive?"

"Why are you upset with me?"

"I'm not upset with you," I said.

"Bullshit. I know you."

"I know you know me. You tell me that all the time." I knew I was being petty, but I was deriving pleasure from being so ridiculous. I had spent my entire life pleasing and accommodating other people, and now I wanted very much to make someone feel uncomfortable, even if—or especially if—that person was Mable.

"This is misdirected anger," she said.

"Oh?"

"Yes, I think the person you should be mad at is Ian."

"Well, you would know."

By now, Fauna and Robbie were on their way back to our table. I had never seen Mable retreat from an argument, so I was surprised when she changed the subject as soon as they sat down. From their point of view, nothing had happened between us. I thought briefly about telling them, but I still felt somehow loyal to Mable and our relationship. I didn't want Robbie and Fauna to see what ugly sort of thing was between us, and I figured that Fauna would be on Mable's side. I didn't know if Robbie would be on my side, or if he would just try to keep the peace. Either way, I imagined that he would be useless.

At some point, the conversation had turned to the tennis match Robbie and Fauna had played that afternoon. Robbie had won all the games except one. He, it turned out, didn't really care about winning. Fauna didn't care so much about winning, but did want others to think she did a good job. It's shallow of me, Fauna said. It quickly became a discussion about the definition of success and winning. Mable began to extol my achievements, my academic successes, and I wondered if she was trying to make amends. She gave the example of a Political Science class we took together senior year in college, in which the professor had excerpted parts of my paper to show everyone. This student is ready to receive their PhD, he had said, before pulling up a slide deck with a few paragraphs I had written. He hadn't revealed my name, but Mable and I had talked enough about the paper beforehand that she knew it was mine. "Brilliant," she said, "Ellie is brilliant."

They all looked at me, as if I should now say something brilliant, or grateful. Instead, I said, "I think I do things just because I'm supposed to. And I don't know if that says anything good about me."

"You mean at school and everything?" asked Robbie.

"Yes, it was never about the actual learning for me. More about the grades."

"I think that's the case with most students," said Fauna.

"That's how I've lived all my life, though," I said. "Not just in school. Everything. External markers of success. I'm doing it right now. I hate my firm, but the thought of quitting feels unbearable." I added, "It's not even like I'm doing well there, especially not since we got here. But without it I have no idea who I'll be."

"Everyone does things because of the status these things confer," said Fauna. "That's normal." When she said this, she glanced briefly down at her hands and then back at me. It was a flutter of a moment, but it made me bold; I felt that she was sharing something she had in common with me.

"But status has been the driving force of everything I've achieved. An inherent desire to be seen as 'good,'" I said. Fauna looked back down at her hands.

"You look at your relationship with yourself as something bad or selfish," said Mable. "Doing that is actually very self-centered, when you think about it."

"So that's my real problem, huh," I said. "Not that I care so much about being good, but that I only worry about this when it comes to my own personal achievements."

"No, you should care less about being good, too," said Mable.

Fauna looked at me again. "Do you feel this way outside of school and your career?" she said.

I decided to say something I never would've said a few days ago, or if I'd been sober. "Maybe this is the reason I got married in the first place. Because it was something you're supposed to do."

"No one feels that way anymore," Mable said. "It's not the nineteen fifties."

"That was me and my first marriage, too," said Fauna, ignoring her.

Out of the corner of my eye, I could see Mable, her forehead bunched together, studying Fauna. It was satisfying seeing her look at Fauna when Fauna was looking only at me.

"I did love Ian, though," I said. "That was real."

"I know you did," Fauna said. "Of course you did."

The waiter stopped by. I said that we were done with our drinks, and we could settle up.

"I've got this," I said to the table, and signed the bill when it came.

"Should we head to dinner?" asked Fauna.

"Sure," said Mable.

We were walking down the gravel path toward the smaller cream-colored building where they served dinner when I said, "You guys go ahead. I forgot I need to write an email for work."

"Aren't you too drunk to do that?" asked Mable, but I had already turned and was walking toward our room. There was a pause and then I heard their footsteps on the gravel as they continued without me. I had headed in the general direction of our rooms but missed the turn that would've actually brought me there, and kept walking until it seemed like I had hit the end of the hotel property. When I reached the security checkpoint, I turned and began retracing my steps.

I could tell I was drunker than I'd realized since every few steps, I took a small stumble. I wasn't aware of people looking at me, though. All I was aware of was that my memory felt powerfully strong. If I wanted to, I felt, I could reach out and touch Ian's skin.

After the second time that I got better grades than Ian, we stopped speaking about them entirely. The week before and the one after they were released, he was nasty to be around, snipping at me if I did any little thing incorrectly. I had my own car at school, but Ian's was newer, and whenever I forgot to fill up the gas tank after borrowing it for an errand, he'd tell me I didn't care about him and his needs. I'm so sorry, I'd reply. I'll go to the station right now. He'd have me over and cook a meal he knew full well I couldn't stomach, chili so spicy that only he could down it and I would resort to ordering takeout. Come on, he'd laugh, at least try to get on my level. He spilled a cup of coffee on my laptop once before grades were released in the fall quarter of our second year, and I knew it was purely accidental, but he bristled when I asked him to help me recover my notes. You should've backed them up more carefully, he said. Let this be a lesson to you. I tried to take it all in stride, aware that in a few weeks, he would be back to his easygoing self. When that happened, he would apologize for the bad mood he'd been in, telling me he would work on it. I promise, he said, I will do better.

Ian and I applied to work for the same judges even though the Stanford clerkship adviser more or less told him that his chances were nonexistent. When we began to hear back, I received offers from more than one judge. He didn't get any. I thought it didn't bother him until we got to my celebration dinner that a friend of ours had organized. It was a potluck, our friends' faces flushed with alcohol and congratulations. Ian popped open a bottle of champagne and held up a glass. He was wearing a gray shirt, his sleeves slightly rolled up. When he had caught everyone's attention, Ian said, A toast to Ellie. Good for the judicial branch for hiring more women, he said, and in particular, women of color. They need to diversify, and it's about time. I blinked, not sure what to say. But then everyone was raising their glasses and the music was turned back on. Ian grabbed me, kissing me on the lips while someone took a picture. One of my female friends had caught my eye after it happened, but I looked away, pretending it didn't bother me.

Later that night, when we were alone, he said matter-of-factly that he was happy he hadn't taken the spot of some woman or minority. He looked like he believed it. This time, I got angry, slamming the dirty plates onto the kitchen counter. Did he realize how offensive his statement was? What about the one at the party? Did he understand how he'd made me feel humiliated in front of all my friends? Immediately, his face fell, and he wrapped his arms around me. You're right, he said, whispering in my ear. You make me a better person. I'm sorry. I'm so proud of you, all your prestigious clerkships.

I thought about what Mable would've done if she'd been at the party. She would've said something cutting and smart in equal measure, been able to pinpoint the reasons why he was wrong. She would've taken it from the personal and into the universal, made an argument he couldn't refute. I thought about how I never told her about any of this, including that when he apologized I had let myself be hugged.

The two years we did long distance, him at a law firm in San Francisco and me clerking in Washington DC, we barely talked about my clerkship. I don't want you to break your confidentiality with the judge, he'd say, before moving on to his day. Of course, I said, thanks for being conscious of that. He visited me only a handful of times those two years, staying only one night, maybe two. Can't wait for you to get out of here, he'd say, gesturing to the small, cramped apartment I shared with my co-clerks. On each visit, I asked him if he wanted to meet my judges. I talk about you all the time, I said. My time here is so limited, I want to relax and spend it with you, he always said. His job kept him busy enough that it made sense, and I felt guilty for pressuring him.

How were you able to stay? I could imagine Mable saying to me. I would've tried to explain that, back then, it felt like normal growing pains. No one is perfect, my mom said when I called her crying once. There must be something you two can do, she went on, to work it out. You saw how hard I had it as a single mother, she said. Do you want that for yourself?

Besides, whenever I thought about the idea of leaving, I could only look at my own flaws. Who was I to be so hard on someone I loved so much? I was too critical of others, too unwilling to forgive, I thought. And I would never forget—would never allow myself to forget—that I'd been the one who pursued him first, attracted to him because of what I perceived to be a vulnerability, an openness. I felt that if I unraveled the relationship, the spool at the center would reveal something shallow and desperate about me.

At a certain point, the sun was starting to set and I realized I must've been walking the grounds for at least an hour. The hotel had turned on the soft lighting that made everything look almost enchanted. I walked by the court where Robbie and Fauna had played tennis earlier, dragging my left hand across the tall wire fence that enclosed the now-empty space. The gravel path was ahead of me. It was quiet and no one was around; I figured all the guests were at dinner. Then I spotted Robbie by the door to one of the courts.

"Here you are," he said as I approached him. We could hear people walking on the nearby path but couldn't see them. The lighting was too soft.

"I wanted to play tennis with you, too. It's not fair you only played with Fauna. You asked Mable and not me." I was so drunk it was easy to ignore how petulant I sounded.

He had changed out of his tennis clothes and was wearing dark slacks and a thin, light gray shirt. Even though he smelled good, like cologne and aftershave, I found myself angry that the appealing animal smell from earlier was gone.

"You're still very drunk, I see," he said.

"So are you." His hair was loose and falling over his forehead, and his eyes were dark and shiny.

He shrugged. "We had more drinks while waiting for you."

I said, "You came to sit with me instead of going back with Fauna to change."

There was a silence and then he said, "I was sent out here to come find you."

"'Sent'? Don't say that."

"Fine, I volunteered."

"You wanted to come find me."

"Maybe."

"Just say it. Say that you wanted to come find me."

"If I say that, will you come with me?"

"Yes," I said.

"I wanted to come find you."

He began to walk toward the gravel path, but I didn't move. I said, "Alone. You wanted to come alone to find me."

"That wasn't the deal."

"You wanted to come alone to find me," I said again.

"I wanted to come alone to find you." He walked back toward me so he was standing only a few inches away.

I'd been holding the fence with my hand as we'd been talking, but now I let go. "I think the courts are closed at night," I said.

"I don't think they lock this door, though."

We looked at each other and then I pushed on the door. He was right. I walked in and he followed me. The door hung open for a moment, but then he closed it behind us.

"Do you remember when you said you were part of my story now?" I asked. I was leaning against the inside of the fence and could feel the chain links digging into my back. It wasn't unpleasant, this feeling.

"I do."

He was standing close to me, my face level with his chest. "If we're going to play, we'll have to be on different sides of the net," I said.

"I know," he said. "I am well aware of the rules of tennis."

Neither of us moved. I stood up on my toes, tilted my head up, and kissed him. We both opened our mouths, and when he pulled away, I let out a small breath.

He took my hand and led me over to a white bench on the side of the court. He let go and sat down. I sat down next to him, our thighs touching.

"What do you want?" he said.

"What do I want? What do I want?" I said. The questions came out like statements. My breathing was sharp, as if I had just finished a long sprint.

"Stop repeating everything. Answer me," he said.

I kissed him again. This time he was more forceful in his response. He began to run his hands through my hair, and then they were behind my neck. I could hear my breath again. I said, "I want this."

We were looking at each other, but it was so dim I could barely make out his face.

"Okay," he finally said. We started kissing again and he put both his hands around my waist and pushed me down so I was now lying on the bench. He was on top of me and he put one of his hands up my dress and then underneath my bra. I pulled up the skirt of my dress and he pulled my underwear down my thighs to my knees. The entire time he was inside of me I kept saying, "Yes." I said it quietly, over and over, like there were no other word I'd ever say again. It felt like "Yes" was the most sublime word ever created.

The meaning, too. At one point I heard him say my name, and to this I could only say, Yes.

When it was over, I said, "I've wanted this more than I've wanted anything in a while." He was still on top of me, and if I wanted to, I could kiss him once more.

"I know." He said this casually, like all of this was normal.

I pressed my forehead against his, and I said, "It's okay. I won't say anything. I don't expect anything either."

He got up. "We should go," he said. "They'll be waiting for us."

Chapter Seventeen

I awoke before dawn and spent most of the next morning lying in bed, replaying the evening in my head. Last night when Robbie and I left the courts and met up with Fauna and Mable, I'd been able to act normally throughout the meal, I thought, and so had Robbie. No one seemed to have noticed. In a way, it was terrifying how easy it was to pretend like nothing had happened.

When I had reassured myself that Fauna and Mable hadn't picked up on it, I let myself think about Robbie. I had no feelings of regret. I had acted on pure desire, basic animal pleasure, and it had been divine.

Around nine I heard Mable wake up, and we headed to breakfast together. On the way, she texted Fauna to see where they were, but there was no response. Last night we had all made plans to go into town for dinner, and when we hadn't heard back by the end of breakfast, Mable figured that Robbie and Fauna wanted the day alone to themselves. This was the first time since we'd met them that they hadn't responded swiftly, and Mable and I seemingly took a silent vow not to discuss this explicitly.

A part of me wondered if Robbie had told Fauna what had happened. I was anxious about this idea, but also exhilarated. I imagined Fauna's face when Robbie broke the news. There was no doubt that Fauna brought out something dangerous in me, but rather than fear it I found myself curious about this new Ellie, admiring her from afar.

Having not heard from them, Mable and I realized we would need to spend the day together. At different points, each of us remarked that we wanted to relax today and how it was nice to be able not to have to talk around good friends all the time. It was obvious to both of us, though, that this wasn't at all what was going on.

Before we left breakfast, we spotted Paul and Bertie across the dining room, and Mable almost leapt out of her chair in excitement, waving them over to join us.

"Bertie here is absolutely dying to go to the spa," said Paul.

Bertie said, "Any interest? Would be nice to have some sort of ladies' day, wouldn't it?"

"I'll go," said Mable. All three of us looked at her. It was as if Bertie and Paul knew how unlike her this was.

"Wonderful! And you, Ellie?" Bertie asked.

"I'll be hanging around the hotel," said Paul. "Happy to entertain myself."

"I'll go," I said, then nodded at Paul. "I mean with you."

"So no spa then?" asked Bertie.

"No," I said.

"Well, this is quite a split then," said Paul. "Each of us pairing off."

"We actually really love to do that," I said. "Mable and I. Meet couples and then split off with them."

"Jesus, Ellie," said Mable.

"We draw the boundaries very clear. The loyalties are even clearer. That way we can perform our respective personalities."

"Excuse me?" asked Bertie. She was trying to flag the waiter and only half paying attention. Paul was now looking at his phone. "What do you mean by that?"

"Oh, nothing," said Mable.

"I mean nothing," I said as Mable let out a long breath.

Paul and I ended up deciding to walk around the hotel grounds, him talking a great deal, I think about his family. He and Bertie had two teenage children who were staying with his parents. We wanted to have a proper holiday, he explained. I didn't offer much about myself, instead asking him open-ended follow-up questions so that he could keep going. I wanted to be like Fauna in that way.

His voice was so comforting that it was easy to think about Robbie while he talked. I watched the memory on replay in my head, and whenever we circled by the courts I entertained the idea of saying to Paul: I had sex there last night.

By noon, Mable and Bertie still weren't back, and Paul and I decided to grab lunch at the restaurant closest to the pool. I ordered freshly caught sole with vegetables and lemon confit, and Paul got a cheeseburger with bacon. Before he handed the menu back to the waiter, he asked me, "Would it be too much if we shared a plate of ceviche?"

"Of course not," I said. While we ate, I continued asking Paul questions about himself while I drifted in and out of memories of last night.

Paul refused to let me pay for lunch, and after I thanked him we sat by the pool, him regaling me with stories about when he and Bertie met. Dinner felt very far away all afternoon, and when it finally became an acceptable time to go shower and change, I was relieved. Paul gave me a long hug and said, "I can tell you're a bit out of sorts, and I do hope everything will be better soon, love." I could have wept in his arms.

Mable and I met Fauna and Robbie outside the hotel in the evening, with Robbie already in the driver's seat of their car with the engine running. He said a quick hello to both of us, and I tried to telegraph that I didn't expect any special treatment from him. Both of them were apologetic, giving us some vague story about why they didn't receive Mable's messages until an hour ago. I waited for Mable to call them out on it, but she didn't; it was incredible how much power they, but specifically Fauna, had over her. I wondered if she was experiencing the same inner turmoil about coming off cool and relaxed as I was. I certainly had more practice at it. Fauna was acting the same to me as she always did, so I felt sure that Robbie hadn't said anything to her.

On the ride, I tried my best to forget about the emails from Marcus I'd gotten right before Mable and I had left our rooms this evening. He'd asked me if everything was okay, since I'd missed the call he'd set up without a word, which he knew was unlike me. I had contemplated sending a response, but what was there to say? I'd missed the call on purpose and had no excuse.

The restaurant, Le Michelangelo, was located on a one-way street in Antibes just a short drive from the hotel. To reach our table, we walked through a front room that had a view into the kitchen and into a cavelike room with a low ceiling and chandeliers. The walls were made of stone and covered in pictures of famous people who had eaten there.

Robbie and Fauna had been to this restaurant many times and ordered for the table: cured ham; crab tartare; sea bream carpaccio; and burrata with tomatoes, basil, and olive oil to start. For our main courses, they chose a black angus filet, ricotta raviolini with truffle oil, and grilled rabbit. They asked for two bottles of wine to begin, and Robbie separately ordered a tequila cocktail made with truffle honey and lime. They seemed determined to keep the night merry, but it felt somehow forced.

When I commented on their festive mood, Fauna smiled and said: "We have to have a good night tonight. It's Robbie's last one here."

"You're leaving?" I somehow got out. It had taken me a few moments to react and then attempt to pretend the news meant little to me.

"Yes," he said. "Fauna had always been going to stay longer." Still, neither of them elaborated on whether he'd been planning to leave tomorrow, or something had happened to cause him to leave abruptly.

"I'll miss him," said Fauna, putting a hand on Robbie's cheek. She was drunk already and her eyes were shiny.

My instinct was to catch Mable's eye, but I knew she wouldn't be looking at me. Instead, I joined them in reminiscing about our time together, as if we were all decades-old friends. Remember when? Did you see her face? I have a picture from that meal, do you want to see? Hahaha.

We were able to stretch out an interaction with another guest at the hotel into an hour-long discussion. There had been an American family here with a daughter, a recent college graduate, who'd eyed Robbie for a few days, then tried to send him a vodka cranberry via the bartender at the hotel bar one evening. None of us were particularly interested in the story when it happened, but we'd all decided it needed to be dissected now.

"We have to do this again," said Robbie as we were finishing the chocolate mousse and lemon meringue he and Fauna had ordered for dessert.

"Yes, we really do," said Fauna.

"Of course," said Mable while I nodded.

It wasn't clear what "this" was referring to, but it was obvious that all of us were lying. We wouldn't travel together ever again, or even get together for a meal. Still, each of us nodded and laughed.

It felt exhausting to keep up, and after Robbie and Fauna picked up the check, to faint protests from Mable and me, I went with him to get the car.

"Is everything okay?" I asked once he'd given his ticket to the valet outside the restaurant.

"It's fine. But I'm leaving in the morning."

"You didn't say anything, right? I didn't, I swear."

"No, I didn't say anything."

"But what happened, then? Why are you leaving?"

The valet brought the car around at that moment and Robbie got into the driver's seat. I took the seat next to him, even though it was Fauna's. I knew we had only a moment before the others would be outside.

"It's time for me and Fauna to move on," he said.

"You left her?"

"We would've never been happy together in the long run. Fauna was willing to say it aloud. I can accept leaving a situation like that."

"That makes it sound like, in actuality, she ended things with you."

"I don't know," he said. "It wasn't that kind of conversation. I wanted to go back to the States, and she was fine with it." He turned up the air conditioning in the car. When he did, I caught a whiff of his aftershave and was reminded of last night. "It's for the best."

"Couldn't you have worked it out? I don't understand," I said. It made no sense, me rooting for the two of them. But the thought of him and Fauna splitting up somehow made me incredibly sad.

"No, it wouldn't have worked out. We want such different things," he said. "I knew that going in. And after what happened between you and me last night, it's become obvious to me that my relationship with Fauna isn't making me happy." He said this softly, and I heard great pain in his voice.

All I could think was that there was no one, not a single other person, who was witnessing this moment except for me. His hands balled up in fists, his scent, the way he looked in this suit, his voice, would only ever happen this once in the car, in France, on this trip, and then it would disappear. This singularity propelled me forward, so close that I could feel his breath against my face.

I kissed him. Cold air from the vents was blowing on my right shoulder, but my right hand was hot and sweaty and I almost slipped on the soft leather of the seat below my palm. For a moment I felt him kissing me back, then I felt his hands on my shoulders, pushing me away.

His face was turned toward me but his body was facing forward. "Shit," he finally said.

"I'm sorry," I said.

"I don't want to hurt you."

"It's okay. I shouldn't have done that just now. I really don't expect anything from last night, I promise."

"I mean it. I care about you a lot, I really do. I'm not just saying it. But I also don't think I can do this with you right now."

"If you care about me at all, you'll stop talking," I said. "Please stop."

I turned to face forward so I didn't have to look at him, and out of the corner of my eye I saw him place both hands on the steering wheel as if he was ready to leave at any moment.

"Okay," he said.

When we'd gotten into the car, he'd closed all the windows so the air conditioning would cool down the interior faster. We hadn't turned on any music, either, and this choice now felt ridiculous. The only sound we could hear now was the murmurs of guests outside, waiting for their cars in front of the restaurant.

I don't know how much time passed until Fauna and Mable finally came out of the restaurant. I immediately got out of the car and into the back seat, even though Fauna hadn't seemed to mind my being in her seat. Robbie's eyes caught mine in the rearview mirror, but Fauna and Mable were too caught up in their conversation to notice. I looked back, but I knew he couldn't see my face clearly in the dark.

The ride home was filled with more of the forced merriment we'd had at dinner, and when we pulled up to the hotel, I could tell everyone wanted to go back to their rooms. Robbie gave his keys to the valet and then gave long hugs to both Mable and me. When he embraced me, I thought maybe I should say something to him but I didn't, and then he started to walk into the hotel with Fauna. The last time I saw him—I knew very clearly it would be the last—he was turned to her, midstep, his arm loose over her shoulders. It was dark outside, and I couldn't make out their expressions.

Back in our rooms, Mable and I got ready for bed quietly. I turned on the television for some background noise. And then when I couldn't stand the silence between us anymore, I walked over to her room and said, "You're mad I went and talked to Robbie in the car, aren't you?"

"I'm not mad," she said.

"Yes, you are."

She was standing in her bathroom with her back to me, brushing her hair, still wet from the shower she'd just taken. She met my eyes in the mirror. "To be mad, I'd have to be surprised. I was anything but that." She paused. "What happened between you two?"

"What?"

"It was obvious last night at dinner that something had happened. And then again in the car tonight. Fauna may not have noticed, but I know you. Did you declare your undying love to him or something?"

"Nothing happened."

"Right."

"Nothing at all happened, and it's actually really offensive to me that you would say such a thing."

She let out a laugh, and it made me feel very alert and alive, as if I had just woken up from a very long sleep. I wanted to hurt her, and I wanted her to hurt me.

I said, "Oh, right. I forgot. I'm the boring, traditional one, the one who only cares about monogamy and marriage. And you're the fun one. Spontaneous, full of life, the one who makes up for all my faults. Did I get that right?"

For a moment, she seemed caught off guard, but then she said, "Of course you'd take his side. I bet you think Robbie was the victim, the one who was wronged by big, bad Fauna."

"He wanted to be with her, and she didn't feel the same way."

"Is that what he told you?" She grinned one of her grins. "I'm sure he's the hero of his own story."

"She ended things with him. That's what he told me."

Mable put down the hairbrush very calmly. "Why is that what you always focus on? Who wanted to leave and who wanted to stay?" She looked at me again in the mirror. "Actually, don't answer that. That'll only make me feel sorrier for you, and the last thing you need right now is more pity. You're drowning in it."

"So this is about Ian?"

"For fuck's sake." She turned to face me now. "How do you view yourself? As Ian's victim? You were silent, you did nothing when he was alive, but not because you were being kind or accommodating. Because you're a coward."

I could only think of violence. I wanted to cut her, gouge her eyes out, grab her by the hair and smash her head against the mirror. "And what are you, Mable? A hypocrite who loves to say just enough so everyone can tell you're a progressive and feminist and a class warrior. Meanwhile, you have no problem with someone else picking up the check for all these meals and this ridiculous hotel. Or being around someone like Fauna. God, it was embarrasing to see you these last few days, tripping over yourself to impress a rich white woman. The Mable I know would fucking hate you."

She stalked past me into the suite's sitting room. I followed her. I felt high from this exchange, rabid even. "Come on, Mable. It's not like you to walk away from a fight. You've got more in you, I know it."

At that she turned around, walking up close to me. Her mouth was partly open, her breath going in and out loudly. When she spoke again, her voice was low. "Your unresolved shit is not just between you and Ian. It's between you and the entire world. It's why you can't bear to leave a job you hate, why you can only be on Robbie's side, why Fauna is a villain to you, and why, even after all this, you still think, deep down inside, that Ian respected you and loved you. That Jeremy did, too." I could feel her breath on my face. "And it's also the same shit that makes me hate being your friend."

"I thought you liked having someone around who you could feel superior to."

"God, fuck you."

"I have done *nothing* to you to give you the right to say that to me."

"So you're the victim again? Let me know when you figure it out so I know what part to play. By the way, your mother would be proud of you. Everything you've ever done is just like she wanted."

"Oh, now the Mable we all know and love is back." I let out a sharp breath. "This is the part where she is cruel but funny, saying whatever she wants as long as it costs her nothing."

She folded her arms, her eyes lit up with anger. "Where's the lie? You're your mother's daughter. You have the job and the money. You even had the powerful white husband."

I took a step back, and reached behind myself with one hand as if to grasp onto a piece of furniture, but there was nothing there. "You've always confused being interesting with being a bitch."

"Let me know when we get to talk about your cruelty, Ellie. We always seem to run out of time for that."

"Tell me one thing I've ever done to hurt you."

"Christ, Ellie. Okay, you want a recent example? Do you remember the first night we were here? When we went to the bar and that guy asked me what I 'did'?"

I blinked once, and then again. I was still catching on to the tail of the memory when she continued. "You said that I write Shit Stories. But I'm guessing the conversation didn't even fucking register to you, since it wasn't about you."

I got out: "I'm sorry, I didn't know what to say. But why are you upset? You and I say that all the time."

"Not with other people, Ellie."

"I just didn't know you would be embarrassed by that. I didn't know you were capable of embarrassment."

"Who am I to you?" Her voice was very cold. "Am I only defined by my relation to you? By being different from you?"

"I could say the same to you."

"No, the difference is that I spent these past few weeks taking care of you. I quit my job, left my life behind, so I could be here for you."

I started laughing. "That's how you see it? That you're doing me a favor? Jesus, Mable. What life did you leave? What job did you leave? You've never finished anything, not even halfway." I went on, "How easy it must be to never have to try, to never actually have to give a fuck. You can spend your whole life feeling superior to everyone else—me especially—because you are the only person in this world who has ever seen the truth. And all the rest of us are just morons, chained up in the cave, watching shadows on the wall. You know the truth, don't you, Mable? Tell me, what is it that you've learned these past few years? All of us are dying to know. Fauna actually agrees with me about you. Yes, we discussed you. She knew you for a few days and could tell right away. That's how obviously broken you are."

Mable's arms were loose at her sides, and one of her hands was visibly shaking. She said, "At least I have opinions and thoughts about the world. I don't just rush straight into accepting things that make me feel good. I actually interrogate things about myself. When I find something I really love, I'll know that it's real. Can you say that? Can you say that anything you ever did was ever real? Or was it just easy?" She was almost panting now. "I'm not sure you've ever actually done anything in your life, only had things happen to you."

These words cut me more sharply than the others had; I could feel my underbelly splitting open and everything inside of me spilling out onto the floor, soft and gleaming. I said the only thing I could think: "You've let me down, too. It's not all on me."

By this point, she had gone back to her bedroom, where she was unzipping her suitcase and pulling back the cover. She looked at me for what felt like a long time and said, "I've never been so disappointed in someone as I am in you."

I began to cry, and so did she. We stayed looking at each other for a minute, me outside the doorway of her room, until she began to fold her clothes and put them in the suitcase. It reminded me of my mother leaving me a few weeks ago, and I began to cry harder.

"Are you leaving?" I asked.

"Yes."

"But then I'll be alone."

She said nothing, just got up and shut the bedroom door. In the morning, she was gone before I woke up.

Chapter Eighteen

I spent the next day trying to pretend that I would be able to stop thinking about what Mable had said or the fact that she was gone. I got up and arrived at breakfast very early so I'd be sure to miss Fauna. When the waiter automatically began to add three more place settings, I told him he didn't need to and then ate a quick meal from the buffet, leaving the table before he could come back to take my order.

At the pool, I settled into a lounge chair out of the way, covering myself with towels so that I couldn't be recognized from afar. I became anxious when people began to sit down in nearby chairs; I thought that Fauna would come over any second and I'd have to explain why Mable was gone, which I didn't have any idea how to do. So I went back to my room and, after an hour of trying to distract myself with television, opened my laptop. There was another email from Michael, the first-year associate, as well as a new one from Marcus. His tone was now hard and even, and I could tell that he was growing weary of defending me to the others. I was debating what to write back when I saw another email in my inbox. It was from Cat.

Ellie, I know I am the last person you want to hear from, but I
wanted to check in on you. At the very least, you should know
that people at work are starting to worry about you.
I also know you haven't said anything to anyone at the firm. You
didn't owe me that, but you did it anyway. Thank you.

I closed Cat's email and then searched my inbox for the recent invitations for the weekly happy hour hosted by the firm at
a nearby bar in the Financial District. I wanted to see the RSVPs.
Usually only the more junior associates attended, and I knew Cat
generally tried her best to make it. She hadn't RSVP'd at all to the
happy hour held right after Ian had died, which was around the
time she started working from home. I pulled up the invitation
from this past week. She had RSVP'd yes, meaning that she was
now back to working at the office.

I forced myself to imagine her at the bar, her long hair tucked
behind one ear, listening to others talk about me. She would be
careful not to insert any opinions about me, but would take part
in the conversation all the same. She'd probably pretend to be concerned for me, worried about my well-being. Because the bar would
get noisier as the evening went on, I imagined her shouting, I really
just hope Ellie is doing okay. I'm worried about her. Others would
find her lack of judgment kind. Then she'd start working on the
draft of this email, writing it and rewriting it until she felt it was
just right. She must've congratulated herself for being the bigger
person, taking the high road.

As these thoughts filled my mind, I wanted to writhe and
scream, pull out my teeth, or call her up and say the foulest things

possible. Mable's absence felt most striking at this point. She would've helped me direct my fury, letting me become the kind of animal I felt like I'd become. I wanted her back with me so badly, and the fact that I was the one who'd pushed her away made me feel sick. I ran into the bathroom and began to dry heave. I panted on the cold floor, my sweat turning from hot to icy. When I could, I stood up to look at myself in the mirror. I really studied myself for the first time in weeks. There was a damp sheen on my face and strands of hair stuck to my cheeks. My mouth was pale and wrinkled and there were wet spots under my armpits and on my stomach and back. I had never looked or felt uglier in my life.

I grabbed my computer and work phone and left my room. Jean-Michel was at the front desk, and although he tried his best to give me a warm greeting, I could tell my appearance frightened him.

"I need to ship something. Right away," I said.

"Of course. Where to?"

"California. San Francisco." I gave him the firm's address and pushed the laptop and phone across the desk to him, as well as a jumble of chargers.

He paused for a moment. "These devices are still on. Shall I turn them off before we place them in the mail?"

"It doesn't matter. Just send them, please," I said, and repeated the address.

"Any note to add to the package?"

I shook my head. He went into the back and returned with a box that had bubble wrap on the inside. He placed everything into it with great care and I wanted to laugh very loudly at his concern that the laptop and cell phone would get knocked around on the trip. He printed out something with the address on it and stuck it onto the top of the package. He was saying something about how long it would take, that it would have to go through customs, and did I want a tracking number? I don't remember exactly what I said, only that I was trying very hard to look normal, to hold my face in the right way.

I must've done fine, or else he was exceedingly polite, because he went to send it off with a smile. I could tell that the other hotel staff were trying very hard to avoid my gaze. I left a handprint on the marble counter.

I went back to my room. It was the afternoon now, and the sun was strong. I knew I was supposed to eat lunch, so I called room service and ordered a blue lobster salad with avocado, pomelo, and honey vinaigrette. It arrived at my door looking pristine. Yet when I lifted a forkful to my mouth, the idea of eating anything made me feel even worse. I placed it outside the door without taking even a bite. Then I went through a series of movements robotically, like I was in the Sims computer game I used to play as a kid. Take a shower, lie in bed, read a book, turn on the television. I executed each command, but felt nothing as I did. I even felt like I was forcing myself to blink and to swallow my saliva.

• • •

I stayed in my room until three in the morning, when I woke up from a brief rest and decided to walk around the grounds. It was still dark besides the lights on the ground every few feet marking my way. I could tell that everything around me was beautiful, although I was unable to take it in. I walked down the gravel road toward the ocean. Behind me, hotel staff on night duty stood at attention inside the glowing lobby. When I reached the end of the path, all I heard was the quiet sloshing of the waves. It seemed as if the ocean, like the other guests, wasn't yet awake either. Behind me I heard the crunch of gravel and turned around. It was Fauna.

"I've never seen you out here before," she said.

"I'm guessing this isn't your first time walking around here at night, then."

"No, I can never sleep. And I like it most at this time. No one else is around. I mean, until now." She was wearing a long dress and flat sandals that had some sort of metallic tinge to the leather. The dress was pale peach, and because the hotel's lobby was lit up behind her, I could see the outline of her legs. Her hair was down, and she had no makeup on.

We fell into step together and went off the gravel path and into the twisting roads within the greenery. Everything around us was trimmed and cut to match the ordered elegance of the hotel. I was wearing sandals, too, and if I stepped too close to the lawn, I could feel the dew of the grass on my ankles and feet.

"Mable left. Maybe you heard," I said.

"I did. She texted me from the airport before she boarded."

"I suspect you have something to say about that." Here, in the middle of the night with no one else around, I felt bolder with her than I had before. "So, go ahead and say it. Let's get it over with."

I felt her glance at me, and I tried to keep my eyes on the road ahead. "I don't really have much to say, at least not what you're guessing I would say."

"But you must have some opinion," I said.

"I do."

"And?"

"Well, that it's quite sad. You two falling out like that. I know how close you were."

"It was my fault, I know that. Even though I think she said some pretty harsh things, too." She looked at me and I met her eyes this time. "But I don't think she was wrong."

She made a low sound in her throat, and I couldn't tell if it was supposed to be a comforting one. Then she said, "What was the fight about?"

"Actually, it started about Robbie. And you."

"I see."

"I don't mind telling you about it, if you want to know."

"I do." Her voice was barely audible over the sound of the sprinklers on a nearby lawn.

"I had sympathy for Robbie when he left. It seemed like you had ended things with him, or even if he technically had been the one to end it, it was because you gave him no choice. Mable told me that my sympathy for Robbie said something not good about me."

We walked for a moment before she replied. "Is that what Robbie said when you talked to him in the car? That I ended things?"

This was the time, if there ever was one, to tell her about what had happened between Robbie and me. Instead, I said, "He said he knew he wouldn't be happy with you."

"Well," she said. "He isn't lying. Not that he would. He isn't a liar."

"But why did Mable act like I was wrong? Or that I had misread the situation?"

"I think she's referring to what I told her about us." She paused for a moment and I thought she wasn't going to say more, but then she continued. "I told her how when I met Robbie, I had just ended my last marriage. I was very vulnerable, not in a good place. Robbie gave me a lot of what I needed, which was kindness and a type of uncomplicated relationship I really longed for at that time."

"Why would you leave that?" This came out more forcefully than I intended. I tried to soften my voice. "I just don't know why you wouldn't want that."

She laughed a bit and put her hand on the back of my head. To someone else, the gesture might have come across as patronizing, but it didn't feel that way to me. It felt like she was nervous, like she wanted to reach out and see if I was really there. "I really loved that about him. But he also didn't like things about me, things that I wasn't willing to change. Or, I guess, things I wasn't willing to give up for what he could offer."

"Was it about money?" I asked.

"Some of it, yes. But the money also represented other things, like what he wanted me, or us, to be. It was something I couldn't fulfill for him, not because I was incapable, but because I'm no longer interested in that." She put a finger in the middle of her lips, as if she were pressing a button. "I'm not sure that makes any sense to you."

"It does, I think," I said. "It also felt as if he liked having you to blame for certain things. Like maybe he got off on feeling a bit resentful."

She let out a real laugh now. "Mable said the same thing. And I bet Mable wouldn't have known you felt the same way. But you two are more alike than either of you think."

"It's easy for me to understand," I said. "I like feeling as if other people are making my choices for me, that I can't help but go along. But that's not really true at all. I have free will."

"Maybe that's true of you sometimes," she said. "But I think you lead the charge when you want to. Like with Mable and your fight." Then she added, "Or with me."

"With you?"

"It's obvious you didn't like me. Or don't like me." I must have seemed surprised, and she added, "You don't try to hide it."

We were now at the end of one of the gardens, and ahead I could see the tennis courts, brown clay with neat white lines. I turned and began to lead us toward another series of gardens. We began walking under an arbor. The air was warm under the long stretches of vines above us, and we could hear each other more easily.

"I do like you," I said, although I think I was partly saying it to myself.

As we walked on, I found the silence between us comfortable and easy, as if we were actually old friends. "Can I ask you something?"

"Sure," she said.

"Can you tell me about your marriages?"

"I had a feeling that was your question. Mable said that you were still curious."

I felt then that my whole adult life would be haunted. Mable was here even when she wasn't. Would Ian be the same? It was easy for me to care what people thought of me, even when they weren't around. Even if they were dead. I didn't like that, and I swallowed this piece of information very forcefully.

Fauna began to tell me about each of her marriages. The first, she said, was to a man she met in college. He was everything she had thought a husband should be: that is, he was nice to her and he had money. You need to understand, she said, that I'm a trust fund kid. Or rather, I am a trust fund woman. One of her parents had been nice and the other rich, but neither was both. He had felt unreal. They lived in a new house, on a block with rules about when you could leave the garbage out by the curb. Both of them had been young, so young, and soon she found that they had nothing to talk about. They didn't care about the same things; they didn't like the same kind of people. I did what I thought I was supposed to do, she told me, but I found I didn't like it at all. Quickly, she said, I fell in love with someone else, which meant I had to leave my first husband. It was obvious to her now that this new relationship was just a reaction to the first one. He had no money at all, and he knew how to talk to her. These two things felt sacrosanct. He was a painter, and his hands were always covered in different colors, something she thought meant he was interesting. He always said yes when she asked him "What if we lived here?" or "What if we did this?" or "What if we became these kind of people now?" This, she thought, was living. She was older than when she got married the first time, but also younger somehow. He drank too much, though, and sometimes disappeared for days at a time, but she was too afraid to ask where he'd been. And just as quickly as it had started, it ended. It was only a twelve-week marriage, she said. And for a long time she was just by herself, which she thought was very nice. Years passed, she said. There were a few people during this time, but no one significant. And then she met the third husband. She felt like this was her first real marriage. I thought I was being wise, she said. After they signed the marriage license, she said aloud: This is the beginning. She didn't expect to change, and neither did he. They were both established with their lives, and really it just meant deciding whose house they liked more. They tried their best together, and he was a good man. A good man, she repeated. He liked to read on Sundays, his feet in her lap. On their kitchen counter they had a stack of recipes printed from the internet that they both enjoyed. They had their own friends, and there were some of each other's they liked more or less, but it wasn't difficult to fit their lives together. It was comfortable, and she is sure she could've lived her life like that. So what happened? I asked. I left, she said, and I'm still not sure why. I hope one day to make sense of it all. It was like there was this version of myself living that life, and I decided that I didn't want to be that version of myself anymore. Not that there was a value judgment, just that I was no longer interested. After I left, that's when I met Robbie.

I took it all in, asking very few questions as she spoke. When she finished, I simply said, "Thank you."

Fauna's story wasn't as unique as I'd expected it to be. I realized that, actually, being divorced three times wasn't all that odd. And yet even though I found what she said somehow familiar, I'd also felt a strong emotional undertow the whole time she was speaking. It wasn't lost on me how similar her reasoning for getting married was to my own choice to marry Ian. I had spent so much of this trip despising her, but I'd failed to recognize that Fauna and I had some things in common.

"All of that, of course, is my own interpretation of events. I'm sure each of my exes would have amendments. Rewrites, even," she said. "So now you know more about my personal life than most. I'm usually a pretty private person." Fauna stopped walking, and I did, too. She looked at me straight on. "Now I get to make you be personal in return. What do you think of your and Mable's friendship?"

I started walking again, and she fell into step. "Well, I think Mable and I are a study in contrasts," I said. "But maybe not as different as I used to think. I don't know. I have to think more about it."

"What about your relationship with Ian?"

"We were different, too. The differences always seemed to me to be good things, strengths that made us better as a couple." After a moment I said, "Ian was also like me, though, in that he cared too much about what others thought. But he only cared because he wanted to know whether they liked him, agreed with him. He saw that as an opportunity."

"Opportunity?"

"A chance for him to get them to do what he wanted or be on his side."

She didn't say anything, which I was glad about. I went on, "I decided a few days ago to try to get over my fear of the ocean. But I don't think that's going to happen." I told her about my failed attempts.

"Well, don't do it that way," she said. "Just get in, your entire body, all at once."

"I don't think I can."

"Then you're not ready."

The sun was starting to come up now, and we could see some hotel staff in the distance, setting up for breakfast service. We walked around for another few minutes before I told Fauna I wanted to go back to my room. She hugged me goodbye, which caught me off guard. I let myself relax into her body. I left her standing by the gravel path, her hand in the air waving to me.

When I returned to the suite, the early-morning sky was tinged with blue. Even though I had taken a shower only a few hours before, I took another. In the shower, I thought only of how the water from the ocean was filtered, cleaned, and funneled into the plumbing, and then the water rushed from the showerhead through the drain and into the pipes and then back into the sea. I stood there until the sound of the water disappeared and it felt like nothing. I brushed my hair and put lotion all over my body, even between my toes. I lay on top of the bed, not bothering to get under the covers. I lay like that for a long time, my hair still wet.

Chapter Nineteen

The next evening, I came back to my room after spending the afternoon by the pool and found the door to the connecting bedroom ajar. The drawers in Mable's room were open, and for a brief moment I thought she had come back. But then I recognized the suitcase.

"Mom?" I called out.

"Ellie," she said from Mable's room. I followed the voice to find her unpacking in there. She was wearing a blue-and-white sundress, and she'd folded the tailored jeans and sweater that she usually flew in into exact thirds on the bed.

"What are you doing here?" Like the last time I'd seen her, I stood in the doorway.

"I came to bring you home," she said. In order to get here from Ohio, she must've gotten on a flight soon after Mable left.

"I don't want to go home."

"Mable called me. She told me how you were doing."

"And how am I doing?"

"According to her, not well."

I went into her room and sat down on the bed, staring at my feet. "Did she say anything else?"

"No, only that she had to leave early to get back to her job. She sent me all the hotel information so I could come."

I ignored Mable's lie and said: "Well, you've certainly made yourself comfortable. For someone who is only here to bring me back home." She was putting on sunscreen, and I spotted a large sun hat on the dresser.

"The tickets I bought us are for tomorrow morning. I figure we still have some time left."

"You seem wracked with concern for me," I said.

With that, she dropped her hands to her side and came over to me. I could smell the chemicals on her skin. "Every time I ask how you're feeling, we just fight."

I closed my eyes and rubbed them hard. She was right, and I knew that if I fell into my usual pattern with her, I would regret it later. "Okay. Fine. I'm sorry."

The scent faded, and I knew she was back at the mirror. After a moment I opened my eyes and said, "Get your suit on and let's go down to the pool. I was just there, and it's not too crowded. It has a nice view of the ocean. You'll like it."

I took her there via the lobby because she wanted to see everything. Jean-Michel was at the front desk, and he looked delighted to see us together. "Ms. Chou called and said your mother would be taking her place," he said to me. He turned to my mom. "Now I see where she gets her smile from. She's been so lovely; you've raised a wonderful daughter."

At the pool, she left her dress on over her bathing suit, just pulling the skirt up so her legs were exposed. She had a light pink pedicure. She drank a cocktail and chatted with the people around us, making friends with a small child who came over to her. When she spoke to the child's father, she gestured over to me with a tilt of her hand, "Oh, that's my daughter."

They smiled and said, "You two look so much alike." I knew this was meant as a compliment.

She said, "Ellie's a top-rate attorney."

"Smart and beautiful," the dad said. "What a woman."

"Yes," my mom said.

She looked radiant, and I told her so, saying that she belonged here. I couldn't read her reaction behind her sunglasses, but she mumbled something and I heard my name twice. We watched the sun set from the pool deck, even though it was getting a bit cold. We covered ourselves with towels like they were blankets.

I decided to take her to dinner at the hotel restaurant that overlooked the ocean, so we went back to our rooms to change. She helped pick out my outfit, a long black sheath dress made from a thin fabric. She wanted to blow-dry my hair and usually I wouldn't let her, but this time I found myself agreeing. The sound of the dryer put a pause on our conversation, but as she ran her hands through my hair, her fingertips touching my scalp, I felt like I could cry.

On our way to dinner, I took her to see the bar in the main building. I didn't see Fauna, or Bertie and Paul, so we didn't stay long. We both had a drink made from champagne, Peachtree liqueur, and peach juice. The bartender explained that the cocktail was designed in the early twentieth century and named after a painter. I enjoyed walking down the gravel path toward the restaurant with my mom; I could feel her awe move through me, and it was easy to pretend that it was also my first time seeing the sun start to set on the ocean, the marvelous grounds. At the restaurant, we got a seat in the corner of the uncovered area. Even though it was now evening, it had been hot that day, and it was still pleasant outside.

We were both looking at our menus when I felt someone come up to the table and smelled that clean scent again. Fauna said hello and introduced herself to my mother, and perhaps sensing my familiarity with her, my mom invited her to join us for dinner. Fauna had on a dress showing off her bare shoulders and arms. She took a seat next to my mom, who was wearing a light blazer that had its sleeves barely pushed up to her elbows. I felt very nervous as we all exchanged pleasantries. It was jarring that two people with such distinct spheres of existence in my mind lived in the same world, let alone were now sitting next to each other.

After the waiter came to take our order, Fauna and my mom began to talk about their lives in a more meaningful way. Fauna asked her about my father, and my mother only shook her head and said: "Ellie never met him. He died when I was still pregnant. Heart attack."

"Did you think of getting remarried?" asked Fauna. "It couldn't have been easy, just the two of you on your own."

"No," said my mom. "I didn't want to get remarried."

I had never heard my mom say this before, and I was surprised. I'd always assumed that she would've jumped at the chance.

"And you?" my mother asked Fauna. "Did you ever marry?"

Fauna began to talk a bit about her marriages, giving my mother a very abridged version of the story I'd heard this morning. In the middle of the second marriage, the waiter came by with our food. Fauna had ordered lamb with squash, goat's cheese, and smoked harissa, while my mother and I had each chosen red mullet, which came with local vegetables, yellow pepper juice, and argan oil. At Fauna's suggestion, we all shared a starter of imperial caviar and a bottle of wine.

At the point when Fauna got to the end of her third marriage, I braced myself for my mom's reaction. But she said, "Of course you left each of them."

"'Of course?'" I said before Fauna could speak.

"What?" my mom asked.

"You said 'of course.'"

"And?"

"That surprises me. That's all," I said.

She looked bemused. Fauna was staring at me, and I knew that I'd just revealed an intimate part of my and my mother's relationship. But it didn't bother me as much as it might have, since I wanted to learn why my mom had said that. In my entire life, I had never, ever heard her speak approvingly of divorce. I said as much, and my mother answered, "One of them wasn't very nice to her. Spending nights away and all that."

"Yes, I know. But what about the other two?" I asked.

"Yes, what *about* the other two?" said Fauna. "I'd like to know I made the right decisions."

My mom said, "Well, with the first one, it sounds like you wanted something more than that life."

"Marriage," said Fauna.

"With him," my mom said.

"I would've thought you would've wanted her to figure it out," I said. "Work it out. Isn't that what you always suggest? 'Something only a mother would tell you.'"

My mom was quiet for a moment and said, "I could've remarried. I had suitors. But I didn't want to."

It was so obvious now that she said it, and yet this had never once occurred to me. I'd never considered that she'd even dated, let alone been the one in control. I said, "Right. Okay."

"And I can say the same, it sounds like, with your final marriage," my mom said to Fauna. "Does that sound right?"

"Yes," said Fauna. "Although ending that one made even less sense."

"Maybe you just aren't the marrying type," said my mother.

"Sounds like it," Fauna said, then shrugged. "Maybe I'll regret it when I'm much older."

My mom shrugged. "Who cares about being the marrying type?"

Hearing this, I couldn't help myself. "Really? You're saying that now? After everything you said about Ian?"

She was quiet and the only sound for a moment was the crash of the waves, the chatter at nearby tables, an old pop song playing on the speakers. Finally, she said, "I'm not proud of all the advice I gave you about Ian."

I let out a laugh that sounded hard and flat, like a coin. "That's one way to put it," I said. "But I never really told you how bad it was either. So you didn't really know."

I looked at Fauna, who was looking at my mom. Because we were in the middle of our meal, Fauna's lipstick was now barely perceptible on her lips, but it had made an imprint on the side of her wineglass.

"What a display we're making of ourselves," my mom said. Neither of us had raised our voices, and none of the guests sitting by us would've noticed anything out of the ordinary. But we've never been so honest with each other before.

Fauna said, "You're both here, aren't you? Both trying. That means something."

We spent the rest of the dinner talking about the past few days. As we did, I felt something shift in the way I looked at my mother. She looked different—not better or worse, but like an actual different human being. If I hadn't known that the person sitting across from me was named Mary Huang, and had in fact given birth to me and raised me, I would've thought her to be an interesting stranger I met on vacation. In a way, Fauna felt more familiar to me than my mom did. Did she always hold her head like that? I found myself wondering. Is that what her hands usually look like in the moonlight? She had been eating small forkfuls of fish, and after each bite, she smoothed out the napkin on her lap with her palms. I couldn't remember if I had ever seen her do this movement before. Every time the song on the speakers changed, she would drum her fingers on the table for a few seconds; I had never seen her respond to music before. When my mother gave her dessert order to the waiter, she pushed her fingertips slightly upward, so they barely grazed her bottom lip. I tried to remember if I had ever seen her move her lips, her fingers, this way, but I came up blank. She was someone altogether different, and yet she was my only family and the reason I existed at all.

At some point the strangeness of my mother became overwhelming, and I excused myself to the restroom. It was a solo bathroom, and inside, I gripped the cold marble of the sink while I let the faucet run. When I opened the door to go back to our table, Fauna was standing right outside. I said, "I'm leaving tomorrow. I don't know if my mom told you that."

"She didn't."

"I was supposed to stay longer. But she wants to take me home."

"I see." Fauna looked around me as if expecting me to move so she could enter.

I said, "I want to stay longer."

"Ah."

"I just feel like I'm not done here."

"Done with what?"

"I don't know. But the thought of going back seems impossible right now."

Fauna leaned against the doorway. The cut of her dress, which looked like silk, accented the curve of her waist. We were so close that I could smell hints of lemon in her perfume. She said, "Go back."

"Why?" I asked.

"I think it's time."

"I was supposed to stay for more days. My suite is booked out for another week at least."

"Ellie," she said. She had straightened herself and was pushing past me into the bathroom. I stepped forward into the doorway out of instinct. "This is just vacation," she said. "This isn't real." She closed the door.

The moment was abrupt and cold. I stared at the bathroom door, waiting for her to open it and return to say something else, to apologize. But she didn't. I became aware of the possibility that everything that had passed between Fauna and me the last few days had not been altogether grounded in reality, but rather what I had wanted it to be. Perhaps our relationship seemed meaningful only because it was meaningful to me. A tunnel opened in my mind. I saw that while she was someone important and defining to me, I might be just another woman she met on vacation, a distant memory in a year, and someone whose name she had trouble recalling in the future. My clumsy and powerful inner narrator, the one that could create entire worlds and feelings that were one-sided, with no footing in what was real or unreal, was dangerous, I saw now.

When I got back to the table, the waiter had brought out our desserts: wild strawberries with yogurt meringue, farm yogurt, and strawberry compote with grenadine; and an order of chocolate with thyme ice cream, chocolate emulsion, and a cacao-nib crumble. Fauna arrived soon after, and we each ordered a glass of dessert wine, too.

After dinner, my mother and I both hugged Fauna, and I wondered if I should say something, a word or phrase that would communicate how I felt after that moment in the bathroom. This meant something to me, I wanted to say. This was real to me, because you were real to me.

Instead, I only said goodbye.

• • •

The next morning, my mom finished up packing for both of us while I settled the hotel bill. The number was astronomically large, big enough to purchase a new car. I pretended that it wasn't a price, but a string of random numbers, like a barcode or part of a telephone number. Immediately after I signed, I pushed the bill across the counter to Jean-Michel.

"I will miss you," he said. "We all will."

I found myself believing him, even though I was sure that I wasn't the first guest who'd heard that. "I will, too," I said.

He stepped around the lobby desk and held out his arms. It was a comfortable hug, even though we hadn't really touched before. "I'm sorry I'm leaving," I said.

"You will come back, won't you?"

"I will try."

The bellhops placed our luggage in the trunk of the rental car and I got into the driver's side, then rolled down the window to say goodbye. My mom sat in the passenger seat. When we reached the security checkpoint, I avoided looking in the rearview mirror. The thought of seeing the hotel recede behind me was excruciating. As I drove, I played the same playlist Mable and I had listened to on the way to the hotel, right after we landed. The songs sounded different now, each lyric more emotional and painful than before. We arrived at the airport with plenty of time to spare.

Chapter Twenty

My mom had booked us both flights from Nice to Paris to San Francisco, and then a one-way for herself back to Cleveland. It was as if she didn't trust that I would actually go home, and the only way to ensure I landed at my destination was if she personally took me there, like an unruly teenager.

After we landed at SFO, I stayed with her for a few hours before her flight to Ohio. We had lunch at a place where the menu seemed to be twenty pages long, and the staff all wore bright green visors that matched their shirts. They were playing loud rock music through the speakers, and we needed to shout to hear each other. We ordered dishes that neither of us could finish; we weren't actually hungry, but it felt like having lunch was the only thing to do in the airport. When it became time for her to exit the international terminal and go to the domestic one, I bought her a sandwich for the flight home. She held the plastic box containing it against her stomach.

"This is it, I guess," I said.

"Yes," she said. I could tell she was searching for words.

"Thank you for coming out there and getting me," I said.

"I figured if I'd called and asked you to come home, you'd have ignored me."

"That's probably right," I said. "I think I would've stayed there until I ran out of money."

There was a loud announcement overhead, something about a flight delay. "And about your job?" my mom asked as soon as it ended. "You think you can say something to them? They've got to understand." On the flight from Paris to San Francisco, I'd admitted to her what had happened with the firm.

I shrugged. "Maybe. In any case, I didn't want to stay there too much longer."

"Cat should be the one who leaves," she said.

"I don't feel as strongly about her anymore. I don't mean to be defeatist. It feels freeing, actually, all things considered."

She shifted the sandwich box in her hands and nodded. "You'll be okay, I think."

At this, I had the strong urge to cry, but I just said, "I hope so." Then, "This is about a decade too late, but I know I gave you a hard time when I was younger."

She looked surprised. "You did give me a hard time."

"I think I'm starting to understand things more as I'm getting older, which means I'm finding it easier to be sympathetic to others. I'm not saying I'm okay with everything that's happened, just that it's easier to understand."

There was nothing else to say, so we hugged goodbye. I thought that I should tell her that I loved her, but it didn't feel right somehow.

. . .

The air inside my house was stale. I opened up all the windows and did a cursory cleaning, wiping down countertops and vacuuming, then collapsed into bed. Even though it wasn't nighttime in France, I fell asleep without any problem.

My sleep had been dreamless, and yet I woke up with great anxiety, covered in a sheen of cold sweat. I felt as though something loud had woken me up, even though I was sure I hadn't heard anything. For a moment, I thought there might have been a small earthquake in San Francisco, my body moving against my will. But what I had sensed as movement was my own heartbeat.

I took a shower and then walked through the house in my towel. In the living room, my feet made wet spots on the navy rug. Ian had bought the rug on a random Saturday afternoon when we'd just moved into our new house. Look at this, he'd said, can you believe it was on sale? Yes, I can, I said. I was laughing and so was he. It felt as if we were in some sort of bad sitcom, the husband with bad taste and the wife who rolled her eyes but learned to deal with it. I found that intellectually embarrassing, yet I received a great deal of pleasure from that interaction. We moved all the furniture to the sides, and he put the rug in the middle of the room. We had dinner on the floor that night.

I pushed the couch over a few inches. There was an indent in the rug from one of the legs of the couch. I put the ball of my right foot into it, balancing all my weight there.

I sat on the living room couch and opened my laptop. I searched online and found a nearby hotel that had an opening for an extended stay and booked it. Then I searched for "real estate agents in San Francisco" and talked to the first person who picked up. "Hello," I said. "I'd like to sell my home."

. . .

The next day, I worked up the courage to call Marcus. I knew that he had every right to be angry, but I held out hope that he had some goodwill left for me.

"Ellie? How are you?" He sounded surprised to hear from me.

"I'm good. Fine."

"We got your laptop and cell phone." I could tell he was smiling on the other end of the line, and that relaxed me.

I let out a long "ha" that sounded a bit like a sigh. "No one has ever done that before, I'm guessing."

"You're a legend around the office now."

"So you're saying it was worth it, then."

He laughed now. "What can I help you with? Don't tell me you want your job back."

I shook my head before I remembered we were on the phone. "No. But I did want to apologize. For flaking out on everything at the end. It wasn't fair of me. I'm sorry."

"It was pretty inconvenient, I won't lie."

"I should've just taken the break, like you said."

"Maybe. Although, I have to say, you sound better now."

"I do?"

"Lighter. You sound lighter."

There was a silence, and for a moment I felt tempted to tell him about what Cat had done. Instead, I said, "Anyway, I just called to apologize."

"Thank you, I appreciate it. What's next for you?" he asked.

"I have absolutely no idea. I'll need to find something soon though, because my health insurance is going to run out."

"Well, for whatever it's worth, I enjoyed working with you. You know, not counting these last few days."

"Thank you."

We spent a few more moments handling some administrative details before we hung up. He reminded me to contact HR to finalize my departure. I spent the rest of the afternoon writing and rewriting a text to Mable, drafting it in a Word document, so she wouldn't see the three dots in the text box appearing and then disappearing.

I wrote different versions of the text. Some of them were more lighthearted. Some were very serious, paragraphs long, dissections of the entire fight. Some were shorter, just asking if we could talk.

Finally I settled on this:

Can we talk? I want to apologize for some things but I don't want to do it over text because all tone will be lost, and I think tone is really important here. And also because I think you deserve to hear it in person. I think we have a lot of stuff to talk about outside of the apology. I hope you know what I mean by that, and if not, I can explain. But again, I don't think text is right for that explanation. Anyway, this is all to say, I really want to talk to you.

I sent it and waited for the small "delivered" sign to appear below my text. She usually responded to texts very quickly, to the point that I'd had to remind her that she was distracting me from my job. But you're always bored there, she'd said. And I'm bored at work, too. When I told her about how I needed to bill my time, she had just shrugged and said, Fine, but it's not like they'll know.

When she didn't respond to this message within ten minutes, I put my phone away and turned on my laptop. I tried to distract myself with some other online searches, but every time I sensed at least ten more minutes had passed, I would check the clock and find out that it hadn't even been five minutes. My hands were clammy. I washed them with hot water, but it didn't help. I turned on the television and decided to catch up on a show I had missed while I was in France. Every few minutes or so, I found myself rewinding it because I was having trouble paying attention to what was happening. I finally turned on the closed captions, just so I could force myself to read the dialogue.

Finally, when it was starting to get dark outside, I got a response. It said:

Yeah, talking is a good idea. Drinks?

I had no idea if it was so short because she'd written it in a rush, or if it was short because she didn't have much to say to me. I decided to believe the former, and we made plans to meet up the next night.

At this point, I realized the check-in time for the hotel I'd reserved nearby had passed. I grabbed my suitcases, still packed from France but now with a few jeans, sweaters, and two jackets thrown in, and headed to the hotel in my car. It was located in the middle of the financial district, just a few blocks from my old firm and Ian's.

A bellman outside took my luggage and led me into a very bright lobby with two fake trees flanking the counter. I gave the man behind the desk my name, and after looking at my two big pieces of luggage, he said, "Quite a long stay. Here to visit family?"

"No, I live here actually," I said. "In San Francisco."

"Oh. I see."

"But I'm moving. Well, I'm hoping to move."

"Uh-huh."

The carpet in my hotel room had a dark pattern, the kind that hid stains well. There was a lamp in the corner and the bedspread looked stiff. I could hear the television in the room next door. I sat on the bed for a long time before I decided to go to sleep.

Chapter Twenty-One

I got to the bar a little earlier than Mable and I had arranged to meet. The only thing I had done during the day was sit on my hotel room bed and scroll through job postings related to the law. I'd used search terms like "legal aid," and "policy." Some of the results were theoretically interesting, but I found myself having no actual interest in any of them. The idea of updating my résumé, writing a cover letter, and going through a series of interviews felt intolerable. It wasn't that I didn't want to work; I longed for something to fill up my days. It was more that every job reminded me somehow of Ian. Every posting was for an office in which we had mutual classmates or friends of ours, or filled with former cocounsel or opposing counsel. They all knew me as Ian's widow. I felt like no matter where I went in San Francisco, I would somehow be defined by him. I even looked up a headhunter Marcus had recommended yesterday. In the picture of her on her website, she had puffy hair and a wide smile, and in her About Me section, she ended most of her sentences with exclamation marks. I looked up the list of offices around the city where she'd placed lawyers and found myself feeling anxious once again.

At our bar, the one that always smelled like ammonia, I ordered a drink and sat down at a booth in the corner. Our usual table was taken, and, anyway, I didn't like the idea of sitting there; it's where Mable had sat the day Ian died. I also thought if she walked in and saw me at that table, she would think I was trying to send her some sign about how everything was okay and normal, and I didn't want to start out on that foot.

She arrived on time, wearing her large black jacket. She always ran cold, and I was guessing that after the heat of the Riviera, San Francisco felt especially cool. She nodded at me from the doorway and then went to the bar and ordered a drink. After the bartender handed her a beer, she came and took a seat across from me, wrapping her jacket around herself more tightly.

"Thanks for coming," I said. I placed my hands around the stem of my wineglass. "I'm sorry for what I said to the man at the bar. The Shit Stories. I know that at this point, an apology might sound pretty empty, but I mean it."

She gave a short nod that gave me no indication of how it had sounded to her, and started folding up her napkin into squares.

I continued, "I've been thinking a lot about all the other stuff you said. About how I was when I was with Ian, and really everyone else."

"And?" she asked, then added, "That sounded harsher than I meant it to be. I'm just genuinely interested in how you've come out of this."

"Ian and I weren't ever equal in the real sense of the term. I always felt smaller than him in some way." She nodded again. I went on, "It feels like you're one of the only people I can be really vulnerable with. And even then, I still feel smaller than you."

"You shouldn't feel that way." She pressed the final fold of her napkin flat against the table. "You think I'm this special person who has these things—gifts, you consider them—that you don't have. You compare yourself to me. But there are times I want to be like you."

I let out a short laugh, then said, "I didn't mean to laugh."

"I mean it. I want to be like you sometimes. You're comfortable with compromise, devotion. With loyalty." A drop of condensation was rolling down the side of her glass, and when it was close to reaching the table she pressed her pointer finger into it. "It's all the same, the way we feel about each other, when you think about it."

"I guess there were some things we just never said to each other."

"No, we didn't." She took off her jacket and let the sleeves fall to the sides of her chair. She was wearing her long-sleeved black shirt, so thin it was almost sheer. She pulled the sleeves over the palms of her hands. "I've been thinking about what you said, too. You're right that I like beginnings. There's so much hope in them. And I can imagine all the problems in an abstract way, a way that's easier for me to accept. To deal with, I guess." She spread out the napkin again and began refolding it. "It's easier not to really try, so I can always have a reason why something didn't work out. I know you've been thinking about how I do this for a while, and truthfully so have I. But we never talked about it. We talked about so many things, and we never talked about the thing I really need to talk about."

"I know," I said. "Sometimes it feels like we never really talked about anything." There was a silence before I said, "I quit my job."

She looked surprised. I told her how I had sent back my laptop and phone, and she started laughing. "Damn, Ellie. Even I've never quit like that."

"It was my moment of strength. Of course, it came at a time of irrationality."

She shrugged. "Hey, how was Fauna? Did you talk to her after I left? I haven't heard from her."

"Actually, yes. There was one night where neither of us could sleep, and we ended up walking the grounds and talking all night."

Her interest was piqued. I could tell that even now, she was hungry for information about Fauna. "What did you talk about?"

"Her three marriages. And a little about you and me, actually. It was right after our fight." I gave her a quick recap of what Fauna had said to me. "And then, when my mom came—"

"I wasn't proud of that, by the way. Calling Mary. But I was worried."

"It's okay, really. I mean, a part of me wishes that's not how it happened. But actually, I found it to be a good moment between my mom and me."

"So, did she meet Fauna, then?" Mable asked.

I told her about the dinner and then how Fauna had been odd and distant outside the bathroom. "It was like we had never had that moment when we talked all night, like I was someone she'd only just met."

"Well, we were just people she'd only just met."

"I know that. But you know what I mean. It wasn't like that either. Have you been in touch with Robbie?"

"No, I think Fauna ended up telling him what I said about him." She grinned. "Doubt he's interested in becoming pen pals."

"What did you say, exactly?"

"That he didn't actually want anything more serious with her. He just wanted to be the one to want more, because he thought it made him interesting."

I was quiet for a moment and then said: "I agree with you about the first part. But I don't think it came from a place of malice. And I don't know if he even knew he was doing it."

"I can't understand people who do things without thinking," she said. "I guess he's a bit of a Rorschach for both of us. Fauna, too."

"Maybe I'll reach out to him," I said. "God, actually no. I take that back. I don't want to."

"Really? You two seemed pretty close."

I nodded. "Your guess was right, by the way. Something did happen between us."

"I knew it."

I told her the story, and when I got to the part about us having sex, she looked amused. But by the time I was describing what happened in the car, she looked sorry for me instead.

"Rough," she said.

"Very."

Mable shrugged. "If you haven't been sexually rejected by a man in a sports car in Antibes, are you even living?"

"I think reaching out would remind me too much of stuff I

don't like about myself. Not very fair to him, I guess," I said. "I need to be alone for a while anyway."

At this point both of us had finished our drinks, and Mable went to get us another round. The bar had filled up significantly at that point, and the bartender took a few minutes before turning his attention to her. When she came back with our drinks and sat down, I said, "I'm going to reach out to Cat, I decided."

"Wow. I didn't expect that." She tilted her head to the side. "That time you totally lost it on her is probably in my top ten moments for you. VIP, truly."

I laughed. "Jesus, I really did cut into her, didn't I? Not like I regret it."

"I couldn't have done better."

She meant it as a compliment, and I took it. I said, "I hated her. I was jealous of her. I was enraged by her. Those feelings still exist, don't get me wrong. But they're more distant now. And what's left is this fascination with her, like as a specimen that Ian was obviously also in love with."

"You really think he loved her, too?" She looked like it had never occurred to her.

"I do. Well, at least, it may as well have been love. It went on for years."

"God, he was a real shithead, wasn't he?" she said.

"You know, it was obvious you hated Jeremy. But I always thought you kind of liked Ian. Approved of him, even. It's not like you ever disagreed with him the way you did with Jeremy—or anything the way you did with Jeremy."

She let out a breath of air with her mouth partially closed, so it sounded like a hiss. "That was intentional. I knew how tough it was for you that I hated Jeremy. And sometimes I just feel like maybe I'm being too hard, you know? It's not like you and I want to be with the same type of person. So with Ian, it's not whether I liked him or didn't like him. It's that I purposefully kept things light. I never wanted him to say something that would anger me, which would compel me to say something to you."

I nodded. "You also assumed that getting to know him better would mean finding out he was bad, though. You didn't see an upside of getting closer to him."

"I was just nervous about it." She took another drink and then said, "Listen, I don't want you to think that all of this, with Jeremy or even Ian, is all on you. That it's all your fault. That's not fair. It's not how I want the world to be; I refuse to think that way. Let the shit lie where it should: at their feet."

She looked impassioned, even mad, and I was reminded of the way she would debate people in our dorm until late at night. I felt a rush of unfettered love for her.

"I appreciate that," I told her. "But I also want to think about my own issues. The ones that do lie at my feet."

"You know, I was thinking the other day about how old you were when you first met Ian. You were like twenty-one, right?"

"Yes. About to turn twenty-two."

"God, think of that. Twenty-two is so young. We didn't know anything at twenty-two. What I'm trying to say, Ellie, is that I don't want you to get the wrong impression."

"I know," I said. "Sometimes I feel really embarrassed when I think of how I was just a few years ago. I really thought I had everything figured out. And I had regret for the earlier version of myself, the one in college. Ages eighteen to twenty-one or something. But now it's the same thing. And I'll probably look back on this time in the future and feel the same about it."

"We aren't that old," said Mable. "Even though we feel like it."

"No," I said, "we aren't."

"The cycle is never-ending," she said. "Well, until we meet the end. You know, *the* end." She grinned with all her teeth, and I did, too.

We decided to order curly fries and shishito peppers, and Mable got a plate of extra-hot chicken wings. As soon as our dishes came out, she said, "It's not that interesting to be divorced as many times as Fauna has. It's actually quite mundane. Everything you told me about her marriages also sounds common. I'm sure if you asked a few of the people here, they would have nearly identical narratives, give or take a few details." She waved around the bar.

"I agree. Once she told me everything, it was like it didn't matter at all."

"Still, I could've sworn that she was someone special when we were there. She works at it," said Mable. "Building up the intrigue and mystery. She doesn't want people to know her."

A server came by to refill our glasses of water, and some of it splashed onto the table. I wiped it up with a napkin and said, "We gave her a lot."

"Stupid of us. We got nothing in return."

"Now you know how I feel all the time," I said.

She let out a short laugh and said, "I got a new job. It was that place I told you about a few months ago, do you remember?" I did. It was a small nonprofit focused on criminal justice reform, and she'd liked their mission but hadn't liked the exact position that they were currently hiring for. "I thought it may have been too late, but it turns out they were still looking for someone." She quickly added, "Do you think it was dumb of me to take a role if it's not exactly the right fit?"

I shook my head, and she said, "I don't know if I ever really gave the job genuine consideration. Anyway, it's good enough. And it's what I need right now."

"Does that mean you're still writing?"

"Yes."

"Can I ask you about it?"

She shrugged, and I said, "Are you still working on the same project?"

"I am. Maybe it'll be something, I don't know."

"I'd like to read it sometime. I just want to know more."

"I want to want that, too."

• • •

Later that night I wrote my email to Cat. I imagined that it would take a while to get down what I wanted to say, the right tone and turns of phrase. But I actually found it very easy. It was as if my subconscious had been drafting this email for a while. I sent this to her work address:

Cat, I want to meet in person and talk. I am sure you have an idea of what you think I'm going to say, but I promise you it's not

that at all. I actually just want to talk. Of course, you don't have
to say yes, but I feel you owe me this, at the very least.

I had barely figured out what to watch on my laptop to distract
myself when I saw a notification on my phone. I'd worried the message might go to her spam folder, since I no longer had a firm email,
but she responded almost immediately saying she would meet me
and proposing three times and places. I could tell that she was eager to talk, too, and I decided then to brace myself for some sort of
teary apology, some monologue begging for forgiveness. I picked a
time, the next night, and a place I'd been to with Mable, but never
with anyone from work.

I texted Mable the screenshots of our exchange, and she responded, Damn, I guess it's happening. I opened my suitcase and
began to lay out possible outfits. What do you wear for a meeting
with your late husband's secret mistress? I texted Mable. I could
tell from her response that she was amused but also understood
that I wanted her to answer the question seriously. She asked for
pictures, and it took me an hour to try on various iterations of outfits and send them her way. During the entire exchange, she was
overly kind, complimentary. Even when I knew an outfit looked
completely wrong, she found something nice to say. In turn, I was
unbelievably grateful, telling her over and over how much I appreciated her help. It was all wrong, the way we were talking to each
other, but I don't think either of us felt we were done atoning for
what we'd said to each other in France.

Seems pretty asinine, I wrote to her in the middle of this, to care about clothes in such a moment. Really shallow, if you ask me. She wrote back: Good thing no one is asking you, least of all me.

When we finally settled on a pair of jeans and a short-sleeved lavender shirt, I pulled back the bedcovers and turned on the hotel's television, conceding defeat on finding anything streaming on my computer that felt right. I flipped through the channels until I found an old movie that was playing. Occasionally, I scrolled through my phone with my right hand. I couldn't focus on either screen.

Chapter Twenty-Two

Ioriginally wanted to show up early to meet Cat, but it rained heavily that morning, which meant that every mode of transportation in San Francisco was slightly stalled. Anyway, I figured that being early would make me seem eager, and I wanted her to be at least a little intimidated. I imagined her sitting at her office all that day, trying to focus on work while counting down the hours to our meeting with dread. I hoped that Marcus had mentioned he'd spoken to me while she was in earshot in the office. I hoped that he'd said I sounded better.

The hotel had speakers that connected to Bluetooth, and while I got ready, I played music on them using my phone. My hands were shaking so much it took me longer than usual to put on mascara. I brushed my hair more than it needed and debated whether I should put on perfume. I couldn't tell if I was feeling this way because of anxiety or because of anger. Mable and I had chosen small gold hoops to go with my outfit, and when I put the earrings in, I worried about accidentally piercing my skin, as improbable as that was.

Mable texted me about an hour before. How are you? she wrote.

I tried to convey my feelings to her, sending her a series of very long texts that mostly focused on how difficult it was for me to decide exactly when to arrive and how to get there. She sent back clear instructions, telling me precisely what to do in short, clear sentences. I appreciated that someone was telling me what to do, and that it was Mable.

When I took the elevator to the lobby of my hotel, I realized that I would still be too early if I left right then. I considered going back to my room, but instead I sat on an uncomfortable chair in the lobby, which was being vacuumed. I searched for Fauna on the internet, this time with the knowledge of her last name. I found next to nothing. Like Robbie, the lone social media account she had was set to private. Requesting to follow either of them was completely out of the question, especially Fauna. After the way we had left in France, I couldn't give her the satisfaction.

On the Muni I took to go meet Cat, I kept my hands balled up in small fists. I was wearing a coat, but I was cold and felt myself shivering. Eventually, I had to expel my energy on something, so I began to crack my fingers slowly and methodically. A woman in a blue jacket sitting close by stared at me. My skin felt damp, and I began to regret that I had decided to put on perfume after all. The scent made me feel sick.

I arrived at the restaurant a few minutes late, and spotted her instantly. It was still early afternoon, so the place was almost empty. She was sitting at a table looking straight ahead at the chair across from her, her face scrunched together with worry.

When I approached and sat down across from her, she smiled, then seemed to immediately regret that decision and tried to relax her face. It only made her features look awkward. The inter-action lasted only the span of a few seconds, but it made me feel powerful.

"I'm so glad you came," she said, after the waiter had come by and we informed him we would only be ordering drinks. He took away the empty plates in front of us, and we both ordered the first glass of white wine listed on their menu. For a moment the waiter seemed to want to suggest other wines, but he only nodded and left.

"I'm the one who asked you to come here," I said.

"Yes, but I was worried you'd change your mind."

"Well, I didn't," I said. It came out a bit harshly, and I was fine with that.

As I suspected, she launched into a long and, at times, tearful apology. She said "sorry" at least five times. She mentioned she was seeing a therapist now. She said she had been reflecting a lot on her choices and that she knew now she needed to work harder at being a good person. I want to be a good person, she said twice. Then she said she wanted to be an ethical person. All of her sentences were simple ones, only independent clauses. At one point, the waiter came back with our drinks, and she didn't seem to care that he was there and kept talking, not touching her glass of wine, while I drank almost half of my own.

I tried to keep my face impassive as she spoke. When it seemed like she was nearing the end, I said, "I didn't ask you to come here because I wanted an apology."

"I didn't think you did. But I wanted to apologize anyway."

"Okay."

"You don't need to forgive me or anything. I don't expect you to."

"That's good because I'm not here to forgive you. I don't know if I can ever do that."

"Right, of course. Obviously. I know that," she said. She finally picked up her wine, and I was thankful that she drank it as quickly as I did.

I realized she was waiting for me to say something. She had clearly gotten out everything she wanted to say to me, and now it was my turn. In this moment, I realized that I had spent so long agonizing about the beginning of our meeting, I hadn't really thought about this next part.

"I wanted to meet because I thought I should know what you were like outside of work. Since you and Ian were so close."

She said, "I'll tell you anything you want."

"I should hope so."

She winced but only tipped her head low, as if she were planning to drink her wine without using her hands.

"Did you ever think about telling me? Like that time we drove to LA for the deposition?"

"I did. I thought about it all the time."

"But you didn't," I said. "Was it because he said he was going to leave me? Or that we were in an open relationship?"

"No. He was very clear he wasn't going to leave you."

This surprised me. I had thought that perhaps Ian had made her a vague promise, and that this had driven the entire affair. "He said that?"

"Yes, he said you were his wife. And that he loved you very much."

"That's rich."

She nodded.

I said, "But then why did you stay with him? What were you getting out of it?"

"I don't know. I mean, I guess I do know, but it's a part of me that I'm not proud of. Not that I'm proud of myself generally."

"Go on."

"It's never bothered me to feel like that. To be someone's second choice. I've felt like this since I could remember. I realize that isn't a good thing, but I can't help it."

"So there wasn't a part of you that thought you could change his mind?"

"Not really." She pulled her lower lip down and to the side, as if someone was pulling on it with a string. She said, "I really loved him. I couldn't bear to end it."

I could see she was telling the truth, and despite everything, I pitied her. She loved him in a way I had never even loved Ian. Or, if I had, that sort of love for him was so far gone at this point I couldn't remember it ever being inside of my body. It may as well never have existed.

"Why did you love him? Transactionally, I mean. I want to know what it is he gave you," I said.

She pushed together her thumbs so hard the flesh under nails turned white. "He made me feel animated. Like I was better than I really was, more powerful. I felt like I could talk to anyone, could laugh off any slight. I know that sounds very simple, but it didn't feel that way at the time."

"I understand that."

"You felt the same way about him?"

I gave her a short nod, my chin moving barely an inch. I don't know if she caught the movement.

She said, "There was this one time when I was having trouble with Brian. You remember when I worked for him?"

I nodded. When Cat started at the firm, she'd been assigned to the Intellectual Property Law group, where Brian was a partner. All I knew was that she hadn't enjoyed working with him.

"They were giving me the most boring work. All drudgery. Basically administrative. Which would've been fine except everyone else was being given better assignments. First passes at briefs, and all that. And Ian—wait. Are you sure you want to hear this?"

Her hand was in mid-gesture when she asked me this. Her eyes were wide and her mouth parted so I could see the top of her bottom teeth. Her expression was soft and open. I could've said anything, and I know she would've accepted it.

I realized that she wasn't being deferential to me just by virtue of our relationship. It was also her very nature; she was a compliant person. Agreement was how she moved through the world, how others had expected her to be all her life, and therefore how she had formed the very outline of her personality. Her language signaled sacrifice, compromise, and settlement. I thought about how Ian would've loved this about her. I thought about how I was, in many ways, the same.

"I do," I said.

"Ian told me exactly what to do. He said to wait until the day after our firm's event celebrating women in the law, where Brian would be making a speech, and then ask him point-blank for the next opportunity to draft a brief. He said it'd make Brian feel big. I would've never thought of something like that myself." She pressed her palms together. "That is horrible to say aloud. Makes me sound like an empty vessel."

If she was waiting for some words of comfort, I didn't offer them. Instead, I said, "And what do you think you gave to him? Besides the illicit sex?"

Cat pushed her lips together. "I think I made him feel powerful. Like he was some kind of god."

"I see."

"I don't mean just because we were having an affair. I mean because of who I am, and who he was."

"I understand that. I do."

I gestured at the waiter for the check. When it came, I pushed it across the table to her and got up. She said, "Right, I'll be getting this."

She looked up at me. "Is that really all you wanted from me?" She had taken her wallet out of her bag and placed it on the table.

"Yes," I said. On my way out, I glanced back at her. She hadn't moved at all, and was staring at the bill as if it contained an unsettling piece of information.

• • •

When I got back to the hotel, I called Mable. In the past hour, I had received multiple texts from her, some of them just a series of question marks. She picked up after the first ring, and I tried to explain everything to her in sufficient detail. When I finished she said, "Well, turns out Cat is more self-reflective than I'd thought."

"I know."

"That whole bit about him getting off on their power dynamic. She got it."

"She's not stupid," I said.

"No, not in this particular way."

"I can't believe she kept on seeing him though he said he wasn't ever going to leave me."

"She doesn't value herself enough, that's for sure," she said. "Not that we should waste our breath feeling bad for her."

"Now that it's over, I'm not sure what I even got out of it. I felt so clear about wanting to talk to her, but now I feel muddled."

"Did you expect talking to her was actually going to make you feel better?"

"I guess I just didn't expect this." I pushed myself under the covers of the bed even though the room was warm. I felt myself overheating but the weight of the duvet felt comforting to me. There was a pause on Mable's end of the line, and I could tell she was debating whether to say something. "Go ahead and say it," I told her. "I'll be okay."

She said, "Did you enjoy hearing that he said he wasn't going to leave you? Like, does he feel different to you now?"

"You mean, did it redeem him somehow?"

"Yes."

"No, I think it makes it so much worse. I would rather he'd been in love with her and planning to leave me."

She was silent for a moment and then said, "Jesus, this is a fucked-up situation."

"You get why I feel that way, though. Right?"

"He's worse this way."

"Exactly. I could understand how someone could fall in love with someone else and decide to end their marriage."

"But that wasn't it at all."

"No," I said.

Mable asked more questions about our meeting: what Cat ordered, what I ordered, whether I thought the waiter was clued in to what was happening. Finally, she said, "Listen, are you busy tomorrow night?"

"No. You want to meet up?"

"Yes. I have this work thing. Would you want to stop by?"

"You're participating in a work happy hour?"

"I know," Mable said, sounding nervous.

I said, "Of course I'll come. Just tell me when and where."

Chapter Twenty-Three

My hotel room had a black wooden table and matching chair next to the window that looked onto the courtyard. I had been sitting there for most of the day doing research on my laptop, not moving much even though the seat was uncomfortable. Next to my computer was the hotel phone, a pad of paper and pen branded with the hotel logo, and a takeout box containing the remnants of a salad I'd bought from one of the chain restaurants on the block. When I picked it up, I was shocked at the length of the line, then remembered that for most people, it was a workday and they were there on their lunch break.

My browser was open to three tabs. The first tab was an email Mable had forwarded to me from her therapist. He had sent her the name of a local therapist he recommended, a woman. The second tab showed the search results for the therapist's name. The third tab contained the results of a search for: "therapy, different types, efficacy."

I pulled up the messages app on my computer and began typing a text to Mable. All the patient reviews for her seem okay. No idea how to tell if she's good otherwise? Almost immediately, she responded, You should call/email first and see if she's taking new patients. Then she texted me a link to the therapist's website. I'd seen it already, so we began to discuss the website's layout choices, the details in her brief bio. In the picture of her on the site, she was sitting in an office chair, a window behind her. She looked to be in her sixties and was wearing a marigold-yellow shirt and beaded earrings that fell to the middle of her neck. I felt that no one who was unkind would look this way.

Mable texted, I like her smile. I said, You know that going to therapy doesn't necessarily mean I'll get better. There's a lot of factors that play into it. She replied, Obviously I know that, I'm the one who told you that. But this is something.

I went to my first tab, minimized the email Mable had forwarded to me, and began drafting a new one. Even though it was only a few lines long, it took me close to twenty minutes to introduce myself, explain how I had found her, and ask if she was taking new patients. It took me a while to decide how to sign off before I settled on: Sincerely, Ellie Huang.

When I was done, I refreshed the browser, went to the sent mail tab, and texted a screenshot of the sent email to Mable, who responded with a series of exclamation marks. Then she said, Can't talk much more, sorry. Heading into a meeting and then need to concentrate on something. See you tonight.

• • •

Mable's happy hour was at a divey bar in the East Bay, not too far from the closest BART station to me in San Francisco. When the BART was underwater, I tried not to think about the fact that we were in a tube hurtling through the Pacific Ocean. Instead, I turned up the music in my headphones so I couldn't hear the train. A toddler and his mother were sitting next to me. He put his hands over his ears and said, "Loud." The mother put her hands over his and he looked up at her and smiled.

It was dark inside the bar and I stood awkwardly by the door for a few minutes before I spotted Mable in a corner, surrounded by a group of people. She was wearing a dark gray dress I didn't recognize. It must've been new. When she saw me, she pulled me into the circle and introduced me to everyone.

After everyone said hello, a tall man with sandy-colored hair started back up on what he was saying before I arrived. He had a firm handshake and said his name was Connor. "I change mine every few months based on my mood," he said to the group.

A woman who'd introduced herself as May said, "Isn't yours a small cartoon cat right now?"

"Like I said," he said. Everyone standing around them laughed. Someone else pulled out a phone and began passing it around the circle, and when it got to me I saw the screen was pulled up to a workplace messaging app. A sketch of a black-and-white cat with oversize tears rolling down its face was above the words "Connor Kerr." An empty circle next to his name indicated that he was currently inactive.

"I still need to pick my picture," said Mable. "I'll start taking suggestions right now."

"What's your mood?" said Connor, pouring beer into a glass from a pitcher on a nearby table then returning to the circle.

"That's a big question," said Mable.

"Well, you're going to need to find some image that perfectly encapsulates who you are," he said.

I walked to the table where Connor had just been standing and poured myself a glass of beer. It was hard to imagine Mable messaging people at a job, asking them questions about projects, conversing with people at meetings, participating in the social structure of this job in a sincere way.

When I found my place next to Mable again, May pulled up her own phone. The picture above her name was of a small white dog. "I got him a few years ago," she said, showing her phone to Mable.

"I don't have any pets," said Mable. "So it's not an option for me."

Connor said, "Like I said, it has to be your mood."

May said, "I've had this one for years."

"That's troubling," said Connor. "You've been in the same mood for years?"

A man wearing a neon-yellow shirt began collecting requests for bar food. He'd been in a nearby group of Mable's other coworkers. Mable started talking to a man from the second group, who'd joined our circle. He had dark black hair parted to one side, and was wearing a thin, bright green windbreaker and white shoes that looked new.

Mable introduced us. His name was Andrew, and when he shook my hand he said, "Can you believe her?"

I said, "All we can do is try to keep up."

"I can imagine," he said.

"Too much for you to handle?"

"Impossible," Mable said.

He looked amused and said, "Of course not." Then he added, "The only thing we had to do to get her to accept our offer this time was to offer her flexible hours."

"I start close to noon," said Mable. "But I stay late."

"I've never managed someone with another career before," he said. "And a writer no less."

"Oh," I finally got out. "You told them about your writing."

"Yes, 'The Something Something stories'?" he said.

"The what?" I asked.

"Ellie knows them by another name," said Mable. "But 'The Tried But Not True Stories' is my working title."

"That's right," he said. "I hope you write a story about us. But also I hope you don't."

"I feel the same way," I said. I paused, and when no one said anything, I realized I was reflexively waiting for Mable to make a joke. But she said, "It's actually mostly about my childhood."

The man raised his hands, wiggling his fingers in a mocking spooky gesture and said, "Childhood. Classic. We all have lots of material there. Doesn't everyone have one good book inside of them?"

"That isn't true in the slightest," said Mable.

"You're the expert," he said.

"Well, I like to think I know something," said Mable.

While Mable talked she looked at me and not Andrew. She was embarrassed about talking about her writing, but there also was something else, something unfamiliar on her face: earnestness. She was being genuine. This made me uncomfortable, too, and neither of us looked at the other as we chatted with Andrew.

For the rest of the happy hour, Mable acted like any other co-worker I interacted with at firm events, which, given how I understood Mable, was not usual at all. Every topic was usually ripe for judgment, her approval or disapproval. But she wasn't offering that this evening; she was on the same plane as them. Most of them seemed to have what she would've once considered conventional lives. Some of them were older than us, in their forties and fifties, and showed us pictures of their children. When Mable looked at the pictures she asked questions about what they were reading, what music they listened to. One person shared that his teenage daughter was having trouble in school. Mable said, "I'm so sorry." I could tell she meant it.

As the happy hour began to wind down, it was clear Mable wanted to stay out with a group of them longer. They invited me warmly to join, but I said I needed to go back into the city. Mable knew I was making an excuse not to stay, but she looked grateful when I said this. It was still new to both of us, this version of her. When I left, she pulled me into a hug and said: It's something.

When I got out of the BART station in San Francisco, I decided to take a walk before going back to my hotel. I could've listened to music, but I took off my headphones and listened to the people talking around me, catching snippets of conversation about their work dramas, the dinners they'd just finished, who they were going home to. A little girl wore bright green boots, a frog's face painted on the tips of her toes.

By the time I arrived back at the hotel lobby, it was dark outside. There were large mirrors by the elevators, and when I waited for one to take me up to my floor, I caught my reflection. My skin

was flushed from the walk, and my eyes were bright. The light of
a nearby lamp gave me a soft glow. Inside my room I took off my
coat and shoes, and then changed into my pajamas. I pulled back
the covers on the bed, stacking all the hotel pillows on one side so I
could sit up, my knees beneath my chin and my phone next to me
on the nightstand. My mom had texted me about something and
I decided to call her, since I knew she'd still be awake. I wanted to
talk to her.

Acknowledgments

I am indebted to Elizabeth Bewley, the greatest agent an author could have. Thank you, Elizabeth, for your advocacy, faith in me, and friendship. Thank you also to the entire team at Sterling Lord Literistic, Inc., including Szilvia Molnar and Amanda Price, for their dedication to this novel.

Thank you to Emily Griffin, whose editorial brilliance and gentleness of heart are unmatched. Every author should be so lucky. Thank you to all at HarperCollins, including Maya Baran, Micaela Carr, Joanne O'Neill, and Lydia Weaver, without whom this book would never have been published.

Thank you to Sally Willcox, Lindsey Staub, and everyone at A3 Artists Agency for believing in me and their unwavering support of this story.

Thank you to Carrie Frye, who was the first person to read this book, and who had confidence in me from the very beginning. Carrie, I would not be a writer if not for you.

Thank you to all who answered my questions as I drafted this novel, including Susan E. Thompson for educating me about law firms and life insurance, and Katie Frederick Jacobson for providing details about the French Riviera, Hotel du Cap-Eden-Roc, and who is responsible for the trip of a lifetime.

Thank you to everyone at Hotel du Cap-Eden-Roc for such a memorable visit that it gifted me a novel. Hotel du Cap is truly un-paralleled in beauty, grandeur, and spectacular service.

Ellie and Mable's visit to the Claude Monet exhibit is based on *Monet: The Late Years* as shown at the de Young in 2019. The quote that Ellie reads is taken from a letter featured in the exhibit written by Monet to Gustave Geffroy. Thank you to curator George T. M. Shackelford, the Fine Arts Museums of San Francisco, and all who worked on this inspiring, exquisite showcase of Monet's work.

Thank you to every early reader of this book for their keen in-sight and generosity of spirit.

A novel cannot be born without a community, nor can a writer endure without friends, and so I will forever be grateful for every person who encourages me. I am especially thankful to my afore-mentioned friends, as well as Tracy Chou, Amanda Glassman, John Kilbane, Daniel Kuo, Michelle Legro, Rebecca Maurer, Kate O'Shaughnessy, Hamida Owusu, Tarana Riddick, John Smolowe, Professor Ronald C. Tyler, Jennifer Zhao, the Housing Team at East Bay Community Law Center, and the members of The Ruby.

Thank you, always, to my family, especially Mom, Dad, and Perry, for whom my writing is eternally intended.

Thank you to every Asian American writer who came before me.

Most of all, thank you to Ben, who remains my greatest cham-pion; and to Maeve, who, more than anyone or anything, has taught me about the astonishing sweetness of life. I love everything about you, Maeve.

About the Author

KATHERINE LIN is an attorney and writer based in the San Francisco Bay Area. She is a graduate of Northwestern University and Stanford Law School. *You Can't Stay Here Forever* is her debut novel.